WOLF TIDE

WOLF TIDE

A NOVEL

by
CATHERINE FOX

The characters and events portrayed in this book are fictitious. Any similarity to real persons, living or dead, is coincidental and not intended by the author.

Text copyright © 2013 Catherine Fox

ISBN-13: 9781490904580
ISBN-10: 1490904581

For my sisters, Grace, Ruth and Hilary,
with love.

CHAPTER ONE

A shout in the night: 'Open up!' Then a fist on the door. Bang-bang-bang! 'Open up! It's the Guard!'

Anabara lurched awake. More hammering. She snatched up her wool robe and stumbled downstairs.

Five officers burst in. Cold night clung to their uniforms. Nets. Iron stunning poles.

'What's going on?'

'Stand back.' A grey-haired one flashed a badge. 'Border Control. Requesting access to your property. We've an illegal alien cornered out the back. Go upstairs, please. Now. Could be dangerous.' He opened the stairs door.

'But—'

He thrust her through. '*Now*, Ms Nolio.' The door closed behind her.

For a moment she stood in the dark stairway, heart galloping. She could hear them in her yard. Shouts. *Over there. Quick! That's it, close in. Net! Net! Net!*

Dear God, what was out there? Some kind of feral Fairy criminal? She fled up the stairs to her room, got back under the quilt. More shouts. What if it overpowered them and broke in? She turned the lamp on to keep fear at bay. Please, please let them catch it.

CATHERINE FOX

Suddenly a scrabbling overhead. It was on her roof!
Anabara bit back a scream. Her eyes locked on to the porthole window in the roof. It doesn't open, it's too small,
nothing can get in!

A hand, clawing. Oh dear God! And a face. A tiny
pointed face.

No! It was a child. A Fairy child. For a second the black
eyes stared into hers. Alien eyes from a different reality,
stranger and wilder than any hawk's. Then the creature was
wrenched off the roof, nails scratching down tiles. Gone.

A cheer from the yard below. Back-slapping. They were
trouping through her house. Job done.

A *child*. Anabara pressed a hand to her mouth. Five men
armed with nets and irons to hunt down a child? She felt
sick.

'Ms Nolio?' a voice called up the stairs. 'All finished now,
thanks.'

She trembled as she made her way back down, knees
buckling on each step.

It was the grey-haired Guard. He saw her face and put
a hand on her arm. 'Sorry, love. I know, I know. Rough
business.'

'But it was a *child*, Officer!'

'Routine precaution. Could have been an assassin using
a cloaking charm.'

'That's ridiculous! How likely is that?'

'Still, safety regs—got to comply. But we got the parents
earlier, so yes, in all probability it was a genuine child.' He
gave her a little squeeze. 'We'll have her back with Mum and
Dad in no time, safe and sound, so don't you fret.'

She snatched her arm away. 'Don't patronise me,
Officer! I know you're going to deport them.'

He looked at her, blew out a sigh. 'Well, let's not get into all that now. It's been a long night. Sorry to drag you out of bed.'

'Don't try and fob me off! They're refugees, they—'

'Now, now.' He had his hand up. 'If they want to cross, they have to go through the proper channels like everyone else, or we'd be overrun. No,' he made for the door. 'Not getting into it with you now. I'm just doing my job. Goodnight, Ms Nolio. Thanks again for your co-operation.'

Co-operation? It felt like collaboration.

She shut the door after him and went back up to bed. It was a long, long time before she fell asleep. And when she finally did—*that* dream again. The one where she'd put the baby in the cellar and forgotten about it. And now it was too late, she knew it must have starved to death.

She lurched awake once more, cold with sweat. Dawn. Pale light through the porthole. In the distance a shrine bell. Gulls keened. A mule cart rumbled past. The city was waking up. Slowly her pulse returned to normal. She stared up at the window. That tiny face. Those black eyes. There was nothing she could have done for it. Nothing. But it still felt like a betrayal.

Anabara opened the top half of her door and looked out across the narrow cobbled street. The houses opposite leaned on one another like drunken sailors. Washer-wenches clomped by in clogs. A pedlar toiled up hill, pack swaying. She stuck her head out and craned up. Bright autumn sun, clouds racing in the blue. On every chimney pot in Larridy the wind flutes sang of the long gone sea. Forget the dream, she told herself, forget the Fairy. It's an amazing morning to be alive on, to be seventeen years old with the whole of your life ahead of you. Be happy! Shirts snapped on a hundred lines. The smell of starch and blueing crept up the hill from the washeries. Then from high up on the city isle's summit she heard the Minstery bells chime for Morning Prayers. Be happy, *be happy*.

But how?—when in her hand was a final reminder from her counsel, demanding an insane, unpayable sum? She gripped her spiky bronze hair. Even at fifty gilders and hour, how could she *possibly* owe him that much? The dream rushed back at her. Oh, for heaven's sake! She didn't even have cellar, let alone a baby to abandon in it!

No, but she had a cupboard under the stairs where for months she'd been shoving her paperwork without even looking at it. All those case notes she'd never got round to writing up. The red-edged bills and menacing letters from the bank, from the Revenue men. Yes, that's what the dream was about; triggered by the trauma of last night's horrible arrest, no doubt. She was such an idiot—she really ought to get on to the filing. Except that now it had turned into the folktale Boagle-man. She'd got to the stage when she was too scared to look. So long as you didn't look, there was still a faint possibility it was still all right. That the baby was alive and well...

Tscha! *Idiot.* She made herself face it. Say she actually was bankrupt. Say she'd spent the last of her inheritance from her parents, that the bailiffs came and took everything, and her landlord threw her out. Not like she'd be homeless, was it, not with the hordes of relatives she'd got. And she could always join the City Guard. Chief Dhalafan would fast-track her application. She could carry on being a detective, only this way she'd have security. Regular income. Colleagues. A pension. She could challenge Border Control policy from the *inside*. Look: going bust could even be a good thing, in the long run.

The bells chimed on. Be happy, be happy.

Instead furious tears welled up. Anabara kicked her door. Blue paint flaked off. Dammit. They were all going to say *I told you so. You're far too young. It's man's work.* Oh, if *only* cousin Linna hadn't left. They'd made such a good team. But Linna wasn't coming back any time soon, not with a baby on the way. *Dammit!* I refuse to be a failure. I just need a big job with a nice fat fee to get me back on my feet. Then I can hire an assistant to sort the cupboard out, and everything will be fine.

But she still couldn't shake off her dream, or her sense of guilt at not helping the Fairy child. It felt like she'd walked through a cobwebby tunnel and the strands were still sticking to her face. The chiming stopped. In desperation she fell back on an old childhood habit. She asked a boon of St Pelago.

I'll go to Prayers, promise. Just send me a job. Please, send me a job. And send me a man while you're at it, she added. (Well, no harm in asking, was there?)

Her hand was still making the threefold sign—forehead, lips, heart—when the messenger appeared.

She heard the boots first. Watched him swagger round the corner. Offcomer of some sort—around 18 or 19, a student from up in the Precincts. Tall. He wore the grey uniform like he was strutting in satin britches. She'd never seen him before. New intake. Probably strayed down here for the legendary washer-wench friendliness. Anabara pretended to study her counsel's bill so he wouldn't catch her staring.

The striding boots halted level with her door. Waited. The baker's sign creaked. A gull mewed.

Then he clicked his tongue as if she were a horse. 'Hey! Pretty girl.'

Up went her chin. She slid the letter in her pocket.

His eyes were black as any Fairy's and twice as bold. Some tribal plainsman, judging by the accent. He approached. 'May I see your titties?'

She gawped. 'No, you may not!'

'No? A man loses nothing by asking. The worse you can do is refuse, hey?'

'Well, you've obviously not met many Gull women!'

'No, never. But you don't look like a Gull, I think.' He rested an arm on her door, stuck his head through and looked her up and down. Then he shook his head. 'You have golden eyes, true, but you are too small, too dark for a Gull.'

She wasn't about to explain her mixed blood to this buffoon.

'Is it true you can fly? Yes? Why you don't talk to me, hey?' He leant closer still. Close enough for her to catch his musky smell. She stood her ground, tried to stare him down. 'Kiss me,' he whispered.

She coloured. 'Tscha!'

At this he laughed. Strong white teeth in his tanned face. One of the front ones was chipped. She could see holes in his earlobes where rings had been stripped out. Where was he from? He spoke Commons fluently enough. 'You live here all alone, pretty girl? Why you have no husband, no father to protect you, hey?'

'I don't *need* protecting,' she snarled. 'I can look after myself, mister!'

'She's fierce!' His laugh rang out in the street again. 'Come, since you are not in the mood for kisses, you may give me directions. I'm looking for...' he drew a letter from inside the breast of his shirt, 'one Anabara Nolio.'

'That's me, clown.' She jerked a thumb at the sign overhead. *Nolio Investigations.* 'Here, give.' She twitched the letter out of his fingers. The envelope bore a black seal: the Minstery triple rings and gull.

'Is from Doctor Scholasticus,' he said. 'He says, come quick-quick.'

Anabara broke the seal and skimmed the circumbendibus prose. It was indeed from the scholasticus. Newly appointed, she'd not met him yet. *Tendered herewith most cordial greetings. If he might humbly prevail upon her. Utmost importance. At a time convenient to her, present herself in the University library. A matter most pressing. He remained in all things her obedient etc.* In other words, quick-quick.

Anabara seized a jacket and left her house, banging the door behind her.

'Why you don't lock your home in the big bad city?' the messenger asked.

'The door's charmed.'

'Charmed!' He stepped away in disgust. 'By a Fay?'

'Excuse me?' She rounded on him. 'We don't say that. We say "person from the Fairy Nations", you racist bigot.'

'Ah, I did not know this.' He raised his hands in mock surrender. 'Don't hurt me, I beg! But what can I say? My countrymen, we have no dealings with these "Persons from the Fairy Nations". To us, their ways are unclean, perverted.' He set off up the hill at a slapping pace.

She tried to rein in her rage. Not fair to take it out on him. Plenty of Larridy folk shared his views.

'So,' he waited for her to catch up. 'You could fly up to the top, hey?'

'Yes.'

'Why don't you?'

She pointed to the *No Flying* sign.

'Hah, rules!' he scoffed. 'You keep the rules, Anabara Nolio? Like a good girl? Why you no fly up the hill?'

Lord, if I had a gilder for every time I'd had this conversation. 'Why don't you run up?'

'Is very steep. Even for me, athlete that I am, running up this hill is hard work.'

'Exactly.'

'Ah, but if I could fly, then I would be always flying.'

She didn't bother to reply. In a minute he'd try and goad her into giving him a demonstration. They all did.

His boots clumped over the cobbles. They followed the old Skuller road as it snailed its way up the hill towards the Precincts. 'They say that Gulls get fat and lazy,' remarked the messenger.

And there it was: the goad.

'Then they can't get off the ground. So maybe you're getting lazy, Anabara Nolio? And fat?'

'How dare you!' She halted by the narrow cut that sliced the hillside clear to the summit, where they hauled the barrows in olden times, now replaced by steps. 'Fat? I can outrun you, any day, *athlete!*'

He laughed.

'I'll prove it!' She pointed to the zigzag ladder of flights. 'You go the quick way—up the Fairy Teeth, there—and I'll go the long way. And *then* we'll see who's fat and lazy!'

'Done!'

'Done! Ready, go!' She set off like a hare.

At the next bend she slowed to the Isle-dweller's steady swinging pace. Skuller Road brought her back past the cut twice more, where she heard the sound of his boots pounding the Fairy Teeth, each time higher, more distant. Finally she dawdled her way across St Pelago Plaza towards the stone gatehouse of the Minstery Precincts.

The messenger stood under a chestnut tree by the marble drinking fountain, arms folded. His shirt was wringing wet. She was betting he'd had his head in the trough.

'Hello!' she called. 'Looks like you won.'

His dark eyes burned. 'You are a bad woman, Anabara Nolio. You make a fool of a stranger.'

'Welcome to Larridy.' *Offcomer,* she didn't add.

He spun on his heel and strode off. That was when she spotted it. Unmistakably, in his cropped fair hair was shaved the spiral of a Minstery novice.

Tscha! The first interesting man she'd met in months, and he was embarking on three years of celibacy.

She watched till he was out of sight. Then came a little spurt of panic: if this was how her prayers for a man were going to be answered, what kind of job was the Saint planning to give her?

CHAPTER TWO

Anabara hesitated in front of the library. She'd spent half her childhood in the Minstery Precincts. This was the first time she'd ever felt nervous up here. She squared her shoulders. I am a warrior from a long line of warriors. On both sides of the family. What can the scholasticus possibly want of me that I cannot achieve? Bring it on.

She found him in the great round reading room. A tall black-skinned Galen. He looked as stiff and lean as a new broom.

'Ah, Ms Nolio.' He shook her hand. 'So grateful to you for coming. I may have a job for you. You deal in security issues, do you not?'

'Yes, that's right.'

'Excellent. Well, the simple fact is this—the security in this library is totally inadequate!'

adequate! adequate! adequate!

Anabara glanced up at the ceiling. Hey, that wasn't a real echo, it was a piss-taking mimic charm! Some student pranksters must have put it there. Had the scholasticus worked it out yet?

She assumed her most business-like manner. 'So, what's the problem, exactly?'

'Well, for a start, this is *not* a lending library, yet it seems clear to me that books are being borrowed willy-nilly.'

Willy-willy-willy! sniggered the echo.

The scholasticus glared up at the vault.

Anabara could feel eyes watching all round the reading room. Students at desks, students behind shelves, up on book ladders, leaning over gallery rails. The stained glass figures in the cupola windows were probably watching too. The scholasticus gestured. 'Come along!'

-long, -dong, -schlong!

Her footfalls sounded on the tiled Round Room floor. The scholasticus moved softly, barefoot of course, his long grey robes whispering. He waved her through a door and shut it behind them. They emerged into the library cloister. Sunshine streamed down into the central courtyard where water tinkled in a porphyry fountain. A leaf drifted down from the cherry tree.

'That *bloody* echo. Forgive me, but I can't hear myself think in there. If your company can deal with that as well, so much the better. You employ someone from the Fairy Nations, I take it? Excellent.'

They turned the first corner and continued along the west side of the cloister.

'Needless to say, you came highly recommended,' said the scholasticus.

Her heart began to patter with excitement. Money, big money. Please, St Pelago.

'And as we will be demanding your full time and attention, we are prepared to pay double your usual rates, to remunerate you for any loss of business that might arise.'

She managed to smile graciously, not punch the air.

He rubbed his bony hands. 'So. Essentially, our goal is a complete overhaul of library security. Initially, what we require is a far-reaching and thorough report into how things stand. And book retrieval. Volumes have, it's clear, gone missing.'

'Have you tried advertising a book recall, no questions asked?'

'Yes, I'm considering an amnesty,' he said, as if he'd rather boil the culprits in oil. 'With all due respect to my honoured predecessor, you *cannot* run an historic library like a gentlemen's club!' he burst out. 'Nobody's done a stock check for generations. We have literally *thousands* of irreplaceable books and manuscripts! Many of which are currently propping open student windows, for all I know! Some of the realm's earliest charters are housed in the underground Stacks! Furthermore—'

'Er, I do know all this, Doctor,' she pointed out.

'Of course you do. Forgive me.' He strode in angry silence until he'd composed himself. 'So as I indicated, what I need is a professional assessment of the scale of the security problem. It's been *woefully* neglected! Our task is complicated by the fact that there are preservation orders on the ancient stained glass charms. And all the external grotesques are Grade 1 listed statuary. But I daresay your associate has all the current heritage legislation at his or her fingertips?'

'Oh, absolutely,' lied Anabara.

'Excellent. And I took the liberty of assuring Chapter that your associates had all the relevant clearance with Border Control...?' A delicate Galen pause. 'The paperwork...?'

'Not a problem!' Did Thwyn even have a Freeman Pass? Oh Lord, how much was a decent forgery going to set her back?

They turned the next corner and started along the north side. 'Do you have any questions?'

'Yes. To be honest, I'm surprised you've asked me, not Carramans.'

'Carramans, yes. That option was indeed discussed. However, Chapter felt strongly that it behooves us to support and encourage new business enterprises in Larridy wherever possible.'

Something wasn't ringing true here. They turned the last corner and headed back towards the entrance of the Round Room.

'Thank you for responding so promptly, Ms Nolio.'

'Well, the messenger said you wanted me to come quick-quick.'

He pursed his lips. 'Needless to say, I made no such remark. They are good-hearted folk, if a trifle forthright, the Zaarzuks. I trust he did not offend you.'

'Zaarzuk!' squawked Anabara. 'He's a *Zaarzuk?*'

'Why yes.' The scholasticus eyed her in surprise. 'We rejoice in ethnic diversity here in the Minstery. And the Zaarzuk people are, as you know, devout followers of The Way. Despite the many frivolous superstitions that adhere to their reputation.'

Anabara got a grip on herself. 'Yes, yes, of course. It's just— He's had his head shaved, *that's* it. You normally look for the long blond hair, don't you? And the eye make-up, ha ha!'

The scholasticus flinched like one who had never in his life looked for long blond hair and eye make-up in another man.

'But obviously I have nothing *against* them.' Would you listen to yourself! Next you'll be saying, *Some of my best friends are Offcomers.* 'So, um,' she concluded.

'I *believe* it is a stylised form of war paint. Not...' The scholasticus cleared his throat. 'Come, let us have the

13

contract drawn up and signed. I took the precaution of asking the scrivener to wait in my study. In case you were at leisure immediately. But there is no hurry.'

Quick-quick. 'My leisure is entirely at your disposal, Dr Scholasticus,' she replied, like a nicely brought up Galen girl.

But I still wonder what you're not telling me, she thought.

Her first challenge was to escape without being buried alive under a slagheap of advice from her Galen relatives. Fortunately there were many secret ways off the Mount. Ledges and tunnels, forgotten snickets, where the gargoyles were so befuddled by erosion you could outwit them.

And, of course, there were the rooftops, where non-Gulls couldn't follow her. Yes, *technically*, flying was prohibited in residential areas, but Anabara only kept that rule when it suited her. And she'd lied to the Zaarzuk: it wasn't really hard work. Not if you were small and light. No worse than running down hill with the wind behind you. Nothing beat that rush. Like diving upward into an airy sea. Rooftops, here we come! Ah, she couldn't believe how well the day was shaping up after that hideous start! Thank you, thank you, St Pel!

Her feet soon found the familiar path, over the grain barn roof. A crumbled grotesque—perhaps it had once been a dragon man?—roused itself to cast a half-hearted block. I'm the Patriarch's niece, she murmured. On Minstery business for the scholasticus. The barrier melted as the dragon man drowsed back asleep. She kissed his sandstone head. Poor old thing, *woefully* neglected, weathered away by the salt air. A thousand years ago not even a gnat would have got past him.

She fluttered down into the alley below and began walking instead. Couldn't risk another flying charge. Her counsel had informed her that unless she settled his bill, he was going to let her rot in the cells the next time she got nicked. But the bastard could wait a bit longer. It went against the grain to pay him, even now she had the money. The alley brought her out eventually into Palatine Square. Junior lawyers flitted on errands through narrow arches between law court and chambers. She skirted the central fountain. Leaves dropped like dead birds from the Candacian plane trees all around.

On the far side stood the black marble pillars of Carraman & Carraman (*For all Your Investigation and Security Needs*). She cupped her hands and peered through the smoked glass. They were going to be livid when they heard she'd got the library job. The occupant of the nearest desk glanced up and gave her the fig. She wagged a finger and mouthed, *I know your mum, Toby Buttery!* He flounced and turned his back on her.

As she hurried on, doubts began to niggle. Why on earth *had* the scholasticus employed her? Because her uncle was the Patriarch? Or was it just newcomer's ignorance? Everyone around here knew that Carramans always handled all the big security contracts in Larridy. They had at least half a dozen highbred Fairies on their pay roll; fire tattoos fore and aft, rapier-sharp psychic skills. She'd kill for just one partner like that. Thwyn was a low-bred, a grumpy old bugger who struggled to cast a simple journeyman charm. But hey. She shook off her anxiety. Surveying the library security—how hard could that be?

A moment later she turned off Skuller into a reeking back alley. Shacks made from scavenged wood and sacking clung to the backs of grander tenements and huddled like tramps under any arch or portico. This was where the blood from the old shambles used to run. Experience had taught her to breathe through her mouth here. The stench of dyers' piss-buckets made your eyes water. And the dog-turd collectors stored their wares in the Slackey, too, before hauling them out to the tanneries.

She squeezed through a group of Tressy rag-pickers. They followed her with their pale grey eyes. Eesh. You weren't supposed to say it, but white-skinned folk always looked to her like plants that had grown under a slab. Pallid and worm-like. Dogs slunk about. Lord, how she hated them. Loathed the little ones, feared the big ones. Couldn't even stand the beloved Gull otter hounds. Tried to hide it, of course.

She came to Thwyn's shack. Something was wrong, she knew it. She pulled aside the tattered sack that served as a door. No blocking charm. The single room had been stripped bare.

And already taken over by a new occupant. A Tressy riverman rose from a low stool on the mud floor. On a rag-pile in the corner, like a blanched pig carcass, lolled a younger man. She could smell fresh-dug earth. And rancid sweat. The elder came and stood in the entrance, staking his claim. Behind her the Tressy women gathered silently.

'Good morning.' Anabara addressed him in Commons. 'Where's the Fairy Thwyn?'

'Gone,' said the man. 'Is gone to Fayland.' He spat.

'Gone home!' Anabara's hand flew to her mouth. No! 'What, permanently?'

The man shrugged. 'He no say. I no ask.'

'When?' Maybe she could still catch him. What date was half-year Crossing-time? 'When did he leave?'

'A week.' He pointed up at the sky. 'New moon.'

Shit! She'd missed him. What the hell was she going to do now? 'He can't have just gone! Why didn't he warn me?'

The women murmured. 'You trouble?' one asked.

'Big trouble,' said Anabara. 'I desperately needed him for a job. There aren't any other Fairies round here, are there?' She brought out a coin.

'Many Fays,' said the women, reaching. 'Fay slaves. They come—'

The man yelled something in Tressy and drove them off like a herd of cows. The women melted into doorways. Anabara pocketed her coin again.

'We are clean people. We no like them kind,' the man told Anabara. 'Dirty Fays. You need human worker, pretty lady. My son, very hard worker. You like?' The son slid over to the door, grinned, toothless.

'No, I need a charm-worker.' Her neck hair began to crawl. 'Who's selling slaves round here?'

The father waggled his head. 'I know nothing about no slaves.'

'Yeah, I bet you don't.'

He bowed and smiled, spreading his hands. 'Is no slaving round here. Bad trade. Very bad. Pretty lady, have a nice day, please. If we see your Fay, we tell him you looking.'

She turned and walked back out of the filth towards the slick commercial district less than fifty yards away. Cheek by jowl. Two sides of the same Larridy coin. Behind her she heard jeering laughter.

CHAPTER THREE

Disaster! Her heart raced as though a cage door had just clanged shut. Thwyn had vanished and now she was trapped in a job she couldn't do. She'd promised the scholasticus she'd be back tomorrow afternoon with her assistant to start work. Where the hell was she going to find another charm-worker at this kind of notice?

Her hand closed round the leather pouch of gilders in her pocket. Take it back. Go straight back up to the library *now*, and tell him that you can't fulfil the contract! But her feet carried on taking her down Skuller towards her house. I'm not giving up yet, she thought. This was make-or-break for her business. Calm down. Think. She still had a bit of time. If she hadn't come up with a solution by tomorrow afternoon, then she'd go back, explain what had happened and pull out. That left her a whole day to find a solution.

Bright sky overhead still, but it felt like the sun had gone in. A burst of rage at Thwyn. The bugger, taking off like that! There was a chance—a very slim chance—some nomad freelancer had come over from the Mainland Fairy tribes, looking for work in Larridy. There might even be another illegal alien who had eluded Border Control, but that was an even longer shot. She could ask around at the docks. But apart from that, nothing.

Nothing except slaves.

Anabara shuddered as she rounded the last bend of Skuller. Slavery. A shameful episode supposedly confined to the pages of history books a hundred years ago, when the Fairy Peoples stopped transporting their criminals to the Human Realm. Everyone knew slaving still went on, though. Terrible business, they said, but what can you do? Like trafficking was the weather and people were powerless in the face of it!

She was back at her house. The charm was jiggered again. She coaxed and pleaded till it till it let her in. Thwyn's workmanship. He was a useless fecker, but what in hell was she going to do without him? She heard the Tressy woman's words again: *Many Fay slaves.* Almost certainly true, but Anabara had never seen a slave. There weren't any in Larridy. She guessed they were sold on and moved out swiftly to the huge anonymous Mainland cities. That was why nice Larridy people were able to act as though the problem didn't exist.

As she cut herself some rye bread and a hunk of cheese, a daydream started to form in her mind. Like the endless daydreams she'd spun as a child, in the chapel built to her parents' memory. She used to sit gazing up at the larger-than-life frescos, and tell them tales of her exploits. The dragons she'd slain, the giants she'd defeated. A hundred and one fantasies of living up to her heroic parents, murdered in the cause of Fairy rights.

This was just another one of those daydreams, she knew that. Because realistically she was never going to buy a slave from some Tressy scumbag, then free him or her to work on an equal footing, was she? Or better still, *doublecross* some scumbag by turning informer, thereby bringing down the whole evil system of slaving and winning worldwide fame and renown! She rolled her eyes. Trying to atone for her passivity last night. Besides, who'd be dumb enough to admit that they owned a trafficked Fairy? Nobody knew nothing about no slaves.

Except the Guard Anti-Trafficking Unit, of course. Charlie Rondo might talk to her. He was a fellow Gull, after all. Or she could sniff around the docks. Slaves had to be shipped and traded somewhere, didn't they? Two birds with one stone: tonight she'd try and pick up some whispers about slaving while she was asking around for an itinerant charm-worker.

In the meantime she had an afternoon to fill. The filing? She got a sudden vivid image of cousin Linna, wagging a finger in her face like an old Gullmother. What if Linna really did come in from the Gull village like she kept threatening, and checked up on her book-keeping? All right, all right. I'll do it. Soon. Tomorrow morning. First thing. But right now, I'm off to the Salt Flats for some flying practice. I need to blow the Slackey out of my hair. She swiftly deposited the cash and the contract in her floor safe and fled.

It was low tide. Gull shepherds on stilts strode like rickety giants along the horizon as they grazed the saltings sheep. The river had dwindled to a mercury ribbon. Mud-larks were scavenging for metal and ancient artifacts. She took a deep breath. Already her soul had begun to unclench. This was where she'd spent the other half of her childhood. From far away came the eerie wail of a great Galen diver. A gust hissed in the ashy reed-heads. Ssssh! She broke into a run. The wind surged behind her, nudging her up off her feet, and she was airborne at last.

Ah, if only she'd been alive when all this was water, before they built the causeway. In a single generation the bay had silted up and the sea vanished. Linking Larridy to the Mainland? Madness. Was there ever a more stubborn island race? A hundred years on and Larridians still went: Offcomer? Chuck a fish-head at him. Huh, forgetting we were all Offcomers ourselves, once upon a time.

High, higher she mounted, until Larridy was a toy city and the flats just a child's drawing, with a ruler-straight causeway, model boats on doodled waterways, and the blobs of Gull villages, marching out west to the distant sea.

Her evening shaped up as she'd expected. A week's rent money gone on drinks for arseholes in the roughest dockside bars in Larridy. Her wealthy thrill-seeking student act was convincing enough to get them talking: trading post out west down river, that was your best option if you wanted a Fay. As to when, ooh, couldn't tell you. Not like they advertise, is it? Best ask around the Tressy rivermen. By one in the morning she reckoned she was done. Too many wide-eyed Offcomer questions and people would start wondering. Mark her down as a snitch. And there was always a chance someone would recognise her, even this far off her patch.

She began the long walk home. Too tired to fly tonight. The wind had dropped. Now and then a breeze drew a faint chord from the flutes. The streets were still lit, but the lamps were fading, their store of sunlight almost spent. Chairmen carried their last fares home. No horses in Larridy, not since they were banned during the Palatinate Wars. Only Zaarzuk chieftains on state visits were granted Freedom to Ride.

Zaarzuks. Lord, that flashing smile, the whispered *Kiss me*. Cocky bastard. Bet he knows what he's doing, though. Unlike the clumsy tongue-tied Gull boys she'd fought off. Literally. What if she'd let him kiss her? Invited him in…?

Tscha! Stop that.

Focus. She still had a charm-worker to find. *Best ask around the Tressy rivermen.* What she'd learned tonight confirmed her suspicions. Some of those big Tressy sailing barges were carrying more than grain in their holds. If she'd found that out in a single evening, the Guard definitely knew about it. Probably had undercover agents in place. She'd have to ask Charlie Rondo.

Or else she'd pole a punt down river some night soon and see if she could locate the trading post. Her heart lurched at the idea. Was it a risk worth running? If only she had a contact who worked the barges.

She rounded the last bend. Stopped short. A man. Waiting on her doorstep. Tall. For a second she thought it was the Zaarzuk. But then the figure shifted and light fell across his face. Tattooed forehead. Long black hair. War feathers. It was a Gull. She started towards him. A long-lost relative from a distant village, probably. But my God, he was handsome. He stood under the last glow of her daylamp like one of the ancient warrior gods come back. Perhaps the Saint was having a second go at answering her prayer?

'Hey, handsome,' she called in Gull.

'Hey, Nan!' He stepped forward. 'Remember me? It's Loxoto. Linna sent me.'

It was the smile she recognised. The sweet shy smile. '*Loxi*!? Oh my God! What are you doing here? Thought you were off at sea!'

'Nah, packed all that in, me. Want to work in Larridy.'

She couldn't stop gawping. *This* was Loxi the bed-wetter? The one we called a mollygull to make him cry? 'Look at you, man. Muscles! All grown up!'

He endured her raptures well, along with the hair tugging and thumping that passed for a Gull greeting. It ended with a hug from him that lifted her clean off her feet.

'Well, come on in!'

Loxi stooped under the low doorway. He looked round him. 'Hey—hull timbers! And this here's a main mast.' He slapped the central wooden upright. 'Man, doesn't it freak you out, living in a wrecker-house?'

'Not really.'

'Who was that Fairy—the one leaving when I arrived?'

Leaving my *house*? She went cold. Another fugitive? Or could it have been Thwyn, still in the Human Realm after all? 'Little bandy bloke?'

He shook his head. 'Female. High bred: saw the fire tatts.'

'What—? No!'

Carramans!

She darted to the cupboard under the stairs. Her chaotic files had been pulled from the shelves and dumped on the floor. Papers tossed and strewn. She shot to the hearth and pulled back the rug to check her floor safe. The charm was sprung. The Fairy hadn't even bothered to cover her tracks. The money was still there, so was the Minstery contract, but the tamper seals were all broken.

The Fairy had read it. Scanned all her secret files. Seen the unpaid bills. The chaos. And she'd gone back to Carraman with a facsimile of everything stored in her cold machine-like brain.

CHAPTER FOUR

L oxi picked up the contract and whistled. 'Woo. Minstery work? Doing all right for yourself, little cousin.'

'Yeah—finally I'm doing so well that Carraman sends his Fairy to bust into my house and see what I'm up to.' She was trembling. How had they found out so fast? She'd told nobody. Someone must be running their gob up on the Mount. Who? And what else did they know—that Thwyn had vanished? That she was basically stuffed?

'What's going on, Nan?' asked Loxi. 'You in trouble? The Gullmothers say you're bankrupt.'

'I'm bloody not!' God, this was a nightmare. What if a rumour of her insolvency reached the scholasticus as well?

'Linna says to tell you you've got to hire me on, eh, so I can do the books.'

'Yeah, well Linna left.' She replaced the contract and slammed the safe. 'So Linna doesn't get a vote any more, does she?' There was a pause. That had come out more bitter than she'd intended.

'Hey, don't be like that, you.' He rubbed her arm. 'She loves Matteo, you know that. She had to leave. Girls all get married in the end, eh.'

'Huh. Not this girl.' With a murmur re-activated the charm. 'And how come the matchmakers aren't on your case?'

He grinned. 'They are. I'm running away. Come on, you. Tell me what's happening. I can see you're worried.'

Should she tell him? Or was that weak? Like she was still was looking round for a man to sort it all out for her?

'C'mon,' he said. 'Give me a job, I'll do it. Anything you ask.'

'You don't know what I'm going to ask yet.'

'It sure as shit won't be the worst I've had to do.'

Suddenly, there he was—the little boy, trembling inside the man. Something cold clutched at her. 'What happened to you on the boats, Loxi?'

But the glimpse was gone. 'It was fine. Just boring. Want to work in the city, me. Aw, give us a job, Nan.' He was starting to wheedle now. Work the eyelashes. Tug her sleeve.

'Stop that!' But the boy had always been impossible to say no to.

'Aw, please? G'wan. I'll do your filing.' He nodded at the cupboard under the stairs. 'Sort that crap out. Got a good head for figures, me. Linna says—'

'God!' she snapped. 'All right. Month's trial period. And I'm the boss.'

Sudden glimmer of hope: she'd take him up to the library tomorrow and say he was her assistant. Fob the scholasticus off for a bit longer while she tried to track down a charm-worker.

Loxi had gone off to his hostel. Anabara lay in her bunk unable to sleep. The moon was setting. She watched it slide across her porthole window, and thought again about that pale pointed face, heard the scratch of nails down her tiles. Maybe this ship-house did freak her out. Sometimes as she drifted asleep the wooden walls of her room seemed to creak and roll on a remembered sea and she'd jerk awake thinking she'd heard the screams of drowning sailors. What if this ship had once carried a cargo of Fairies in her hold? Stowed among the grain sacks, in iron cages no bigger than barrels. Like the slave Loxi had stumbled across.

'My folks sent me away to make a man of me,' he'd burst out. 'And look! I come home a bigger sissy than ever. Nan, I see his eyes in the dark, watching. I know he's coming for me.'

'Loxi, even if he escapes, there's no way he's coming back looking for some insignificant Gull deckhand. And he *won't* escape. The irons will see to that. Hey. It's over Loxi. You're a good person.'

'Aw shit. See? Still a crybaby.' His smudged the tears away. 'I love you, Nan. You were always kind to me.'

She hooted. 'I used to tie you up and play human sacrifices with you!'

'Yeah, but at least you let me play.'

The games we played. God, I was a monster. If he loves me, he must have forgotten. It was clear to her, suddenly, just how tough his childhood must have been. No place for sensitive boy in a world of otter hunting and bare knuckle boxing. Well, she'd be kind to him this time round. He had vowed he'd do anything, but after witnessing him in that state she hadn't mentioned what she was planning. No, if she was going off a-hunting for Fairies, she was going to do it by herself. He'd helped enough without realising: she knew now when and where the next slave auction would be held.

And in any case, there were some things a girl could do better on her own. Better than any man. I can do this, she told herself. I can, I can.

Silence.

Tick, tick, said the clock on the study mantelpiece. Ten past two.

The scholasticus rubbed his bony hands together. His gaze skimmed Loxi, then fled back to his book shelves. 'I daresay Ms Nolio has outlined our situation here?' he remarked to a volume of Early Candacian Love Songs.

For God's sake. It was like she'd brought a well-behaved warhorse into the Precincts and announced it would be assisting in her investigation.

'Yeah,' said Loxi.

'Splendid.' The scholasticus plucked a parchment from his desk. 'Now, I have here a list of alumni still living in Larridy who might have honoured themselves with borrowing rights. I wondered if, perhaps, Mr Laitolo might...? Unless...?'

Trying to decide: was it racist to ask if the savage could read? Anabara took the parchment and handed it to Loxi. 'Off you go. Ask them if they've got any overdue library books.'

The scholasticus wrung his hands and twitched.

'Don't worry, he can read,' Anabara reassured him once Loxi had gone. 'And he doesn't normally bite people's ears off unless they insult his ancestors, ha ha!' There was a pause. Anabara made a note not to attempt humour with the scholasticus again.

'Am I correct in assuming you are sub-contracting this work to Mr Laitolo?' he asked. 'That is to say, you are not expecting the library to, ah...?'

'His wages will be paid by my company, yes.' God, what a flea-skinner. 'By the way, I'm still sorting some visa issues regarding my new Fairy associate. Bureaucratic cock-up. You know what Border Control are like.'

He inclined his head.

Crap. He doesn't believe me. 'Right. Um, I'll just get up on to the library roof, then, and er, do a preliminary check on external security.'

She'd been up here often as a child. Many an illegal hooley match round the hallowed chimney pots with assorted hardscrabble Gull cousins. And then there was that scorching summer day when the lead burned her bare feet and she and Linna had tied Loxi to the lightning conductor as storm clouds boiled up on the horizon...

She went round the huge cupola from mullion to mullion. The windows housed squadrons of saints and angels who—theoretically—guarded the library below. Fierce eyes swiveled to watch her progress along the parapet. Did they recognise her, the evil minx who tortured weeping little boys? They had been designed as free-walking figures, able to leave their frames and fight to defend the library. But after centuries of neglect they had seized up.

Anabara's conscience suddenly attacked her. What was she playing at, pretending she knew about restoration work? Even if Thwyn hadn't skedaddled, he'd never have had the technical knowledge to write a proper report.

She gazed out in despair. From up here you could just see the sea, a bright band on the western horizon. Somewhere over there towards the Larrus delta was where she'd be heading tomorrow night, relying on her childhood river craft. Looking for the slave auction. Her heart gave a lurch. She was mad even to think of it! Even if by some miracle she found the auction and sweet-talked the Tressy dealers into selling her a slave, where would that get her? Heritage work like this required a team of skilled Fairy artisans. Instead, she'd be down several hundred gilders, and saddled with some lummox too thick to charm the lid on a biscuit barrel.

Except... Except... This was her last chance to rescue her business. And maybe there was something deeper going on as well. She took a deep breath. I'm going to try, she decided. It's what my parents would have done. For once I'll be doing something worthy of them, not just standing by while Border Control forcibly repatriates desperate refugees. I know I can't bring down the whole evil system of slaving, but I can make a difference to one life. I can free one slave. *Or die trying*—was she brave enough for that?

Anabara got to her feet before her resolve could waver. She glided down from one roof level to the next, until she was above a small courtyard.

Hah, look at that—the Zaarzuk, pacing with his head in a book! Ancient Galen grammar, she was betting. The pale spiral of scalp showed in the blond stubble. He was in novice robes now. Barefoot.

She sprang down, startling him. 'Good day, mister. Still sulking?'

He drew himself up. 'A Zaarzuk does not sulk! He broods, dark and dangerous. While he whets his scimitar and plans revenge!'

'So it's true—you really are a Zaarzuk?'

'Truly, I am a Zaarzuk. Ah! She smiles at last. This pleases you?' He grinned and tucked the grammar into his rope girdle. 'You think naughty-naughty things?'

'I do not!' She tried, but he was impossible to scowl at. 'It's just your reputation, that's all.'

'The filthy Zaarzuks, yes?' His big laugh rang out. 'Come, tell me what people say.'

That you kiss with your tongues. That you pierce your parts with gold rings to enhance a girl's pleasure. 'Oh, that you're liars and thieves and braggarts, that you sleep on the stable floor with your horses. That you treat your dogs better than your women.'

'Not so! These are lies.'

'And when I was a little girl the Gullmothers told us if we got out of bed after lights out, the horsemen would get us.'

'Ah yes. We do this,' he agreed. 'If we catch bad girls in the dark, it is our duty to take them back to bed.'

'Na, ah.' She laughed and shook her head. 'My cousin Linna and I were forever trying it. You never came.'

'We were remiss!' He smote his chest. 'What can I say? Try it tonight and I will be there.'

'You,' she stabbed a finger at him, 'are supposed to be celibate, mister.'

He caught her hand. 'But what of my honour? I, Tadzar Dal Ramek, would die a thousand deaths sooner than shirk my Zaarzuk duty! Truly.' His other hand slid round her waist, gathered her close. He put his lips to her ear and murmured, 'Three years! This is too long to keep my poor stallion penned in his stable.'

Anabara just had time for a jolt of shock, when a silent figure appeared.

The Zaarzuk sprang back. His book tumbled to the floor. 'Master!' He bowed and retrieved his grammar. 'I was explaining Ms Nolio some aspects of the Zaarzuk culture.'

The Master of Novices regarded him steadily, till the Zaarzuk lowered his gaze.

'The Patriarch wishes to see you,' said the Master. 'Not you, brother. The Patriarch wishes to see his niece.'

At this, the Zaarzuk's eyes widened. He let fly some guttural exclamation.

30

Crack! went the Master's staff on the flagstones. 'Dal Ramek, this is a holy place. Seek pardon for sullying it.'

The Zaarzuk dropped and did obeisance, palms and forehead on the stone, arse in the air. And there he would have to remain—a tempting target for any passing student boot—till the Master saw fit to release him, or the next service bell rang.

'Come, Ms Nolio. I will accompany you.' He led her out of the courtyard.

She glanced back at the Zaarzuk. 'You can't just leave him there!'

He raised a Galen eyebrow. 'Ms Nolio, do I tell you how to run your business?'

'Only all the time!'

When they'd safely rounded the corner he grinned and broke into Gull: 'Well, that's what big brothers are for, eh.'

'Yanni, Yanni!' She flung herself into his arms. Nobody could hug like Yannick. 'So go on—who is he? Why's he a novice, not an ordinary student?'

'You know I can't discuss him with you.' Yanni hesitated. 'But as your big brother, I'd warn you to be careful. If I didn't know you'd immediately treat it as a challenge, that is,' he added with another smile.

'Fine. I'll be careful. Anyway, it was nothing.' Stop blushing.

He hesitated again. 'Ana, look, my task is to turn scholars into warriors, and warriors into scholars. Not all my charge find their path equally smooth, that's all.'

'And he's going to find it tough, you mean?'

But he wouldn't answer. Just hugged her tight again. They walked arm-in-arm down the stone walkway towards the Patriarch's quarters in the old palace.

CHAPTER FIVE

'Uncle Téador!' She smiled up into his beloved face. The Patriarch was a typical lean dark-skinned Galen, like the scholasticus. 'How was the trip?'

'Productive, I think.' He bent to kiss her forehead. 'Let's sit, and I will show you my new treasure.'

This was their ritual each time he returned from a long state visit. One day she'd grow out of it. Maybe when she was ninety. His apartment was a cavernous museum of a place. Against the walls stood cabinets full of curious gifts from around the globe—treasures from earlier journeys. They sat on the fur hearth rug. A hundred miniature silver bears had died for this particular Palatine whim. Drowned in barrels so their precious pelts weren't damaged.

'Hey, guess what?' she said. 'I landed the library security contract.' He nodded. Yes, of course the Patriarch knew that. He knew everything. She teetered on the brink of blurting out her woes. But he had enough to worry about, fundamentalists on one hand, atheists on the other. Instead she said: 'Just to alert you, the new scholasticus is considering an overdue library book amnesty.'

The Patriarch sat very still. He did not permit his eyes to swivel to his shelves.

'Now's your chance to sneak them all back, uncle,' she whispered.

'How well you know me!' He laughed and clapped his hands. 'And now, the treasure. You'll like this.' From the pocket of his robes he drew what looked like a small slab of dark glass. 'The latest toy from Galencia University.'

'What is it?'

'A writing tablet.' He slid a small white-steel pen from a slot in the side. 'If you write a message, then your words will appear on another tablet, many miles away.'

'You're kidding!'

'Not at all. One day everyone will have one of these, apparently. They are already very popular. The prototypes keep going astray, much to the frustration of the scholars. Who knows what secret networks already exist? Watch.'

He traced the pen across the glass. Letters appeared as if below the surface. *From Téador Yannick IX, to Professor Eldondor, greetings.* They slowly faded. And then—impossible!—a reply wrote itself: *Greetings, my Lord Patriarch. I trust your journey home was pleasant?*

'What? No way!' Her flesh crawled. 'Is it charmed? How does it work?'

'Well now, that's something for your cousin Rodania to answer. The scholars kindly explained to me—in layman's language—that it exploits the principles of theoretical numerology that underlie Fairy psycho-mechanics, and hence the universe itself.'

'Huh. Maths. Everything's maths, isn't it?' Thinking: Rodania, everything's Rodania. But that would grieve him.

'Yes. Maths explains all. Though so far they haven't said why it does. So I'm not out of a job yet. Let me compose a farewell, and then you may tell me your news.' He wrote swiftly on the tablet, then put it away again in his pocket. 'Now, how are you? You seem troubled, my dear, despite this good fortune with the library work.'

'My stupid Fairy associate's vanished, so I can't fulfil the contract!' She pressed her hand to her mouth. 'Sorry. I'm still all churned up. The night before last Border Control came after a Fairy fugitive who was hiding in my back yard. I know they have a job to do, but it was all so… brutal.' She felt herself wobbling on the edge of tears. 'It was only a *child*, uncle.'

He laid a hand on her arm, but said nothing. Just waited. He knew there was more. She drew a breath and blurted: 'I've *got* to do something! Tomorrow night I'm going to punt down river to the delta island. To a slave auction. I'm going to buy a Fairy slave and free them to work for me.'

There, she sounded exactly like her six year old self, boasting of dragon-slaying again! But his silence clothed the preposterous claim with truth: she really *was* going to attempt this.

He took both her hands in his. 'Dearest, dearest dear. I'm a selfish old man and I don't want to lose you. This is a mad and reckless quest. But I sense you must attempt it. May the Lord of Light guide you.'

'I'll be careful, uncle.' Please tell me not to go. Forbid it, make me promise.

He kissed her forehead again. 'I have something for you. It was your mother's. I dreamt about it last night, so perhaps this is the time.' He got to his feet.

She watched as he crossed the room and opened a drawer in the magnificent Palatine desk. His lips moved, unlocking a charm. Something precious then. A flash of silver. He shut the drawer and came and sat again.

'Here.'

From the chain swung a single dark green gem the size of a walnut. Like a clot, ugly. Carved, or natural? She turned it this way and that, then suddenly, it was a curled up figure. 'Woo! It kind of jumped into focus. What is it supposed to be? A Fairy?'

'Yes. Very ancient, or that's my feeling. What do you make of it?'

She shook her head. 'Is it a good thing?'

'Hmm. It doesn't feel evil. Powerful perhaps, but not evil. It's yours to look after. See what you make of it. Or what it wants to do.'

She shivered. 'You think it has a will?'

'Well, most ancient Fairy artifacts have something of the soul embedded in them, don't they?'

'Where did Mum get it?'

'She was given it, that's all I know.'

'Did she wear it?'

'Yes. Two Fairy messengers brought it when they came with the news. Now, this is something I have never spoken of to anyone else, Anabara: they also brought me a *paran*. A narrow ceremonial blade made of incandescent white-steel. Something I'd heard of, but prayed never to see. It hurt my eyes just to look at it. Assassins wield them—the pure-bred fire lords. You've seen Fairy fire markings? Well, these creatures are all fire.'

'Why did they bring it? Were they assassins?' To her dismay a tear trickled down his lined cheek. 'Uncle!'

'No, they were just ordinary folk from the clan bound to protect your parents. They were expecting me to kill them. Lots were drawn and these two were chosen.' He wiped his eyes. 'I sent them back home with their *paran*. Of course I did. Their death wasn't going to bring your dear parents back. But from the Fairy perspective there is still a double blood debt. They have no grasp of forgiveness. If it takes a thousand generations they will carry on trying to honour it.'

Outside the big Minstery bell began to toll. Midday Prayers. They got to their feet. Her uncle fastened the chain round her neck. She felt his fingers tremble.

'Uncle, will it be… all right?' She wasn't sure what she meant. Everything, perhaps.

The bell tolled. Tolled again. The stone lay cold against her breastbone.

'Yes.'

'You really believe that?'

He was silent so long she wondered if silence was his answer. But then, as if a single feather had drifted down on to the scales, he said again, 'Yes.'

This was her comfort in the dark: that someone knew where she was. Someone was praying for her.

She traveled by little tributaries and Gull-made ditches, heading towards the river island in the last big bend before the waters fanned out into the delta. To anyone but a Gull there were few landmarks out there in the salt flats: the island was the only reliable one. Behind her the racket of Larridy dwindled, though the occasional drunken shout still scarred the night. Groom parties, brawling locals, ensuring the Guard was over-stretched and that no patrol would be out here in the wastes at market time.

Downstream she punted, with no more sound than a jumping fish. On each side there lay the endless salt furze, and every so often the dark shape of a dragon tree. The saltings sheep had all been folded hours ago. Dog kelp thick as eels tangled her pole. God, it was harder work than she remembered. Her arms ached. More than once her feet slid and her heart lurched. Blisters formed on her palms. The brine got in, smarted. Before long she began to fear she hadn't left herself enough time. Not a breath of wind. The rushes stood motionless. Just the trickle of water, the suck of pole in mud, and her ragged breathing.

She'd joined the river Larrus now—surely she must be close. Or had she forgotten how far it was? What if the riverscape had changed since she played down here as a child? What if, after all this, she missed the market? Well, that would be her answer: it was not meant to be.

But just as she was allowing herself to think *Oh well*—a noise.

Voices in the distance. Or one voice, chanting. The auctioneer? Round the next bend she caught a glow on the horizon, and mast tops. Her heart began to race. Yes, she recognised it now—the island was after the next bend. She let the punt drift on the current for the last quarter of a mile, steering with the pole. Minutes passed. The chanting rose to a climax. Stopped. Then came a general hubbub. Shouts. The noise of iron scraping on wood. Was it over? Her knees shook. She steered to the bank, wedged the pole in, got off and squatted, head down, waiting for the sickness to pass.

She stood up. A huge old dragon tree reared above her. The perfect vantage point. One bound and she'd be up there. Go on. Do it. You'll be able to see everything from up there. Yes, but I'll be visible too. Heart and mind were a clamour of fear. She called up her brother's training. Calm. Focus. The eye of the archer, nothing but you and the target. Nothing else, just you and the target. Her pulse slowed, the rushing in her ears stopped.

Calm.

In that split second she heard him. His blow went wide, and she was off through the furze like a fox. He came after her. Two of them now. Crashing. Yelling. Ha, she could out-run these oafs.

But they were driving her ahead of them. Too late she realised it. Next moment she burst through the low cover into the open. A ring of torches. Men loading a barge. Cages.

Hands grabbed her. A rag was flung over her head, pulled tight. She clawed at it, at the hands. Useless. Save your energy. They dragged her stumbling through the shrubby roots. A clearing. Sandy underfoot. The rag was ripped off.

Tressy rivermen standing round a brazier. They stared. Yabbered in Tressy. What is this? A spy? Yabber yabber.

'Who's in charge here?' she demanded. Silence. 'Get your filthy hands off me! I want to know who's in charge!'

A tall pale man stepped forward. He had blank fish eyes. Eyes like moonstone marbles. Like the Boagle-man. Pelago! Was he blind? No, he was staring right at her.

'I am in charge. Why are you here, demy?' His voice was silky soft.

'Why do you think? I wish to purchase a slave.'

There was an astounded laugh from the rabble, then silence. The man had a hand raised.

'The lady wishes to purchase a slave,' he said. 'Does the lady have money?'

Hands groped. She smacked at them. A gesture from the leader, and the hands retreated. He had the eyes of something that fed on cruelty. Saint Pelago aid me!

She put up her chin. 'Assuredly, I have money. One does not go to market penniless.'

Laughter again.

Was this the way to play it? Like grandmama terrorising shopkeepers? 'Well? Speak up! Have you the goods, riverman, or are you wasting my time?'

The man smiled. 'You are a brave little lady, to come here all alone.'

'Who says I'm alone?'

They consulted in Tressy. 'My men say you came alone, in a Gull boat. The lookout saw you half a league off. Yes, you are all alone, my lady.'

'But not unprotected.' Oh dear God, protect me.

More crowing. The man raised a hand. Silence.

'You have powerful friends, perhaps, who know where you are?'

'Do you think I'm a fool? Of course my family knows where I am. Come! My patience is wearing thin. Show me your goods, or detain me no longer.' It was slipping from her. Her bluster wasn't working.

A man slunk up to the leader. Spoke in his ear. Shit, it was that slug from the Slackey. What was he saying?—she's a Guard spy, came snooping round yesterday, kill her now! She'd have to make a break for it. Fly? They might not know she could. She coiled to spring.

But a hand grabbed her arm. She turned. The slug son. He smiled his gummy smile. All around her they smiled. She could smell them, smell their thoughts: What order shall we have her in? When will my turn be? Who gets to finish her off?

I'm going to die.

A strange calm surprised her. The feather drifting down, this way, that way, on the air. And she thought: Well, even this long night will have an end. It will pass away like everything else.

The leader barked an order. A flurry. Clang of iron. Dread kicked back in. She'd fight. Die fighting. Some of them would lose their jewels tonight. Oh, pray God someone found her body. Yanni, Uncle Téador, I'm sorry.

But the leader turned to her, inclined his head in a slight bow. 'My lady, you have arrived somewhat late. Our business here is completed. All we have left is one poor specimen that no-one would buy. Normally I would not insult your intelligence by showing him to you. But perhaps your need is urgent?'

So that's what the slug was telling him: she's desperate for Fay help. Her knees almost buckled with relief. 'Very well. Bring him to me. If he is biddable, I will consider it.'

The man smiled his gentle smile. 'They are all biddable, my lady. We have seen to that.' He snapped his fingers. A slimy bundle was flung at his feet. 'Get up, Fay.'

She watched. The rags stirred. Her heart sang with horror. Hands emerged. Iron embedded in the flesh. The creature dragged itself to its knees. Raised its filthy head. Looked up at her with dead eyes.

The man kicked it. 'I said, get up.'

The Fairy got to its feet. Tall. It stood like a hollow tree. There was nothing there, no hope, no spark.

'Well?' said the man. 'A poor specimen, as I warned you, my lady.'

'Good God!' She gathered her grandmama's manner about herself. 'You have nothing else?'

He turned up his palms. 'The lady came late.'

She eyed the creature and tried to sneer. 'It looks fit for nothing!'

'It no dead yet,' hissed one. 'You feed, it wake up plenty.'

'Hmmph.' She surveyed the creature from another angle. He was motionless. Was he even breathing? 'Of what sort is he?'

'Scum.'

'Filth.'

'Filthy Fay-dog.'

The leader raised a hand. Silence. 'I will not lie to you, my lady. He's not in the best of shape. But he is hardy, of working stock. And as my compatriot observes, he will revive if you feed him. So. A good strong slave goes for a thousand gilders. What say you may take him off my hands for five?'

'Five hundred? Barefaced robbery!'

He kicked the slave who collapsed back into a heap of rags. 'No? As you will. I had hoped you might spare me an unpleasant task, my lady.' His hand wandered to a knife hilt at his belt.

Her scalp crawled. 'That, if I may say so, is your problem.' She tapped her foot, pursed her lips. 'However, as you surmise, my needs are pressing. I'll give you a hundred and fifty.'

'Four hundred.'

'Two hundred. It's all I have with me, take it or leave it.'

'Done.'

'Done—though I must be mad. The creature's at death's door.'

'He's stout enough.' The man bent, seized the slave by his hair and pulled his head back. 'Open your mouth, Fay.' Anabara flinched as he drove a stick between the creature's jaws. 'See?' He peeled back the upper lip to show the empty canine sockets. 'Freshly de-fanged. They'll grow back, but any horse doctor will pull them for a fee. We'll just de-tongue him for you, and he's all yours.'

A man approached with a pair of long-armed cutters. Another drew a red hot iron from the brazier.

'No!' cried Anabara.

They froze.

'I... He's no use to me if he can't talk!'

But the leader gave a nod. The man with the cutters seized the Fairy by the jaw.

'Stop!' screamed Anabara. 'Do that, and the deal's off. I can't run my business with a dumb slave!'

The leader stared his blank stare. The red hot iron glowed. Then he shrugged. 'As you wish, my lady. But he's a liar and he'll try to charm you. They all do.'

'That's my affair.'

The man with the cutters flung the Fairy back on to the ground. He lay without moving.

'Maybe she like tongue,' sniggered someone.

'Dirty Fay-whore,' whispered another.

'You need to sign the papers,' said the leader. 'We can't let him go intact unless you sign. The risk, my lady. We have to cover ourselves.' He produced a greasy paper in Tressy. God knew what she'd be signing.

'By all means.' She groped in her pocket. Something, anything in High Galen. There—the final demand from her counsel. It would serve. One of her business cards fluttered to the ground. Let it lie. 'If I could just ask you to sign this receipt?'

Silence.

'What's the problem? This is a business expense,' she snapped. 'Sign here. I don't want trouble with the Revenue men.'

The man stared again. What new plan was crawling across his mind? He waved away Butros's bill, pocketed his parchment. 'Come. This is a friendly transaction. We are merely helping one another out, as one business person to another. What need for paperwork among friends?'

'What indeed?' She put away the bill and drew out her leather purse. 'Here. Two hundred gilders.'

He took the pouch and tossed it to a henchman. 'Count it.'

They all stood as the gold chinked. A hump-backed moon inched above the horizon. She became aware of other sounds, shouts, oars in sockets, a ragged snatch of work shanty. They were making ready to put to. How many slaves were being shipped away tonight?

That was when she knew she was being doublecrossed. It was too easy. Here's your slave, my lady, you are free to go. She'd seen too much. Yes, they'd let her go, but some tragic accident would overtake her up river. Who knew what would happen to the poor Fairy.

Powerful friends.

'*Would* you hurry it up?' she rapped out. 'My uncle is expecting me for Last Prayers. The Patriarch does not like to be kept waiting.'

A ripple swept round the group. A superstitious hand made the threefold sign. The leader's pale eyes were on her. He beckoned the slug. They conferred. Please, please. Anabara felt sweat trickle cold between her shoulder blades. Chink, chink, chink went the gold coins. Silence. A nod from the counter.

The leader turned to her. 'The money is good. The Patriarch your uncle need not be kept waiting, my lady.' He bowed. 'I wish you joy of your slave. On your feet Fay.' He hauled the creature up by his hair, thrust his face close to Anabara. 'Look. This is your new mistress, Fay. Obey her.'

Anabara stared into the Fairy's face. His black eyes were on her throat, dead as pebbles. Then with a jerk she realised: they were locked on the amulet.

'Come, slave.' She turned to leave. 'I am already late, thanks to these buffoons.'

The man shoved, and the Fairy stumbled after her. 'You!' he summoned the slug. 'Accompany them back to her boat. A pleasure doing business with you, my lady.' He bowed.

'Likewise, I'm sure.'

'A friendly warning: he is a dirty treacherous Fay. Treat him as you would a cur, and do not make the mistake of thinking he's human.' He smiled one final lingering smile. 'I hope you enjoy your Last Prayers.'

CHAPTER SIX

The journey back was a sick blur. The Fairy fell into the punt and never moved. She battled the current. When would the pursuit would begin? She saw those moonstone eyes, the little smile: Yes, we have given her enough time to hope. After her, men!

Faster, faster! Every tendon screamed. She fought till she had nothing left, then fought on. Clawing her way past one bend, then another, eyes straining for the lights of Larridy, begging the Saint for aid, and terror, terror at her back. Last Prayers. That smile. He meant these to be her last prayers.

Another bend. One more. Then suddenly her will broke. The pole slithered from her grip and fell with a clatter across the boat. She collapsed, sobbing. I can't, I can't. Now the river would sweep them back. I tried my best. Yanni, I tried my best.

It was several moments before it registered. They were not moving. The punt had drifted sideways, but they were not going downstream. The tide. The tide had turned!

She sobbed. Made the triple sign. Raised her head. And there was the moon, riding up the heavens. The sky was crowded with stars. One dropped, silent. It left behind a brief slit of fire. The tears of St Pelago. She heard the soft trickle of water. And maybe that was a light, a faint glow in the east? Maybe they weren't far off after all.

Slowly she got back to her feet, braced her wobbling knees. Somehow got the pole upright and gripped it with her raw hands. The Fairy lay, a bundle of rags in the shadows.

'Nearly home now,' she said. 'Nearly home. It will be all right.'

There was no reply.

Larridy at last. She bumped the punt into the nearest jetty, fumbled the rope round a mooring pin. Didn't matter, bound to be some uncle's or cousin's place. There was the Gullgate. A short walk and they'd be home.

'Here we are,' she whispered. 'Are you awake?'

There was no sound, no movement. Let him not be dead. She couldn't bring herself to touch the heap of rags and find out.

'Are you all right?'

Nothing.

She should have brought food and water for it. She'd let it die. 'Wake up!' she cried desperately. 'Get up! We can't stay here!'

The rags stirred, thank God.

'Come on, we have to walk now. Quick! They might be after us.' She lurched out of the boat on to the jetty. The creature crawled after her. 'I'm sorry. I should have brought food. There's some at home. It's not far.'

Still he said nothing.

'Can you speak? Do you understand Commons?'

Nothing.

'Speak to me!'

She heard a whisper. No more than a dead leaf blown across a flagstone: 'Yes mistress.'

Of course: he was a slave. He needed commands.

'Come. Follow me.' She began to totter towards the Gullgate lights. Behind her she could hear the poor creature's dragging steps. Tears began to roll down her cheeks. She rubbed them away. As soon as she got in she'd put an end to this obscenity. Cut those manacles off.

They passed under the arch and stumbled up the Skuller Road. Nearly home. It will be all right. Nearly home. The washeries stood dark and silent. Nobody was awake. Empty laundry lines criss-crossed the sky.

There it was, there was her little house. She swallowed a sob. Never knew I was so feeble. But it was done. They'd made it home. She leant on the door. It swung open. The charm had stopped working altogether.

'Here we are. Safe now. Will you come in?'

But the slave stood like a broken post on the doorstep.

'Come in!' she ordered.

He staggered over the threshold, into the room, eyes blank.

'*Guest, you are welcome to my home*,' said Anabara in her schoolgirl Fairy.

A quiver ran through him at the sound of his Father-tongue. But there was no other response.

'Right. Well. First things first.' She blundered to the cupboard under the stairs and fetched out the long-armed bolt cutters. They looked strange to her, remote, blades still in their grease. Like an object recalled from childhood. Was it only that afternoon she'd bought them?

At the sight the Fairy fell groveling on his face. He pawed at her feet.

'Stop that!' She flinched away. 'What's wrong?'

He raised his head, slid a finger across his lips, promising silence.

'Oh, my God, I wouldn't do that!' She dropped the cutters and squatted beside him. 'I'm not going to hurt you. These are to cut off the irons. I want to free you.' Why wasn't he saying anything? Because he was not allowed, of course. 'Talk to me! Ask me your questions!'

'Who sent you?' he whispered.

'Nobody. I came of my own accord.'

'Who knows of this?'

'Just my uncle, the Patriarch. Nobody else.'

'Why would you free me?'

'Because I will never, never keep a slave, that's why. All I want is a business partner.' Damn it, she was crying again. She wiped her eyes on her sleeve. 'Look, I run an investigation company. I've got a big job on, and my Fairy colleague's disappeared. I need someone who can work charms. Security charms. Can you do that? Tell me if you can do that!'

'I can.'

It was probably a lie. Who wouldn't lie at a moment like this? 'Never mind. I'll free you anyway. And if you decide you want to work for me, you'll just have to do your best. All right? Say something!'

He swayed. 'What are your terms, mistress?'

'My terms!' Her mind shrilled in terror. Why hadn't she prepared? Even lawyers sometimes missed loopholes and ended up signing their lives away. *He is a treacherous lying Fay, don't make the mistake of thinking he's human.* Quickly! But she was lightheaded with exhaustion. I have nothing left to care with. Let him do what he likes.

She heard her mouth formulating sentences as they knelt together on the floor: 'Well, you would work for me and… and seek to promote the prosperity of my business. I'd be in charge, but you can have your own area of responsibility, which would be security… stuff. But, um, if I ask you something, you must always tell me the truth—you need to promise that.' Her mind went blank. What else? Think! 'Oh, and I'll pay you a fair wage. And you can stay here if you want. There's a spare room. Will that do?'

There was a long silence.

'Have I forgotten anything?' No answer. 'I command you to tell me at once if I've forgotten something!'

'You have forgotten to say I must not kill you,' he whispered.

'Shit!' Her heart bounced against her ribs. 'Thanks. Um, you are also to promise that you won't kill me. In fact, you must promise that you will do me no harm whatsoever.' She groped for legal-sounding phrases. 'Or cause any third party or inanimate object to kill me or do me harm. The same goes for any member of my family. You mustn't harm them or cause them to be harmed. Whatsoever. In perpetuity.' That *had* to cover it. 'What do you say? Tell me.'

Another silence. 'If you will free me,' he whispered at last, 'I will agree to your terms, mistress. A handshake will bind me to it. Except for this—you will pay me no wages until I have paid back your two hundred gilders.' He swayed again.

'No no, don't be silly. I'm more than happy to—'

He fell back unconscious.

'Oh my God, are you all right? Shit!' His eyes were open, staring at the ceiling. She should have fed him! What the

CATHERINE FOX

hell did they eat? Cream and honey, like the old tales said?
She lurched to the pantry for a jug of milk.
'Here. Drink this! Drink it!'
But his eyes had glazed. He was dying.
'No! You can't die!' She was going to have to touch him.
She slid a cringing hand under his neck and raised his head
and shoulders. A scream of horror nearly escaped her. He
weighed nothing! A sack of gull quills and dried cuttlefish.
Hollow. They really were hollow as dead flies. Her hand
waggled as she put the lip of the jug to his mouth, tilted it.
Milk rushed everywhere. Was any going in?
Suddenly he spluttered. Then reared up, seized the jug
and drank. Drank it dry. Light came back to his eyes.
'Ready?' She put the jug aside.
He wiped his mouth and stripped off his ragged shirt.
Skin and bones. When had the bastards last fed him? He
held out his right hand.
She grasped the cutters and took his hand. No! She
gagged. The flesh was already growing over the iron.
'It's going to hurt. I'm sorry.'
He made no sound as she set to work, gouging the blades
into his palm. Was there no end to this night's horrors? His
blood spilled out like liquid opals, ran down the cutter arms,
over her hands. She gagged again. Her fingers slipped. Deeper,
she'd have to cut the flesh away to get enough purchase. Her
own blistered palms started to bleed. Still he made no sound.
But then, they never did. There, she'd got a hold now. She
gripped the handles. Bore down. But she wasn't strong enough.
'Give me strength!' she sobbed. 'Please, St Pelago, please.'
Then with a dull *nick!* she was through. They wrangled
together with the spiked iron loop and at last he ripped his
hand free. The manacle fell with a clunk.

50

And still the Fairy said nothing, simply held out his left hand.

One last push, she told herself. Save us, I sound like a midwife. There was surely enough gore, enough anguish. But what was she birthing? Who even cared any more? She gripped her cutters and began again.

Nick!

The second iron dropped to the floor.

A sigh. The Fairy raised both mangled hands aloft. He gazed at them, turned them this way, that way. Blood ran down his forearms, drip, drip, from his elbows on to the floor. Suddenly he cocked his head. Listened. She heard him hiss.

Then he turned his gaze on her.

No, he wasn't human. Whatever it was looking out at her through those eyes, it was not human. But he won't kill me. We have a deal. Fairies never go back on a deal.

Except—oh dear God!—they had not yet shaken hands.

'No!'

Too late. The Fairy bared his fangs—they'd grown back! He snarled at her in Fairy: *You are a* something.

'No. Please!'

'You are a simpleton,' he repeated in High Galen. 'Quickly!' He seized her as she tried to crawl away.

'Please don't kill me!'

'Give me your hand!' Their palms slithered in his blood as he gripped her. 'I agree to your terms.'

'What?'

'This solemn contract binds us, Anabara Nolio.'

Oh dear God, what was he, that he knew her name?

'Quickly! Repeat my words!'

'What… what should I call you?'

'You freed me, you must name me. Now. The first thing you think of.'

'Um... Thwyn?'

'The first!' He gripped her hand so hard she cried out. 'That was the second.'

She cowered. Fiery light rippled under his skin. This was no lowborn Fay scum. 'But the first was just a... a thing, not name.' That thing the Patriarch had prayed he'd never see.

He shook her. 'Say it!'

'*Paran.* This solemn contract binds us, Paran.'

He released her hand and stood. 'Get up. They are coming.'

'Coming? Now?'

'Now—as you waste time.' He hauled her to her feet. She cried out again—monstrous impossible strength! 'They are at the Gullgate. They intend to seize me and cage me again. And school you never to open your lips to a soul.'

'Oh my God!' She made the sign. 'Then why did they let us go?'

'To bring the fear into your home.'

'But— How do they know where I live?'

He kicked the irons. 'Tracking charms.'

'Get rid of them! Oh God save us!' she wept. 'We've got to hide!' But where? They'd break the door down, ransack the place. 'Out the back. To the Precincts.'

He caught her arm. 'Too late. They are in the street. Hush now! You should sleep.'

'*Sleep?* Are you mad? I'm—'

Sunshine was streaming in through her porthole window. Anabara stretched under her feather quilt. God, she was stiff. What was wrong with her? She felt like a tenderized steak. Bad dreams, too. A night full of them. Running from Tressy rivermen or something. Punting against the tide. She had a feeling it had ended badly. Ah well. Just her subconscious going over the worries of the day; the whole library fiasco, and whether she was mad to risk a trip to the—

Wait. What day is this?

As if in answer, the Minstery bells began to peal. One after another the city's shrine bells picked up the sound. Sunday! She sat up. Hell, her hands hurt—a mass of raw blisters. And they were covered in some kind of silvery stuff. She froze. There was something she was not quite catching hold of. Some eel of a dream—there! But again it slipped from her. She pushed back the quilt and got out of bed. Ow, ow, ow. Saints in heaven, she was still in her clothes. They were filthy. *What the hell was I doing last night? Rolling in a pig trough? Was I drunk?*

She was halfway down the stairs when the memory burst over her. She sank on to the step. The nightmare played back. Every detail. There was no waking out of this. The Fairy, that bundle of rags she'd bought—oh sweet Saint Pelago, what kind of thing was he? His name was Paran— her own stupid fault. Why did she have to go and think that word? Ill-omened, ill-omened. *Why am I such a fool?* If only Linna was still here to save me from myself!

The events of the night flickered again like sheet lightning across her closed eyes. But there was a blank at the end. She remembered her panic—the men were coming, they were in the street. What had happened next? Had she been knocked out? How could she possibly have slept? Unless— Had the Fairy charmed her? She began to tremble. And the deal—what stream of folly had she blurted out? Even Butros with all his legal wizardry wasn't going to be able to extricate her from this mess! And even now the creature was down-stairs, waiting for her.

Well, she couldn't sit here for the rest of her life. It must be faced sometime, whatever it was. Let's get it over with. She hauled herself up and hobbled down the rest of the stairs. He won't harm me. He cannot harm me. Please don't let him harm me. She took a breath and opened the door.

Yes, he was waiting for her.

Clean and dressed. Where had he found clothes? She'd heard somewhere that the manacles made them all look identical, but even now he was free he still looked... nondescript. Like, well, your average lowbred. He was neither fair nor dark. Not tall, not short, not ugly, not beautiful.

'*Good morning, slept you well?*' Lord, she sounded like her old *Other Tongues* primer. 'Sorry, is it all right if we speak Commons? Or Galen? I'm afraid I always messed about in Fairy lessons.'

'Galen.'

'Thanks. Listen, last night: what—'

'Stop.' He came close and looked down into her eyes. He *was* tall. She must have forgotten. 'I am bound by your terms to answer with the truth.' His speech was soft and uninflected. As expressionless as his face. 'Be sure you wish to hear the truth before you ask me anything.'

Not human, she thought again, not human. Black eyes, taut skin across angular features—that's what made them look so hungry. Predatory. That, and the zigzag teeth.

'Did the rivermen come for us?' she whispered.

'Yes.'

'But you charmed me so that I slept through it?'

'Yes.'

He must have carried her to bed! Hollow, but freakishly strong, strong as soldier ants. Don't think of it. 'What... happened to them?'

His eyelids flickered. Quickly. Like a lizard's.

'No!' She backed away. 'That's fine. Don't tell me.' But now the not knowing was worse. Horror upon horror unfolded in her imagination. She squashed the images to the back of her mind. 'What if they send someone else? My door—'

'I've charmed it. And the windows. Nothing can enter here with ill intent.'

'Thanks.' Her lips quivered. 'Sorry. I'm not normally this pathetic.' If she was hoping for reassurance it was in vain. 'I should probably eat something. Are you hungry?'

'I ate last night.'

'Good! Excellent!' *The hearts of his enemies!* 'Well, I'll just, um, get some clean clothes and head for the bathhouse. I need to...' She gestured at herself.

'A word before you go. You need not fear me.'

'Yes, absolutely. I know that. You promised not to harm me.' She put on a smile.

'And yet you do fear. You fear I am a monster. That I eat the hearts of my enemies. That I killed those men in ways too horrible to imagine. Isn't that what you're thinking? Small wonder you fear!'

'I'm sorry.' This was mortifying. 'It's just that... Look, I genuinely believed I wasn't prejudiced. But clearly I am. All the old myths keep rearing their heads. Sorry.'

He reached out to her. 'Feel.'

Do it. She made herself take his arm in both hands. The weight of it shocked her. And the skin was... non-human.

Like... What was it like? Yes—the animal man, came to school with his menagerie, gave her the big snake to hold, dense coils, supple strength under her fingers.

'Right. Not hollow, then.' She tried again to smile. 'Sorry. I'm an idiot.'

'The mind plays tricks.'

'Yes.' She let go of him, managed not to wipe her palms. 'I hope you're not in too much pain. Your hands. Where I had to cut them.'

He held them both out to her, turning them over. Palms, backs, no scars, nothing.

'But—'

'It was a long night,' he said. 'The mind plays tricks.'

'Weird.' She shook her head. 'I'll probably feel better when I've eaten. Then we should talk about—'

'Tomorrow,' he said. 'This is the Day of Rest.'

A short way up Skuller she found a low windowsill and sat to eat the breakfast she'd bought. The bells had fallen silent. The righteous were at prayers and the unrighteous were in bed, or sleeping it off in the Guard cells. Or re-hashing last night in the bathhouse. Sundays in the steam room, that was where you picked up the juiciest gossip. Yeah, and she'd be the hot topic today, turning up in this state.

She took a sip of chocolate and leant her head back against the closed shutters of the cobbler's. High cloud in the blue this morning. Wisps, like carded cobwebs. Well, I'm still here. The sun is still shining. And I still haven't a clue what I'm going to do. But thank you. She drank some more chocolate and turned her attention to food.

What the hell was this stuff on her hands? Like she'd been massacring snails in her sleep. Suddenly her memory

churned. Her palms were slippery on some tool, there was
something she was wrestling to do. *Give me strength!* She felt
again the jolt of that dull *nick!*

It was Fairy blood! The chocolate slopped. She almost
dropped her honeycake. Her heart battered in her chest
like a caged pigeon. The mind plays tricks? No, the Fairy
was playing tricks on her mind. But how? He'd promised
not to lie to her—that was in the deal. You must tell me
the truth, that was what she'd said. Uh oh—he hadn't lied.
Just made her think she was imagining things. Treacherous
as serpents. They all were. Or was that just more ignorant
prejudice?

Well, one thing was certain—she'd feel better after she'd
eaten. She peeled back the paper and devoured the honeycake, careful not to touch it with her fingers. What were the
properties of Fairy blood? No, she wasn't even going to let
herself think about it. A Larridy gull swooped down. She
drained her drink, and tossed him the last crust. He seized
it and soared off.

There, the simple homely magic of hot chocolate and
honeycake! And a long hot soak and a massage would cure
anything else. She levered herself back to her feet and
limped up the hill to the bathhouse. She'd worry about this
later.

CHAPTER SEVEN

The sun shone through turquoise glass of the dome. It was like the seabed down here in the steamy twilight. The bathers might have been mermaids. On the walls of the hot rooms mosaics glittered, scenes from ancient Gull mythology—the whale gods, the first warriors arriving in their longboats and driving out the demons of Larridy long before the first Galens arrived.

Anabara drifted in and out of sleep as she lay on the marble slab. Now and then the shrieks of the washer-girls echoed from the women's beauty room as they painted one another's toenails, and gossiped about their conquests. She'd had to endure Jennet Pettyfrock's tiny piggy eyes scrutinizing her in the foyer. Asking her if she'd enjoyed a nice bit of rough last night. Silly cow. She'd flirt with a temple door if it had a knob on. Couldn't credit that there were other ways of measuring success than how popular you were with men.

But in here it was still. Still as the ocean floor, with the waves lapping, the soft hands moving in ripples over her body. Gentle today. The Candacian bath attendants always sensed what you needed. Afterwards she drowsed in the lounging room, skin glistening with almond oil. The scent of verbena and poplar drifted from the censers. Let me lie here forever. Far away the Minstery bells were pealing again for service end.

Uncle Téador! She had to get a message to him to say she was all right.

The jolt set her pulse racing once more. I should get back, she thought. But home was not home any more. Not with that *thing* in her house. Why had she said he could stay with her? Pity, perhaps. That bedraggled broken wretch. And now it was clean and clothed. It stood up on its hind legs and addressed her in High Galen in its sssoft snake-like voice. It would not lie, but it would deceive her in a thousand ways until she feared she was going mad.

And tomorrow she would have to go with him to the library. Another cold wash of dread: the scholasticus was going to ask for his papers. Paran was no longer an illegal slave, but he had no Freeman Pass. Good forgeries took time. And how was Loxi going to react to his new workmate? He must never find out Paran was an ex-slave, or he'd flip. Oh God, was nothing ever going to be straightforward again?

Yanni. Yanni would know what to do. No! She'd vowed to when she set up her business that she would not keep running to big brother to sort the world out for her. And Uncle Téador was already carrying all the woes of The Way on his shoulders. It wasn't fair to drag him into this. Grandmama? No way! Linna had enough to think about with the baby coming. Loxi was part of the problem. Cousin Rodania? Huh. Anabara would rather sit bare-arsed on a sea urchin than go to Ms Perfect for assistance. I have no-one, no-one to confide in.

Feeling a tide of *Poor Little Orphan Me* about to engulf her, she got up and returned to the changing room to dress. Please, St Pelago, I just need a friendly ear. A shoulder to cry on. She made her way up the marble steps (ow, ow, ow!) to the foyer.

A nickering laugh echoed.

Quick as a flash Anabara ducked into an archway. Great. Old Pel was still having fun with her prayers: here was a shoulder to cry on. Silk-clad, perfumed with civet and endlessly, fatally, sympathetic. But Anabara had learnt the hard way that short of shouting your secrets into the Minstery's great bass wind flute, there was no better way of broadcasting them than by confiding in grandmama's equerry.

She peeped out. Yes, there went Enobar, with another pretty boy in tow. Dammit! It was that stuck-up little git, Toby Buttery! A thought struck her: had Enobar—that fount of all gossip—got wind of her library contract and blabbed? Was *that* how Carraman's were keeping tabs on her doings up on the Mount—pillow talk? I will fecking kill Enobar. She seethed till they had disappeared into the men's quarters. Then she crept from the bathhouse.

Outside the noonday glare made her eyes ache. She stopped at the Messenger Booth and wrote a note to Uncle Téador, to be delivered at once, then continued home. There was that gull again. It wheeled round, then came in to land on the dome of a tiny shrine. One of the city's many; squeezed into a crack between the houses on either side. Anabara must have walked past a hundred times without a second thought. She peered in through the arched doorway. It was no bigger than a sedan chair. A one person shrine. On impulse she made the sign and went inside.

The stone seat was cold. A votive candle flickered. Above it was a mosaic of St Pelago preaching on a pile of tiny skulls. Telling the Gull people that the Lord of Light asked only for their love. It was artisan-made, a crude piece of work compared with the bathhouse mosaics, built in memory of some long-dead Larridy ironmonger. The Saint glared at her with mad little stone eyes.

'Stop that,' she told him. 'I'm here, aren't I?'

Was she expecting some kind of vision? Her mother, like Uncle Téador, had been a great visionary. But visions tended to come after long periods of meditation—not Anabara's strongest suit. More Gull than Galen in her bloodstream. She'd always been better at scrapping than praying. Yanni had grown up in the Minstery precincts, of course, and being 13 years older than her, he'd known their parents, been shaped by them. She had no memories, no real sense of what they were actually like. They were as holy and two-dimensional in her mind as their frescoes.

But here was a question: would she have been a better person if her father's mother had not stomped up the hill and demanded an equal share in her son's orphaned baby daughter? Woo! The clash of the grandmothers! Granny Gull had died not long after. Anabara couldn't remember her. There was no telling how different it might all have been, but for Granny Nolio's intervention. *I might have been another Rodania, unlocking the secrets of the universe with the mighty key of my intellect.*

St Pelago nailed her with his ironmonger gaze. He doubted that.

Nah, you're right. I'd still be me. No visions for the likes of Nan Nolio. Pointless sitting here waiting for one. But she still couldn't face going home. The Fairy lurked like a poisonous spider in the corner of her mind, all the more terrifying because she couldn't see him. Her hand went to the strange amulet. She closed her fingers round the knobbled stone. Perhaps her mother had done the same in moments of hesitation, or despair. This whole thing is too big for me, she thought. I can't do it.

But you can do the next thing.

Anabara froze. Was that her own mind answering her? Or had the thought come from outside—from the Saint? She stared at him. He stared back. How could you tell? But it was true: she *could* bring herself to go home. She *could* face the Fairy. Do the next thing. Yes, and then the thing after. And then the one after that. That was all anyone could ever do, come to think of it, even the greatest of all visionaries.

It's really very simple, she told the mosaic Saint. It's all just made up of tiny little pieces. One after another after another. And in the end, there will be a picture.

Please let there be a picture.

She creaked to her feet and left the shrine. Above the gull mounted on white wings, high, higher, then off into the blue.

Well, that massage must have done the trick, astonishingly. The following morning she woke free from aches and pains. Even her blistered hands were nearly healed. Bizarre. But the Day of Rest was over. The time for talking had come.

So Anabara talked. She talked about her business. She gave a potted history of the City of Larridy. She talked about the University and the Minstery. She talked about the role of the City Guard, the set-up at the library, the heritage problems.

The Fairy listened. Or she hoped he was listening. He might have been off in the marzipan mines of Tara-doodle for all she knew. Lord, would she ever get used to this absence of expression, this stare that made you feel like a total feather-head?

'So.' She made her tone business-like. 'Any questions?'

'Yes. What are we waiting for?'

Anabara flushed with indignation. 'We're waiting for my cousin, actually. He works for me. Does the accounts, handles the admin side of things.'

Damn, Gull timekeeping was not going to look snappy and professional here. (When does the meeting start? When everyone's here, eh.) But then she heard footsteps, and there was Loxi—with a huge pile of books.

'Man, am I the best book-finder in the world, or what? Woo!' He dumped them on her table with a grin. He hadn't spotted the Fairy sitting in the shadows. 'They were falling over themselves not to look racist. Couldn't give me the books fast enough. I deserve a raise, me.'

'Hey, well done!' She squeezed his arm. 'Loxi, I want you to meet—'

She got no further.

Loxi dropped like he'd been scythed. 'Don't let him kill me!'

'What? Get up, you soft lump!' She turned to the Fairy and switched back to Galen. 'Paran, I am *so* sorry. Loxi, *come out.*'

But he stayed curled under the table, whimpering in terror.

She cuffed him. 'Listen to me Loxi, he won't harm you. It's in the deal. You're my kinsman. *He can't harm you.*' She was ready to cry with mortification. She turned to Paran again. 'I'm sorry. He's not normally... he's had some bad experiences.'

'Fetch me a drink of water, Gull,' said the Fairy to Loxi.

What the hell was this—some kind of bizarre Fairy ritual? 'Why?'

'He's foresworn.'

'Impossible! When? How?'

With a hiss the Fairy bared his fangs.

'Oh my God, Loxi, get him a drink. Quickly!'

She had to fill the glass at the pump, clamp Loxi's fingers round it, haul him across the room by his ear. There wasn't much water left in it when finally Loxi held out the glass. The Fairy took it, drank. He set the glass down. Then he took a step towards Loxi.

Out like a snuffed candle. The Fairy caught him as he fell.

'What happened? What the—? Oh dear God!' shouted Anabara. 'What have you done to him? You're not supposed to harm my family! He's my *cousin*! Shit! Don't *ever* bare your teeth in my sight again!'

'Hush!' He stood holding Loxi—all six foot of Gull warrior—like he was a child's raggedy doll. He murmured something in his own tongue. Then he blew into Loxi's face. The black lashes fluttered.

No! Was he charming him? Into—? Another old tale sprang into her head. Oh Pelago, Auntie will kill me. 'Put him down!'

'He'll sleep while the charm works.'

'What charm? Make it stop! No! What are you trying to do to him?'

'Sweeten his memory, nothing more.' He blew again. 'The rivermen used him cruelly.'

It all fell into place. 'That was *you* he found in the grain hold?'

'I wondered if I dreamt him. He pushed a wet rag through the bars for me to suck on. He promised to come back with water. But they caught him.'

Pelago! She made the sign. 'What did they do to him?'

'They tied him to the cage and went for their master.'

'The one with the… eyes?'

'The same. He ordered his men to thrust your cousin into the cage, so they could watch the sport. He explained to the boy all the things Fays like to do. How long it would take him to die. Your cousin wept and begged in terror. So of his kindness the master offered a choice of bed-fellow: himself, or the Fay.' The Fairy paused. 'I'll tell you more if you wish.'

She shook her head. Pressed her fist to her mouth. Poor, poor Loxi. 'Please put him down.'

'Ah, look—the charm works.' Loxi smiled in his sleep. 'I should warn you, your thoughts are daubed a yard high on the wall of your mind.'

'What thoughts?'

He laid Loxi on the hearth rug and smoothed the hair back from his forehead. Then he stood. Expressionless as ever. 'Don't worry. I have not charmed your kinsman into a mollyboy.'

She shut her eyes. I'm not prejudiced, I'm not! she wanted to shout. 'Look, no offence to your heritage. I mean, come *on*, half my Galen friends… But it's not part of Gull culture. It just doesn't happen.'

'Truly? I wonder at that.'

'Believe me, it's totally alien. In the old days the village elders would stick mollies in barrels of broken glass and roll them down Skuller. That was the punishment.'

He stared. 'I no longer wonder at it.'

After a pause she said, 'That was hundreds of years back, obviously. There's no law against it any more. But Gulls are very traditional people, that's all I'm trying to say.'

A sob shook her. That's why that monster made Loxi 'choose'. He knew it would destroy his pride. Well, let me daub *this* on the wall of my mind: I'll get him. So help me, St Pelago—one day he'll face justice for what he's done.

But if the Fairy perceived her vow he made no sign. Perhaps he didn't care? Of course he doesn't care, idiot. They're incapable of empathy with humans. Not like us, not like us, remember? Although he'd seemed almost gentle just now. Yeah—right after he'd bared his fangs at us! Over a poxy glass of water! What was she supposed to think? This was like a nightmare game of death chess, with secret rules but no clues. Her hand went to the amulet.

Instantly the Fairy's eyes were her.

Her pulse leapt. 'This? It was my mother's.'

'Yes.'

'You knew that?'

'It's in your thought.'

'Tscha!' In letters a yard high. 'Do you know what it is?'

'Yes.'

'Well? Are you going to tell me?'

'No.'

She laughed in surprise. You bloody are, mister! 'I insist you tell me the truth.'

'Have a care. You put me in a double bind—I promised to do you no harm.'

'The truth will harm me? Oh, what *is* this thing? Get it off me!' Her fingers scrabbled at the clasp. But then she steadied herself. Her mother had worn it. The Patriarch himself had fastened it round her neck. How could it be evil? She scowled at the Fairy. 'But I want to know. I just hate not knowing stuff.'

'Well, I hope you will bear that trial,' he replied, 'since I should hate to cut off my right ear.'

'What?' she shrieked. 'I never specified any such thing!'

'I am well aware of that. It's the default penalty.'

She gripped her hair in both hands. 'This is a total fecking nightmare.'

'Indeed it is. I have never encountered so botched and reckless deal in my life.'

'Hey, the circumstances weren't exactly brilliant, if you remember!' she burst out. 'I deserve a bit more recognition round here!'

There was a long silence. Like he was performing some complex calculation—totting up the Favours Received column, balancing it against Trouble Caused. The result appeared to be: No, she deserved nothing.

'Look,' he said, 'your cousin wakes.'

Loxi stirred.

'Hey, Loxi.' She nudged him with her toe. 'Shift your arse.'

'Hmmm?' He opened his eyes. Frowned. 'Man, what happened?'

'You passed out, you lummox.'

'I did?' Then he caught sight of the Fairy and sat bolt upright. 'No!'

The Fairy knelt. Stared into Loxi's face. 'You've fulfilled your promise. All's well.'

Loxi nodded, eyes round.

'Will you shake hands?' Another nod. Loxi reached out a trembling hand and the Fairy clasped it. 'Those were dark times. We will not dwell on them any more.'

Loxi nodded again.

'See?' said the Fairy. 'Your worst fear came for you, but you've lived to tell the tale. The world will seem brighter now. Come, on your feet. There's work to do.'

'Yes, right, so here's the plan,' said Anabara, to remind them she was boss. 'We head up to the Library now, where you can hand in the books, Loxi. Then I introduce you to the scholasticus,' she turned to the Fairy, 'and he'll tell you about the security issues, at great length, probably. Oh, and there's a mimic charm somewhere in the vault that he wants us to get rid of. Meanwhile, I will be making a few enquiries. There's something weird going on with this contract. I get the feeling I'm being set up. Any questions?'

'How are you planning to explain my presence?' asked the Fairy.

Planning! Lord, I don't know—with some lie or other. 'I'll just say you're my new associate.' What if they ran into some jumped-up *Papers, Please!* Guard, though? Well, she couldn't worry about everything all at once. Her fingers brushed the amulet. Just do the next thing.

Loxi edged away from the Fairy. 'What's the situation with Carramans, eh?' he whispered.

'Use Galen or Commons,' she whispered back. 'We need Paran to understand us, eh.' But even as she was saying it, she was seized by the conviction the Fairy could follow every word.

'Are Carramans still on to you?' Loxi asked in his lazy Gull-accented Galen.

'I don't know. But I reckon I've found out how they're getting their information!' Her eyes flashed. 'A little shite I was at school with called Toby Buttery, he works for Carraman's, and he's going with Enobar. Enobar? Candacian-Galen demy. Grandmama's equerry.'

'Heard of him, yeah.'

'Enobar, the town-crier. Honestly, I could kill him.'

'Or I could,' suggested the Fairy.

The room turned into an echoing cavern. Beside her Loxi moaned.

'No! It's just a *saying.*' Her heart boomed like a death drum. 'I didn't mean it literally! No killing anyone—got that? Saints in heaven, I *love* Enobar!'

'Ah,' said the Fairy. 'Then I will forbear.'

'Oh for God's sake, Loxi—head between your knees.' She shoved him into the nearest chair.

The Fairy stared down. 'He's very tender-hearted.'

Is he? Or could it be *you* that's a Grade A fecking psychopath?

All in all, the day was shaping up rather well.

CHAPTER EIGHT

They got to the Precincts without further incident. Loxi kept several yards between him and his new colleague. Still, no moronic bigots spat at Paran and called him a dirty Fay, so she wasn't obliged to kick any heads in. They entered the library. Loxi handed in the pile of books. The scholasticus fluttered his hands in delight, then he turned his attention to Paran.

Loxi edged away to round up more volumes. But before he could escape, Anabara grabbed his arm. 'So he's a *Fairy*. Just get over it. You're showing me up.'

'He stares at me, him,' he muttered. 'Like a gannet watching a sandwich.'

'*All* Fairies look like that,' she hissed, 'it's just their bone structure.'

When she returned to the main desk, the scholasticus was parading his linguistic prowess. Anabara struggled to follow the rapid Fairy dialect he was using. The echo minced round the vault, two seconds behind. The students were smirking. Pity to disable the charm, really. She scanned round, wondering where it was hidden, and caught sight of the Zaarzuk. He winked at her from the top of ladder. Consulting bound volumes of *The Journal of Advanced Clinical Psycho-Medicine*? Very likely. Enjoying the view down blouse fronts was her bet. She turned her back and made herself focus. The scholasticus was still going strong. Here and there she caught the odd word—*books, very difficult, old*—but most of the conversation was beyond her. Conversation? Monologue. The Fairy was giving him the gannet treatment.

But then there was a pause. The scholasticus repeated his question. Something, something, *papers?*

'Ah, yes, about that,' she began.

But to her amazement, the Fairy drew a booklet from his pocket. My God, it was never a Freeman Pass?

The scholasticus took it. 'Let's see: *This is to certify that the Fairy (artisan class) known as **Paran a'Menehaïn**,'* he read, *'is hereby granted the freedom of the City Isle of Larridy, in the Federation of Mainland States, to reside and work within the borders thereof.'* He skimmed to the end, checked the dates, the official border seal and the bearer likeness, then handed it back. 'Well, that seems to be in order.'

Order, order, order! bleated the echo.

The scholasticus glared up at it. 'I'll be delighted to hear the last of that.'

Prat, twat!

Anabara snorted. A herd of pigs chased round the vault. She patted her chest. 'Sorry. Got a cough.'

'I'll check the exterior charms first, Doctor.' And the Fairy was gone before the scholasticus was halfway through his ornate valediction.

Anabara hurried after him into the library cloister.

'Paran, wait.' He turned. 'Show me that pass.'

The Fairy handed it to her.

She flicked through. Top end forgery 'Bloody hell. How did you get it done so fast? Who made it?' He waited. Giving her time to retract the questions? 'I want to know the truth.'

'Ignorance may be expedient,' he said.

'The truth. Now.'

'Very well. I acquired this last night. The owner no longer needs it.'

'And you've doctored it? Paran, it may fool the scholasticus, but that's the first thing the Guards look for! The Psych Unit always scan for charms.'

'They won't find any. The pass is unaltered. The charm's in the beholder's eye.'

He does *perception* work?! La la la. Not even going to *think* about this. 'Um, that's very impressive, but technically, not legal.'

He stared.

'Well, it's psychological fraud, isn't it? "Invading and distorting another person's reality".'

Still staring.

'Right. Well anyway. Obviously I'm relieved you've sorted the ID problem, so I'm prepared to skate over this one. But if you could just bear that in mind in future? That we need to operate within the law?' She got an urge to knock on his skull and say, *Hello?* 'Whose was it?'

He took the pass back and pocketed it. More staring, but she didn't back down. He shrugged. 'As you please. It belonged to one Thwyn Brakstone.'

'What, *my* Thwyn? But how did he get home without it?'

'He didn't.'

Her breath caught. Water tinkled in the fountain. Cherry leaves lay all around, as though some scarlet bird had been plucked by a hawk. This can't be happening. 'He's dead, isn't he?' she heard herself say.

'Yes.'

The hair on her neck crawled. 'Did you kill him?'

'Not I.' The Fairy curled his lip. 'He was fortunate there.'

'*Fortunate?*' Her voice echoed round the Cloister.

'Yes indeed. Not to fall into my hands,' said the Fairy. 'I would have kept him alive. A day for every day I spent on that ship. "Your" Thwyn was a blood-traitor and a master charm-smith.'

'What are you talking about? He was useless.'

'Not so. You've seen Brakstone's handiwork—those cunning spiked manacles. It seems he tired of his trade. He turned informer, sought Guard protection. But he was double-crossed. The slavers slit his throat. His body lies under the floor of his hovel.'

'Oh my God.' The world went glassy. She was staring at a picture. In the picture was a fountain, a cherry tree. Egrets. A nondescript Fairy. What had she got caught up in? 'How do you know all this?'

'Oh, I learnt it from the rivermen. They are careless with their tongues.'

Another leaf broke from a twig. She watched it drift down. Thwyn. A collaborator. Dead. 'We should report his murder.'

He searched her face. Or her mind. 'I honour your vow to avenge your cousin, but there are swifter and surer ways to punish the rivermen than this.'

'No,' she said, 'it's more, I can't just walk away from a murder. As a citizen of Larridy. Paran, we've got to report it. They cut his throat in cold blood!' The blank stare. 'Look, maybe he deserved it, but that's not for us to decide. We can't go around dishing out vengeance, or we'll end up back in the dark age. That's what the courts are for, the whole criminal justice system.' Hello? 'Listen, if you're going to work for me, you've *got* to understand that.'

'This is not your battle. Keep out of it.'

'It's *everyone's* battle, standing up against violence and injustice. My parents died for it.'

'Ah!' He touched his forehead, bowed. 'Then of course.'

Shit. Now he thinks it's a blood vendetta. But she was too weary to argue any more.

'Are we finished?' he asked. 'If so, I will assess the charm-work.'

'Fine. Do that.'

He slipped away between the arches. A shadow, a movement in the corner of the eye, something you might have imagined.

Anabara sat on the ledge of the nearest arch and watched the fountain. She was shaking. Freeing him was meant to be a simple act of kindness. What had she unleashed? Another half-remembered image slithered through her mind. Something she'd seen in that moment of deal making. But what was it? Gone again.

One thing was clear, though: from now on, life was going to be like walking through a busy market with an naked blade in her hand. She'd have to be watchful every second. A careless outburst: *I could kill Enobar...* Oh dear God in heaven, I can't live like this. What am I going to do?

The next thing. You can always do the next thing.

Which was to report Thwyn's murder. Obviously the Guards would ask how she knew. Keeping Paran out of this was essential, or she'd end up being prosecuted for illegally liberating an enslaved person. She'd have to claim it was a rumour from her lowlife contacts. Would they buy that? Maybe she'd contact Charlie Rondo. A fellow Gull would accept an anonymous tip-off. Yes, find Charlie—that was what she'd do. She leant her forehead against the stone arch and tried to summon the strength for the next thing: her civic duty.

But an entirely different thing came to her instead. Striding briskly.

'Ah, there you are. Grandmama's looking for you, Anabara.'

Rodania. As usual Anabara felt like a squat yellow poison toad beside her.

'Oh hello, Rodi. Tell her I'm on my way. Couple of things I need to sort out first.'

'No, sorry. I know you'll just slide off. Come along, please.' She had the secret passwords of time and space to crack, and here was Anabara being tiresome. 'She's worried about you.'

'So what? She always is.'

'More than usual.' Rodania folded up her tall frame and sank to the ledge. She crossed her ankles. Kept her knees together like a lady should. Anabara felt like poking a big hole in those flawless silk stockings. 'It's about this library business,' her cousin said.

Aha, so she *was* being set up. 'What's the gossip then?'

Her cousin leant close and dropped her voice. 'Basically, it's the new scholasticus. Trying to save money. He's paying you a third of what Carraman quoted for the job.'

'What?! He approached Carraman first?'

'Of course. There's no way anyone expects you to be able to handle this.'

'Thanks!'

'And as to that new associate you've acquired—who *is* he? I saw him skulking about just now. I hope he's not charging you much, because frankly—'

'Let's see if he can actually do the charm work, shall we, before we completely write him off?'

'I'm trying to tell you—nobody *expects* you to do the work! Which is just as well—he's a only lowbred worker, you can tell by looking. If he says otherwise, he's lying. Does he have any highbred fire markings? No. Well, there you are then. Look, if you want my opinion—'

'I don't.'

'—you'll bow to the inevitable. Everyone knows there's got to be a huge fundraising drive to finance proper heritage-standard Fairy artisans. Chapter has kept on leaving it for the next generation and hoping the problem will go away. The new scholasticus has finally grasped the nettle. He needs a report quickly, then he can get on with applying for grants before the deadline. It's just a hoop he has to jump through, and you're a lot cheaper than Carramans. Look, I can write it for you, if you like.'

'Write it *for* me!' squeaked Anabara. 'You are unbelievable!'

'Well, whatever. A report's all the scholasticus wants, if you'd only listen. Nobody expects your company to do any actual restoration. You should have asked for more money, mind you. That's what Grandmama says, anyway.'

'Thank you for conveying her views.' She gave a bright smile. 'Now I can get on with running my business without having to visit her.'

'You're hopeless. Why do you have to be so prickly the whole time? We're *trying* to help.'

'Do I barge into your laboratory and try to help you?'

Her cousin laughed. 'Forgive me. But frankly, the thought of you and advanced theoretical psycho-mechanics…'

'Exactly. Ditto *you* and investigation work.'

'Well, this is getting us nowhere.' Rodania rose gracefully and smoothed her academic gown. 'I'll tell Grandmama you're busy, but that you'll call tomorrow. May I say that?'

'No. Butt out.' An image flashed into her head: Uncle Téador looking grieved. 'Look, sorry, but I've had a rough couple of days. This is turning into a total nightmare. And don't say "Told you so," or I may have to...' *Kill you!* She closed her eyes. Careful, careful!

Rodania sat again and laid a hand on her arm. 'Ana, are you coping with all this? Don't be cross, I just want to help. If I can, of course.'

Anabara sagged, allowed herself to relent a little. 'Thanks. You've already helped, actually. Confirmed my suspicions about the whole library deal.'

'Good.' Rodania beamed. 'If I hear anything else, I'll pass it on.'

Nothing a good Galen girl liked better than to be useful. Must exploit that. 'I might need to pick your brains about perception charms sometime.'

'Why?'

'Just something that's cropped up.'

'Ana, if your Fairy's claiming he can do perception work, he's definitely lying. He'd either have to be an elf prince or some kind of elite mind warrior. Honestly, you've got to crack down on him, or he'll—'

'Ta dah! And *this* is why I never consult you, Rodi-kins. You instantly leap to conclusions and start telling me what to do.'

'Fine!'

They glared at one another.

Although dammit, the conclusion she'd leapt to was pretty much correct. Mind warrior? Oh shit.

'Well, anyway,' sniffed Rodania, 'if he can do serious perception work he'll have a *paran*, which I very much doubt!'

'What?' The world had gone echoey again.

'A *paran*—a ceremonial knife. It's—'

'I *know* what it is, for feck's sake.'

'You don't have to yell at me!'

'Sorry. It's just, his name's Paran.'

Rodania rolled her eyes. 'Then he's *definitely* a charlatan. Oh come on, Ana, that's a little boy's fantasy name! Ooh, look at me, I'm Super Assassin! If he was genuine, no way would he call himself that.'

'Yeah, you're probably right.'

'Don't trust him an inch.'

'Believe me, I don't.'

A bell tolled. Midday Prayers. Could this get any worse?

She caught a look on her cousin's face. One she recognised from girlhood, when they were battling to decide who had the greatest imaginary powers.

'I just get a bit jealous sometimes,' she muttered.

'Of me!' said Anabara. 'No way.'

'Well, I get fed up with being the good girl. You seem to have so much fun.'

Anabara thought about the last 48 hours. The nightmare out on the salt flats. Her lovely Super Assassin housemate. Not forgetting murder.

Her pulse kicked up again. It was no good, she had to report it.

'Fun. Not the word I'd use. But thanks.' She got to her feet. 'Give me a head start before you let Enobar loose?'

'Oh, I'll say I couldn't find you.'

Anabara wagged a finger. 'St Pelago will hear you fibbing!'

'He's heard worse in his time.'

'He surely has.'

The next thing proved elusive. Charlie was not in the station. Nor was he at any of the usual Guard lunchtime bars.

She spent a pointless afternoon tramping the streets of Larridy trying to locate him. By the time dusk was falling she was starting to panic. She'd have to go and take her chances with whoever was on the front desk.

But a bite to eat wouldn't go amiss. She was only a few minutes from home.

And there was the next thing, waiting on her doorstep. Charlie. And another officer. A woman. Tall, man-like. Anabara hadn't seen her before. Some light-skinned Offcomer.

'Hey, Nan,' said Charlie. She could see a slick of sweat on his face in the daylamp's glow. 'We'd like you to come with us to the station.'

That was when she spotted the windowless Guard litter. The uniformed bearers in the shadow. Her heart began to race.

'What's this about?'

'We'll explain when we're there, eh.'

'Am I being arrested?'

'Na, ah. Just a couple of questions.' With every passing second he seemed more agitated. 'Come on, eh.'

All the while the strange woman officer stood there, pale and silent.

'Sorry. I know my rights, Charlie.'

Then the other officer stepped forward. She had a big face, like a reflection in a spoon back. Eyes like sea gooseberries, a nose that had been broken more than once.

'Let me explain about your rights, girly,' she whispered. 'We don't give a shit about them.'

And she slapped her face. Before Anabara had time to react, the bearers seized her and bundled her into the litter. The door slammed. She heard the charm click into place.

'Nice work.' A hand smacked the roof and the litter lurched up from the ground. 'Take her away, boys.'

CHAPTER NINE

Anabara braced hands and feet against the sides of the litter. Nothing to hang on to. Bastards were giving her a rough ride, too. Careening round corners. Clouting walls. She could smell the piss and fear of previous occupants.

I can't believe I let them take me so easily! All very well to say she'd been caught by surprise. How much of her training was intended for exactly that?—the surprise attack. Shameful! But that a Guard should strike her, that a *woman* should strike her. It felt like a betrayal. And Charlie, a fellow Gull, turning a blind eye. You are toast, Rondo. I'm going to—

The Fairy flashed into her mind.

Well, anyway, I'm going to tell your mum.

And she was going to come out fighting, that was for sure. Bloke-woman was going to get her ugly nose bust one more time.

Wait. That was what the woman wanted, wasn't it? An excuse to whack her in the cells for assaulting a Guard. Time to use your brain not your fists. So what was this about?

It had to be about Thwyn. They'd found his body. Standard procedure would be to question his associates, rule them out of their enquiry. So why the hell were they roughing her up? No!—she was seriously a *suspect?* Impossible!

What evidence did they think they had? But then her pulse began to race. Was someone framing her?

Suddenly it looked suicidal to report Thwyn's death. *Ignorance may be expedient.* She should have listened. Anabara drew a deep breath. Silence was her only option now. No matter what, she must keep her mouth shut until she had her Butros with her. It wasn't like this was ancient Palatinate Larridy. Bloke-woman was hardly going to make herself a necklace of Anabara's toenails. Besides, the minute Chief Dhalafan heard of this—

Douff!

Anabara lay winded. The bastards had dropped the litter. Slowly her lungs unclenched and the air creaked back in. Yes, she'd heard they did that to tricky customers. Round the back of the Guard Station.

They left her trapped in the dark stinking box for a long, long time. No way of gauging how long. But finally, footsteps. She heard the charm ratchet back. A hand reached in, seized her and dragged her out. Bloke-woman.

'Oh, are we here already?' said Anabara. 'I must have dropped off.'

'Smart arse.' Grip like a bull crab round her upper arm. Light on her feet for such a big woman. A fighter, then. Probably Boggan wrestling. Anabara was marched on her stiff legs towards a side door. By-passing the front desk. Not good. Down a narrow corridor, blinking in the harsh light. Doors on each side. Barred windows.

There was Charlie. His lips moved, unlocking a door charm. She was sent sprawling into a windowless interrogation room. A low stool for her. Two chairs for them. They came in. The door clanged to.

Charlie helped her up. No prizes for guessing which one was playing Nice Guard tonight.

'You haven't arrested me,' she said. 'You haven't charged me. I am entitled to send a message, and to have my Counsel present—'

This time she was ready. Open-palmed cuff round the head, like the Gullmothers dished out.

'You haven't awested me,' mimicked the woman in an ickle voice. 'I'm entitled to thend a methage.'

'Uh, Ma'am, point of information?' muttered Charlie. 'She *is* entitled to...'

The woman rounded on him. Shriveled his nuts with a single look.

Suddenly Anabara got it: Ma'am was the mother of all Gullmothers. Charlie was man enough to face down any male authority figure on earth. But he could no more defy Ma'am than pick himself up in a bucket. He shot Anabara a pleading look.

'Get a message to my Grandmother, eh,' she snarled in Gull.

'What? What did she say?' demanded the woman.

'Ma'am, she ah, insulted my manhood.'

'Did she now. Insulting an officer of the Guard. We'll add that to a charge of failure to cooperate with an ongoing investigation, shall we?'

My God. How anyone could have got to adulthood and not lost that whiny Bogganburg accent was beyond Anabara. Thick as pigshit, that's how Bog-whackers sounded.

The woman turned to Charlie. 'Officer Rondo, run and get a glass of water for Princess Gob-shite.'

'Uh, Ma'am, thing is, there's supposed to be two of us present at all times during—'

'THAT'S AN ORDER!'

He saluted. 'Ma'am!'

The door shut. Bloke-woman smiled. She had yellow mule's teeth in her big face. It was like being interrogated by a Wolf Tide jack-o-lantern. 'Look at that! Just the two of us. Any idea what this is about, gobby?'

'I am entitled to send a message and to have my Counsel present—'

She reached out and took Anabara's nose between her knuckles and twisted. 'Sorry, what was that?'

Anabara's eyes watered. Calm. Stay calm. Do *not* lose your temper.

'Listen, lovey.' She gave another twist, came in close with the bulging eyes. 'As a so-called detective, you've probably clocked I'm not from round here. Which means I don't give a shit who your powerful relatives are. You may also have spotted that Mummy's boy has stepped out of the room. Now, I can send him on an errand to Tara-doodle if I want, so a really good strategy would be to start answering my questions.' She let go. 'Sit.'

Anabara sat on the stool. She wiped the tears from her face. Sniffed.

Bloke-woman plonked her broad arse in one of the chairs. 'When did you last visit the Slackey?'

'I'm entitled to send one message and—'

Another cuff. Anabara clenched her teeth. Kept her temper. Just.

The woman sneered. 'And they told me you were a fighter.'

Charlie returned.

'Thank you, officer,' said Ma'am, taking the glass. 'Go ahead—act dumb, but you were seen by dozens of witnesses. What took a stuck-up little princess like you into the Slackey?'

'I am entitled to send—'

She dashed the water into Anabara's face. Oh please. Do we have to be this predictable? Anabara mopped herself with her sleeve. What was *with* this woman? She was acting like someone was marking her out of ten for her Nasty Guard performance.

'Ma'am!' protested Charlie.

Ma'am turned the ball-shriveling stare on him again. 'Why don't you go and find some reports to write up, like a good boy?'

'But—'

'DO IT!'

He snapped another salute. 'Ma'am!'

The woman turned to Anabara again. Behind her back Charlie gave a swift thumbs-up before he vanished. Yeah, suck on *that*, Offcomer, thought Anabara. Help was on the way.

'Can you account for your movements over last week end? Let's hope so—because this is a murder investigation I'm in charge of here.' She leant close and whispered, 'This is where you gasp and say, "Murder? I don't know what you're talking about, detective!"'

'No,' said Anabara. 'This is where I say, "I am entitled—"'

And so it went on, with minor variations, until at last, Anabara heard what she'd been waiting for: the unmistakable sound of a high-powered Don't-Feck-With-Me Galen lawyer knocking Guard heads together.

I demand to see my client immediately! NOW, or I'll have you demoted so fast your ears pop, sunshine!

'What the hell?' Bloke-woman got to her feet.

'Well look at that!' said Anabara. 'Just the two of us in the interrogation room! Isn't that illegal?'

It took Butros approximately one minute to spring her. Threats whistled like crossbow shafts. Woo!

'Come, Ms Nolio. We're done here.' Butros turned on his heel in swirl of red legal silk.

'Well, Ma'am, this was lovely,' said Anabara brightly. 'We must do it again some time.'

'Trust me, I'm looking forward to it,' snarled the woman.

Butros wheeled back round. 'Did I just hear you threatening my client, detective?'

'You did not.'

A bout of professional eyeball-wrestling. Then: 'Good.'

Quite how you could get so much menace into one word Anabara had no idea. They probably taught a course on it at Galencia Law School. Butros Kaledh had graduated top of his year there a decade ago. After graduating top with his undergraduate degree here at St Pelago's. Butros Kaledh had to be top of everything, or there was hell to pay.

He swept through the station like a big pissed-off black and crimson vampire bat. Anabara scuttled in the wake of his billowing robes. It felt like a silly dream. Like she was drunk. Tipsy with relief, probably. She kept wanting to giggle.

There was Chief Dhalafan in a dinner suit and academic robes, talking to a black-uniformed psych. Yes, that was right—somewhere in some far-off universe it was University Matriculation Feast tonight. Uncle Hector Dhalafan would have been dining on High Table with grandmama. Not a real uncle, of course, just an old family friend. She tried to catch his eye, but Butros jerked his head for her to catch up. Never mind. She'd rat bloke-woman out to the Chief tomorrow instead. Make her start caring who Anabara's powerful friends and relatives were!

Charlie had gone to ground like the coward he was. She caught a few smirks as they passed the front desk. Maybe Ma'am wasn't popular with the locals. Of course she wasn't. Chuck a fish head at her! Anabara choked back another giggle. They went down the steps, crossed the forecourt and were out in the street. A sleek ebony palanquin was waiting.

'I thought you'd be glad of a ride,' said Butros. He opened the door for her. 'No extra charge.'

'Thanks.' She leant back against the plush squabs. Yes, on the whole she preferred *this* end of the legal system. It smelt of chypre not piss. Tiny daylamps glowed in the pleated silk ceiling, turning the litter into a rosy cave, and a music charm was playing Fairy madrigals.

Butros got in beside her and a lackey closed the door. He was one of Grandmama's beautiful talented young men. She collected them the way other old ladies collected stray cats.

'Look, thanks for coming out like this,' she said. 'What time is it?'

'Just gone one in the morning.'

'Lord, no wonder I'm starving! Can we grab something to eat? But I suppose we should talk first.'

'I confess, I was hoping we might,' he said. 'Since this really wasn't altogether convenient.'

She could smell bathhouse oil. Diamond studs glinted in his ears. 'Gosh, hope I didn't interrupt anything important.'

He arched an exquisite eyebrow. 'Tell me—without too many egregious lies—what this is all about.'

'Well, going by what bloke-woman said, it's a—'

'Detective Mooby, please.'

'Mooby!' Anabara snorted. 'Is that her name?'

'No, Anabara,' he said, 'her name is Detective Goat-banger. What did Mooby tell you?'

'She— Hey, we're going up hill!' cried Anabara. 'No! I am *not* going to Grandmama's! I don't *believe* this! Stop! I'm not a child!' she shrieked. 'Butros, you're *my* Counsel. *I* pay you, so you follow *my* orders, not hers!'

He winced. 'Don't yell, please. I know this will come as a shock, but I have lots and lots of clients, all of whom expect me to follow their orders. And talking of paying…?' Again, the eyebrow.

She just stopped herself—he spent too many hours each week in the combat room. It would be safer to smack a cobra. 'I was *actually* about to settle your bill.'

'I don't doubt it for a moment.' He patted her hand. 'Let's get back to Detective Butch, the Bog-whacker.'

'It's *Mooby*, you racist man-whore. And I'm *not* talking to you.'

'What an eccentric approach to adopt with your Counsel. Did Mooby tell you it was a murder investigation?'

'Can't remember.'

'What did she ask you?'

'Wasn't listening.'

'What's she got on you?'

'Dunno.'

'You are absolutely my favourite client, of course,' he purred—like a panther giving its prey a ten second head start. 'But I'm beginning to ask myself why I didn't just stay in the bathhouse.'

She gave him the fig.

'You are all joy.' He settled back into the velvet and closed his eyes. 'I'll send you my bill.'

The palanquin was still gliding up Skuller. She knew she was being an ass. She was in dire need of his advice and expertise. But his high-handedness was insufferable.

Delivering her to grandmama like a naughty schoolgirl! She gritted her teeth.

'Sorry.'

He opened one green-amber eye. 'Continue.'

'You're right, Mooby did tell me it was a murder investigation. She kept on asking when I was last in the Slackey, and what I was doing over the week end. But I genuinely don't know what she's got on me, other than he was my business associate. Believe it or not, I was on my way to report it when they grabbed me.'

Voom! Back on full legal alert. 'Report what?'

'Well, his murder, obviously. An informant told me he'd had his throat cut by the slavers, and his body was under the floor of his shack.'

A very long silence followed this. 'Oh shit.'

'What?'

'Sorry, let's be clear here: who are we talking about?'

'Thwyn Brakstone, of course.'

He drummed his fingers. She could almost hear the thoughts zipping like killer hornets round his mind. 'What did you tell Mooby?'

'Nothing. Just kept reciting my rights.'

'Thank God for that. Your informant—was he or she confessing to the murder?' She shook her head. 'Have you seen the body? The murder weapon?'

'No.'

'So you don't actually know any of it's true.'

'No. But—'

'Anabara, you don't *know* this. It's hearsay. You have no duty to pass on unsubstantiated rumours to the Guard.' The palanquin made a smooth right hand turn. Probably passing through the Minstery gatehouse arch. 'As your Counsel,

I strongly advise you to remain silent. Leave this with me. I'll see what I can find out. I hope to God he's not dead.'

'Butros, you're scaring me!' She grabbed his silk-clad arm. 'What's going on? Someone *else* has been murdered?'

'Yes. Two bodies were found by a mud-lark at low tide late last night. Probably killed somewhere else, then dumped.'

'Oh my God! Who were they?'

'Their names haven't been released yet. But they were Tressy rivermen. My source says they choked on their own blood.'

Everything went glassy again. 'But how could that happen?' she whispered.

'The murderer cut out their tongues.'

CHAPTER TEN

Oh, I learnt it from the rivermen, whispered Paran in her memory. *They are careless with their tongues.*

She began to shake. 'Oh God, Butros, I think I know who killed them.'

Butros tugged the silk bell rope. The palanquin halted. He murmured new directions to the bearers, and they set off again.

'Change of plan. Grandmama can wait till the morning. I'll send a message.' He put a hand on her arm, but asked no more questions until they were safely in his apartment overlooking Palatine Square.

She had known Butros more than half her life, but she'd never been up here before. Nobody had. He was psychotically private. He conducted his business in his Chambers, his pleasure in the bathhouse. But here she was, in his reclining room, surrounded by understated good taste that murmured *fifty gilders an hour.* She lay on a low couch while he brought her bread, olives, cheese, wine. The best of everything. She couldn't do justice to it. The fact that he'd brought her here told her she was in deep trouble.

'Right. Let's hear it,' he said.

'But you'll just run to grandmama!' Dammit, stop crying. She blew her nose.

'I think you must be confusing me with Enobar. Talk.'

So she told him everything. The library contract, Thwyn's disappearance, Loxi's nightmare year on the boats, the slave market, her fears about Paran. He listened without gasps and reproaches, pressing her only on the legal details of her deal with the Fairy. Then he was silent. Thinking. For what felt like a month.

Eventually he said, 'Well, there's a hair-raising tale. Looks like you're right, someone's trying to frame you. My money's on the rivermen. Their leader, whom you so chillingly describe, is one Semmayit Golar. Owns a palace over on the Mainland, protected by razor webs and thought-activated psycho-charms, courtesy of a certain Larridy security firm with whom he has business dealings. Allegedly. Golar also has a pack of Tressy wolf hounds roaming his grounds. Avoid him.' He drummed his fingers again. 'So, that deal of yours definitely bars the Fay from doing you any harm?'

'The *Fairy*, Butros. Yes, definitely. Plus he can't harm any member of my family.'

'Well, that's about half the population of Larridy covered. Do *not* ask him for the truth until I've had a chance to speak to him. Describe him, please.'

'Oh, you know, typical Fairy worker. Kind of…' What the hell *did* he look like?

'Distinguishing features? Any fire tattoos?'

'No. Wait…' What was it she was so nearly, nearly remembering?

Butros sighed. 'Remind me never to call you as a witness. Don't worry, I'll have him located. Paran. Cute name.'

'I couldn't help it!' She braced herself for more blighting sarcasm. 'Butros, do you think he actually could be… an elite mind warrior?'

'Why yes! What other explanation could there possibly be?—other than you ballsed up the deal and he's playing you like a tinker's fiddle.'

'Yes, but what about the Freeman Pass?'

'Did he actually *claim* he'd performed a perception charm on it?'

She thought back. 'Good point. He said "the charm's in the beholder's eye."'

'Then I think, on balance, we can assume he stole the pass, and he's just your average lying gutter weasel.'

'My God, you are *such* a bigot, Butros!' Still, she had to admit it was a relief. 'Do you think Loxi and I should go to the Guard and lay evidence against Golar?'

'Not till I've got a better picture of what's going on. Tell Mr. Laitolo to keep his mouth shut and make an appointment to see me. I suggest you try to carry on as normal,' he said. 'Look, I know you're scared the Fay killed them—'

'FAIRY!'

'—but this has all the hallmarks of a tribal killing.'

'Well, I just hope you're right, that's all.'

'They were probably informants. The tongues will have been sent to their families. All of which leaves me wondering what Mooby's got on you.' More finger drumming. 'Hmm. Anyway, for now, stay alert, keep out of the Slackey, and don't make yourself an easy target.'

'You think I'm in danger?'

'Just a precaution. For your ears only, there's talk of corruption. That's why Mooby's been brought in to head up the anti-trafficking unit.'

'The City Guard are involved? You're kidding!'

'Then why do the tip-offs always come too late? Why are no big arrests ever made? These questions are certainly being asked over in Mainland Federation Guard HQ.'

They were?

'Do you keep abreast of inter-state politics at all?'

'Naturally,' she lied.

The eyebrow. 'Then *naturally* you'll know the Federation is getting impatient with Larridy acting like it's still a Palatinate and a law unto itself. Hence the likes of Ms Mooby, kicking ass without fear or favour. But she'll back off you, now there's the possibility of legal action.'

'*Possibility*? I'm damn well pressing charges! She—'

'Think, please. What if someone high up in the Guard wants to see her booted back to Bogganburg in disgrace? She's one ugly bad-tempered mare, but at least she's on the level. Never fear, I'll keep her on a short leash.' He yawned, and stretched. 'Bedtime. I'm in Court early. Grandmama is expecting you at 10. Tell her your Counsel has forbidden you to discuss this highly sensitive case with anyone.'

'Seriously? She won't understand. And Enobar will be hopping mad.'

A small smile. 'A day in which I annoy Enobar is a day not wasted. Let me show you to your room. Don't be afraid. This whole place is charmed as tight as a drum.'

'Thanks, Butros.'

He flicked her cheek with a finger. 'Sleep well.'

Anabara woke early to the sound of rain against the window. It was nearly light. She pulled on yesterday's clothes. Butros had already set off for his Chambers, so she left him a thank you note like a good Galen girl, and let herself out of his apartment. The door closed behind her. Charms activated. State-of-the-art security, so powerful she got a momentary brain-fuzz off the force field. God, the man was paranoid.

She went down the marble stairs. Not too stiff, considering what she'd been through in the last few days. Her hands had completely healed. Some serious training was overdue all the same. No way would anyone catch her napping like that again.

Out in Palatine Square the wet cobbles shone. Rain whispered in the plane trees, dripped from the last yellow leaves which hung as big as dragon's paws. The wind flutes were silent, but the weather was gearing up for the equinoctial storms. Only a couple of days now till Wolf Tide.

She headed for the Precincts. The gatehouse doors stood open. Chestnut hulls lay on the flagstones like tiny hedgehogs. She saw other silent figures in the morning gloom, all heading towards the same quadrangle for the Dawn Song. If any of them were tourists expecting some kind of choral rendition, they'd be in for a surprise.

In St Dalfinia Senior Women's Bathhouse Anabara changed into her white martial suit. She walked barefoot across the rainy courtyard and took up her position among the other high-ranked warriors. The Master of Novices called them to order. First the formal bows, then with a slow circling move the Dawn Song began. Spectators always commented on how graceful and flowing the silent routine looked. Yeah, thought Anabara—flowing gracefully from *We take down the opponent* into *and now we break his neck!*

The rain fell, fine, relentless. She felt it trickle down inside her collar. Breathe, focus. Inhabit each move fully. But her thoughts rambled, bleating and idiotic as saltings sheep. *Smack that cow Mooby's head in. Paran. Was the Zaarzuk here? Grandmama. I'm soaked.* She was powerless to round them up.

What a total travesty that was, she thought when it was over. She turned to slip away, but not fast enough. Her name was called. She clenched her teeth, approached the Master, bowed.

'Ms Nolio, where's your focus this morning?' he asked.

Behind him the novices were all earwigging. The Zaarzuk grinned.

Anabara bowed to the Master again. 'If you lecture me in front of these pillocks,' she whispered in Gull, 'I'm going to lie on the floor and kick and scream.'

He considered this. Inclined his head. 'You need some sparring practice. Come.' He began to walk towards the combat hall. She fell into step beside him. 'Had a bad night, you? You'll feel better when you've kicked seven kinds of crap out of me, eh.'

Yeah, he was right. That felt better. A thirty minute bout of crap-kicking sorted her head out the way meditation never did. And now she was twiddling her thumbs till her appointment with grandmama. Reclining in a silk robe in the bathhouse. Nice long soak, a massage, and now a lounge. The student quarters were fairly basic, but no expense was ever spared for the Precinct's elite. A music charm played theorbo concertos, incense rose from the censers, and she'd sent the bathhouse girl off to fetch her some clean clothes from grandmama's. Well, no point being a stuck-up little princess if you didn't milk it now and then.

This morning she was the only one reclining among the purple velvet cushions. Laid out on the low marble slab beside her was breakfast. All the meanies had provided was a few pathetic baskets of fresh bread, some platters of cold meat and fish, bowls of fruit, mounds of frivolous patisserie.

Oh well, I can always ring the little bell and send the girl for more, thought Anabara.

She poured some chocolate and was about to select a pastry when—there!—something moved.

Her pulse raced. Someone was in here. A man. Golar! Behind that carved screen. Between her and the door. *Stay alert. Don't make yourself an easy target.* No other exit. The windows were high, narrow. A weapon. The water flagon. Pelago, let him not have a crossbow!

Her fingers closed round the vessel's neck. Focus. Keep him in your peripheral vision. Wait for his move.

She could hear him breathing.

Then a voice whispered, 'Psst, pretty girl!'

Dear God! She released the flagon. That *fecking* Zaarzuk.

His appeared from behind the screen, grinning. 'I see you fighting the Master. Hey, you fight very good. For a girl.' She was trembling with rage. And the tidal wave of relief. He crossed swiftly and knelt before her. 'Hey, hey. I frightened you? I'm sorry.'

She shoved him away. 'Just *feck* off, idiot! This isn't some stupid game!'

He smote his forehead. 'I am a big idiot, like you say. Forgive me. You think, for real, someone is hunting you?' His eyes flashed. 'Only tell me his name, and you shall have his jewels for knacker-ackers and his head for your gatepost!'

'Clown.' She steadied her breathing. 'It's nothing. Work stuff. Now get out. You shouldn't be here.'

'Tell me about your work. I can help, maybe?'

'No way.'

'Ach, God's love! Pity me. I kick my heels here, I weep for boredom. I miss my horse, I miss my dogs. Am I a schoolboy? Give me man's work and I will do it. Tell me: this

Fay—Fairy—of yours. He mends the ancient charms of the library, yes?'

'Yes.' Or pretends to. 'Out. Now.'

'I go, I go. But the library, you know it has tunnels with many thousand, thousand books? Some say twenty leagues, like a maze, all under here.' He rapped his knuckles on the marble floor.

'Yes, the Stacks. What about them?'

'There are ghosts down there.'

'Tscha!'

'Would I lie to you? Ghosts of Fays. Fairies. I have seen their lights.'

'No you haven't. Students aren't allowed in the Stacks.'

'What can I say?' He turned up his palms. 'I am a Zaarzuk. I go where I am not allowed. I see a sign, *Forbidden* and pff! I must go there.'

'Really? I hadn't noticed that.' Stop encouraging him. She tried to frown. 'Look, seriously, if you're caught in here—'

He shrugged. 'Then I take my punishment. Who is this great dumb Gull you bring to the library, hey? I hate this man. All the girls are lusting for him. They steal books on purpose, so he must come to fetch them back. I think maybe you keep his picture in this?' He flicked the amulet with his finger. 'Maybe he's your lover?'

'None of your business.' She slapped his hand away. 'Now get out, or I'll tell the Master.'

'You would betray me?' He seized her hand and tucked it inside his robe, pressed it to his heart. Her breath caught. God, the taut muscle of his chest. 'You feel it beat, yes? The Master, he has no heartbeat. He has no passions, no weakness like other men.'

Wrong, she thought. Yanni had no defence against her girlish pouting and tantrums. Admittedly, these weren't ideal tactics for a Zaarzuk warrior.

'Why you smile?' He raised her hand to his lips, but she snatched it away. 'He works me, he beats me with his stick, he gives me nothing but water and oats. What, am I his mule?' He gazed at the feast.

Anabara sighed. 'Go on then.'

He kissed his finger tips, and fell to it.

Well, the man surely had an appetite. She lounged back among the cushions and watched as he devoured more than she usually ate in a week—bread, cheese, meat, more bread, cakes, great drafts of pomegranate juice. He smacked his lips, he groaned with pleasure. Yanni was clearly starving him.

Finally he wiped his mouth, sighed, and gave her a flashing smile.

'Finished?'

'I pause for breath.' He pointed to the pastries. 'What you call these, hey?'

A spot of Offcomer-baiting was called for here. 'Well, the little round ones are harlot's navels,' she lied.

He worked the tip of his tongue into his chipped front tooth. 'Yes, I know this sweetmeat.'

I bet. 'Those ones there are tart's thighs.'

'These I know also. They fall apart very easy.'

She guffawed. 'And the ones with cherries on top are maidenheads. Help yourself.'

'Help myself?' He reclined suddenly, facing her. Mouth inches from hers. 'A man does not help himself to a maidenhead. It must be given him as a gift, yes?'

'Na ah.' She laughed. 'You'll be waiting a long— Woo! Get off, you ape!'

'Come, let me try how sweet the cherry is.' Stop giggling, idiot, sling him out! But the heat and hardness of him, through the thin silk. 'You make me have these tarts instead?' he asked, 'these harlots?' His mouth. Too close.

Oh dear Lord.

It was true.

That *was* how those filthy Zaarzuks kissed. Like this. And this. And—

A shriek echoed round the room. The girl dropped the pile of clothes and fled.

Anabara squirmed underneath him, tried to thrust him off. 'Get out!' An alarm bell started clanging. 'Get out, get *out!*'

But the Zaarzuk only laughed at her panic. He twitched her robe open, and sprang back out of reach. 'Hah, two pretty peaches! These I will have later.'

'You—!' She clutched the silk round herself. 'Arsehole!'

He scooped up a handful of pastries and swaggered from the lounge to meet his punishment.

CHAPTER ELEVEN

I meant to do that. It was a tactic. Create huge rumpus,
distract grandmama from murder enquiry.

Aw Go-o-od. This was *so* mortifying. Anabara sat huddled on the library roof, her chin on her knees. Silver ropes
of rain shimmered their way across the salt flats. The only
person in history to be banned from the St Dalfinia Senior
Women's Bathhouse for lewd behaviour.

But we were only kissing, for God's sake. If it's lewd
behaviour you want, check out the Senior *Men's* Bathhouse!
Talk about double standards!

Nevertheless, Ms Nolio, you are banned. Furthermore,
you should consider yourself fortunate your contract with
the library has not been terminated. Said the Dean of
Women. (Also known as Aunt Léanora.)

Yes, it would blow over; the worst of the nudging and
sniggering would pass. And no doubt she could have Butros
kick up a legal stink about gender discrimination and get
the ban reversed. But she would for evermore be pointed
out as that detective who'd been surprised in the bathhouse
under a Zaarzuk. God, nobody was going to take her seriously ever again!

She thunked her forehead. What's the *matter* with you?
Encouraging him with your smutty jokes and giggling, then

expecting him to listen when you tell him to get out! Oh why was she so crap at the whole man thing? Screwed by her mixed heritage, that's why. Everyone kept giving the poor motherless Anabara the benefit of their advice. The Galen women told her to assert her right to physical love without shame (well, unless that contravened University regulations). Then along came the Gullmothers to tell her that only dirty sluts didn't save themselves for their husband on their wedding night!

Small wonder she was so clueless. Helpless in the hands of a greedy wicked Zaarzuk who knew exactly what he was about. Did she love him? No. Yes. No. *No*! Stupid and pointless to fall for him. Not like she was going to ride off into the sunset and become a Zaarzuk bride, was it! Learn his language and his ways. Be treated worse than his dog.

And then there was the thought of Yanni. She wrung her hands. Anything else she could brazen out. He'd said nothing, but he was incandescent. This was what had driven her up here on to the roof. She was trying to get a grip before facing grandmama. It wasn't working. Instead, she found herself two seconds from howling in misery. She flapped her hands in front of her eyes to urge back the rising tide of tears. No good.

She scrambled to her feet. Then her heart lurched as if she'd lost her footing. Paran. Watching from the top of the library dome. God, that's all I need. My lovely associate: at best a liar, at worst a killer.

He sprang down, skimmed silently across the wet roof tops towards her. It hit her: I've spent my whole life trying to be pro-Fairy because of my parents. But I hate them. I hate the creepy way they move. I hate the way they stare. I hate the way they talk. I hate every horrible slinking lying thing about them. I know I shouldn't, but I do. There. I'm worse than Butros, she thought. At least Butros isn't a hypocrite.

The Fairy dropped to her side. Stared. Waited.

She cleared her throat. 'How's the charm-work going? Any progress?'

'Yes.'

Lying gutter weasel. Playing you like a tinker's fiddle. She'd got to master the art of pinning him down. 'Specifically,' she said, 'what progress have you made with the library's ancient stained glass window charms?'

Pause. That was another thing she hated—the time lag before he answered.

Every.

Bloody.

Conversation.

'Specifically,' he replied, 'I have repaired the defence charms on seven of the twelve stained glass windows in the Library Round Room dome of St Pelago's University, in the City Isle of Larridy.'

For a fleeting second Anabara wondered if he was taking the piss. But they had no sense of humour, of course. Then she thought: hang on, *repaired?* He'd *repaired* them? Impossible, he—

Pin him down, *pin him down.* 'When you say "repaired", what do you mean, exactly?'

Stare. 'I mean, I have restored them to good condition and working order. Set them to rights. Mended them. Renovated, revivified, re-pristinated them,' he said. 'Is my meaning still obscure?'

Shit—the preservation orders! What kind of a bodged job had he done? 'Aargh! Stop mending them!'

'No.'

'Paran, these are priceless heritage-listed artifacts, not shop fronts! You can't just wade in and charm the crap out of them! Stop working on them this minute!' He shook his head. 'Hey! The deal says I'm the boss.'

'The deal also says I have "my own area of responsibility". Namely—' he curled his lip '—security "stuff".'

'Well, the deal ALSO says you have to promote the wellbeing of my business!' she yelled in panic. 'We're just supposed to be doing a preliminary report, here! If you knacker those windows, my professional reputation goes up in flames!'

'Ah—your professional reputation! I was forgetting,' said the Fairy. 'Perhaps I, too, could enhance it by cavorting naked with a dirty horseboy in the public bathhouse?'

Her cheeks blazed. '*What* did you say?'

'I said, perhaps—'

'I heard you, bog scum! I'll toss you off the fecking roof if you talk to me like that! First off, I didn't *cavort naked* with him; secondly, we call them *Zaarzuks*; and thirdly, it wasn't the *public* bathhouse!'

A long silence. Long enough for Anabara to recite the 'doing her no harm' clause to herself several times. And to reconsider the bog scum remark.

'A word of advice,' said the Fairy. 'Don't defend yourself like that. You'll only magnify your folly.'

'I don't need your advice.'

The three-quarters bell began to chime. Grandmama.

She made a belated stab at dignity. 'I apologise for losing my temper. We'll have to discuss the windows later, as I have an appointment. One other thing—my Counsel wants to see you. He'll explain why. His name's Butros Kaledh and I'd appreciate it if you told him the truth.'

'Butros Kaledh.' Pause. Another curl of the lip. 'Is he a kinsman of yours?'

Ba-boom! went her heart. 'Why do you ask that?'

'Oh, curiosity.'

Rain pattered on the tiles all around. She could read nothing in those jet-black eyes. 'Listen, I love Butros, all right? He's like family. I'd be beside myself if anything bad happened to him.'

'Ah!' said the Fairy. 'Then we must hope he is careful.' He turned to leave.

'Paran, listen to me!' she called after him. 'You can't just... just go around killing people. You've got to promise— What?'

He was pointing to the side of his head. 'My right ear. I am attached to it. I prefer to remain so.'

With that, he was off over the rooftops like a grey spider.

Grins on every side. It was like those nightmares where you're walking to school and for some reason you've got no clothes on. Go on, say something, she urged them. Say one word and I'll kick your teeth in. She passed a knot of male students outside the buttery. One of them clicked his tongue like a horse trotting. Blood rushed to her cheeks. Right! But as she turned, the Fairy's words flashed into her mind: *You'll only magnify your folly.* Paran had given her good advice once before and she'd ignored him. She clenched her fists and walked on. Snickering followed her down the length of the marble arcade.

And now there was the 'What Are We Going To Do About Anabara?' committee to face. Which influential VIPs had grandmama assembled this time for the emergency Governors' Meeting? The university Vice Chancellor? The High Sheriff of Larridy? God?

Enobar would be wetting himself with excitement. Maybe I'll get Paran to kill him after all. Anabara thunked her forehead again. Don't joke about it! If you tried to be funny, even intelligent highbred Fairies stared like you'd lifted a leg and farted. They could grasp the idea of humour conceptually, but they drew back in disgust whenever it occurred. She doubted Paran even got the concept. He was the most literal-minded moron she'd ever met. *I LOVE ENOBAR*, she daubed in letters a yard high.

And she did. In spite of everything, she loved him. Partly because he was a fellow demy. His father was Galen, his mother Candacian. Shorter than most Galens, slight, totally exquisite to look at with his honey skin, his curls, his slanting dark eyes. Grandmama had poached him three years back from the Candacian Embassy, where he had been a trainee attaché. He came with glowing references. Of course he did! According to Butros, Enobar had been about one week away from getting fired for his inability to keep his big mouth shut. Or tell the truth when it was open. Enobar was 19 years old and in the humour stakes, the total opposite of a Fairy—he thought everything was a joke. And Anabara just knew today's gag was going to be: *Did you hear the one about the Patriarch's niece and the Zaarzuk?*

She rounded the corner beside the library.

What the hell?

Blood rushed back to her face. The scholasticus—with Carraman Senior and a highbred female Fairy. Probably the one Loxi had seen busting into Anabara's house. All three stared at her as though they had heard the joke, and frankly, it was about as big and clever as a whoopee cushion. Carraman fingered his silver-topped ebony cane. His eyes slid over her damp clothes, grubby from the library roof, and he sneered. The Fairy's tattoos rippled with liquid fire. She didn't sneer, but she emanated menace, like a bottled thunderstorm.

Then the scholasticus inclined his head, and the three passed on in silence. The ten o'clock bell began to ring. Golar, she thought suddenly. *A certain Larridy security firm with whom he has business dealings.* Allegedly. What was going on? Was Carraman part of the plot to frame her? She stared after them and felt an icicle of fear slip into her chest. But there was no time to puzzle over it now. She sped towards the Senior Staff quarters and up the shallow marble stairs.

The door chime faded. She heard the flutter of silk, the tinkle of anklets, as bare feet padded to the door. Enobar let her in.

'I'm not telling you anything,' she said. 'Who's here?'

'Just me and her ladyship,' he whispered. 'But you are *so* going to tell me *everything.* Oh my God, oh my God—was he masterful? Did he—'

She smacked him aside and went through to the reclining room. 'Grandmama!'

'Darling!' A whirlwind of embroidered kaftan and Anabara was in the matriarchal bosom, cheek ground against a tangle of pearls and gold. Jessamine enveloped her and she was two years old again.

'You poor, poor child! This is an *outrage!* What was Léonora *thinking?*' Anabara was crushed even tighter. Grandmama's nasty little hairless dog yipped around their ankles. 'Come, sit with me, my darling, and tell me all about it. Enobar, a tisane. And some almond biscuits.'

They sank into the velvet depths of the couch. Anabara kicked off her boots and tucked her feet under her. The dog sprang up. She shoveled it into grandmama's lap and wiped her hands. The thing looked like a raw offal sausage with a ginger moustache.

'I make a point of never criticizing my successor,' began Grandmama—Anabara knew better than to glance Enobar's way at this piece of monumental self-delusion— 'but I would *not* have made such an absurd song and dance were *I* still dean. A quiet word, that's all that was required.' She adjusted her peacock feather turban, and petted the dog. Dame Ferdinora Bharossa had the nose of a sorceress, and her eyes were a terrifying poison green in her dark face. Her reputation as a hex-caster was formidable. Completely unfounded, but formidable.

'As if we were not all aware how much "hospitality" goes on in the men's bathhouse!' she snorted.

Enobar was lurking in the kitchen doorway behind grandmama's back. Mouthing, *Is it true? The gold rings?* Anabara gave him the fig. He tossed his black ringlets.

'Don't worry.' Grandmama stroked Anabara's cheek. 'I'll have Butros sort this out, my darling. Well! A Zaarzuk is a splendid choice! In fact, you could scarcely have done better, I think.'

'Actually, grandmama, we didn't—'

'True, they are a byword for lechery, but highborn Galen women have taken Zaarzuk lovers in the past. Queen Zephnia, for example...' Anabara tried to focus on the *Zaarzuk Consorts Down the Ages* lecture, but Enobar was posing in the doorway with a cucumber by way of illustration. 'Well, it's true,' concluded grandmama. 'I don't know *why* you find this so amusing, Anabara.' She turned. 'Where's that tisane?'

Enobar whisked out of sight, then came back with the tray. 'I totally agree, mistress.' He set down the tea and perched on a stool at grandmama's feet like another pampered lap-dog. 'But unfortunately, Tadzar Dal Ramek is a novice.'

'That's easily remedied: he must enroll as an ordinary undergraduate,' decided grandmama. 'I will speak to Yannick.'

'No!' Anabara flushed. 'Please don't get involved. The Zaarzuk is *not* my lover and he's not going to be. So can we *please* move on?'

'Very well, my dear, but you have no need to be ashamed of the uninhibited pursuit of self-expression.' Grandmama gestured and Enobar poured the lime blossom tea. 'With all due respect to the traditions of your father's people, the fettishising of female chastity is both archaic and repressive. You are seventeen! It's time you gained some experience, my dear. What about that ravishing Gull boy?'

For God's sake! Anabara loved her grandmama dearly, but now and then a disloyal thought flashed through her head. How on earth had this shocking old woman produced three such saintly children? One Patriarch, one starched-up Dean of Women and one martyr! 'Loxi and I are *business partners*, grandmama. You know what you think about mixing business and pleasure.'

'Oh,' said grandmama. 'Well, we'll put him on my pay roll instead. I'm sure Enobar can find a job for him.'

'Oh, mistress!' Enobar crossed his eyes and gave a happy shiver. 'I know the exact job I'd like to give him!'

Anabara leant forward and hissed, 'He's a *Gull*, you jackass!'

'Did you realise, the poor boy has been living in some *frightful* cockroach-infested hostel, six to a room?' asked grandmama. 'Of course, I had him brought up here to my guest quarters the instant I heard about it.'

'You did *what?*' No need to ask whose idea that had been!
Right. When Mother Laitolo comes storming in to punch
my lights out, I will be referring her to *you.* But Enobar was
too absorbed in admiring his buffed nails to catch her eye.

'Well, never mind all this. My darling, what is this *terrible*
business with the Guard? I could not believe my ears when
the messenger came last night!'

'Thank you for rescuing me, but I'm sorry,' said Anabara.
'Butros has forbidden me to discuss this highly sensitive case
with anyone.'

'Yes, yes, of course he has,' soothed grandmama, 'but
that doesn't mean *me.*'

It took several minutes to convince her that this was,
indeed, what Butros had meant. While they argued, Enobar
picked up his beribboned lute and began plucking chords.

'Well,' said grandmama eventually, 'Butros knows best,
but—I saw that, Enobar!—but I shall have a quiet word
with Chief Dhalafan, all the same. He was telling me at
the Feast only yesterday that some *dreadful* Boggan woman
has been foisted on them by the Mainlanders. These
Offcomers, they *mean* well, he said, but they do *not* understand our ways. Don't worry, Hector Dhalafan will sort it all
out, my darling.'

Anabara gave way. It was usually better to nominate something for grandmama to help you with, otherwise she got
frustrated and started to help behind your back. 'Thanks,
grandmama. That would be wonderful.' She kissed the old
woman's cheek.

There were three more lectures to sit through: *How
to Handle Lowbred Fairy Associates, Reasons Anabara Should
Resume her Academic Career,* and *What the Scholasticus Wants
and Why.* Then she had to fend off all Enobar's persuasive

wiles as he walked with her to the Library. She threw him a crumb of gossip—a description of Butros's apartment.

'No!' He clapped a hand to his mouth in glee. 'Mirrors on the *ceiling*? Oh my God, oh my God, it sounds like a Bogganburg bordello! I won't tell a soul.'

The lie would be all round Larridy by nightfall. Serve Butros right. If he hadn't installed a highly illegal memory-wipe charm on his door, she wouldn't have been forced to make it all up, would she?

It was lunchtime. Now would be a good time to track down the mimic-charm in the Round Room ceiling. And maybe have a nose around in the Stacks and see what this ghost nonsense was all about. She entered the library foyer and headed across the chess-board floor to the Round Room.

Her way was immediately blocked by a large black-robed beadle. Part Gull, by the look of him. 'Sorry, Ms Nolio. Can't go in there. My orders are to escort you away from the library. The scholasticus will see you in his study.'

No! How *dare* the scholasticus humiliate her publicly like this! No point taking it out on the messenger, though. They set off. The beadle's heavy tread echoed in the foyer. They climbed the sweeping staircase. I'm about to be fired, she thought. Well, that explained Carraman's presence. Her mind bristled with law suits. I'll bloody see you in court, you devious, double-dealing, fecking... fecking... *librarian!*

The beadle rang the bell, then bowed. Anabara glared. Hope you enjoyed your moment of power, you sad small person.

'Just doing my job, Ms Nolio.' He glanced left and right. Murmured in Gull, 'Kick his bony arse, eh.'

CHAPTER TWELVE

'I demand an explanation, Doctor!' barked Anabara, getting in first.

It was clear from his prim face what the explanation was: she had brought the Library into disrepute by her lewdness and made a fool of him in front of his colleagues in Chapter. He was not man enough to say this out loud, though.

'I have taken professional advice.' He wasn't looking at her. For fear of contracting the lewdness germ. 'In the light of which—'

'What, from Carraman?'

'That doesn't concern you!' he snapped. 'The Library will be making alternative security arrangements from now on. So if your associate would kindly expedite his report on the state of the ancient charms, we will wind up your contract.'

'Let me get this straight—you're firing me?'

'Please don't make this difficult for yourself, Ms Nolio.' He opened the door. 'That will be all.'

Anabara's temper flared. 'You want us to leave the job half done? We are long past the report stage, doctor. My associate has already repaired seven of the windows.'

'What?' He forgot himself and looked at her. 'He has done *what* to them?'

'*Repaired*,' said Anabara. 'Restored them to good condition and working order. Renovated, re-pristinated them. Which bit didn't you follow?'

The scholasticus closed the door and sat down hard on the nearest chair. He got out a white handkerchief and blotted his forehead. 'Well. Good gracious. Are you sure?'

'Absolutely.' She could always change her name and flee the country.

'Well, good gracious me. I had not thought... I was told... Well, this is thrilling news indeed! You *are* confident that the work complies with the current heritage legislation?'

'Absolutely.' Mngaargh.

'And I trust there has been no, ah... escalation of costs?'

'My agency prides itself on sticking to an agreed a fee, Doctor.' That's right—we're lewd, but we're cheap. 'So *if* you'd to allow me back in the Library?'

'Of course, of course! I apologise for the, ah, misunderstanding.' He scuttled to his desk, snatched up a quill and began to scribble on a slip of headed parchment. Now his precious budget was safe, she could probably prance nude on High Table with a rose in her teeth. 'There. That should suffice.' He handed it to her. 'Again, my apologies. I'm afraid I had not appreciated that Mr a'Menehaïn was so highly skilled an artisan.'

She treated him to grandmama's haughtiest stare. 'I only employ the best, doctor. And now I propose to take a swift look round the Stacks, and—'

'No!' His eyes darted to the door.

'I'm sorry?'

Tick, tick, went the clock.

The scholasticus swallowed. Blotted his forehead again. 'You can't. That is to say, the Master of Stacks assures me

there are no security issues with the underground book
depository. You will find plenty to keep you occupied in the
Round Room. The mimic charm, for instance.' He opened
the door for her once more. 'May I just reiterate how grateful I am for all your hard work, Ms Nolio?'

'It's a pleasure, Doctor.'

She headed straight for the Stacks. The door was protected
by a top of the range sentinel charm. Carraman's best. Again,
a question mark sprang into her mind. What was Caraman's
role in all this? Just trying to claw back the business he'd lost
to her? His sentinel charm trounced her, anyway. In vain
she presented her permission slip from the scholasticus and
recited the names of her important relatives. *No Unauthorised
Access,* said the sign. *By order of the Master of Stacks.*

The Master of Stacks? Anabara could vaguely picture
him, another skinny spider-legged Galen, but with a stoop
like he was carrying an invisible water-bucket in each hand.
What the hell did he have to say to anything, though? Why
was the scholasticus so freaked out at the thought of her
investigating the Stacks? Once again she missed Linna.
She'd have cooked up some devious scheme for by-passing
official channels. So far Loxi had shown no flair for devi-
ousness. But she had another useful cousin, didn't she?
Rodania. Groan. Anabara left the library, hit the rooftops
and sprang from building to building until she reached the
scientific quarters.

Rodania was far too polite to allude to Anabara's disgrace, but she oozed disapproval. No doubt she whole-
heartedly endorsed of the Dean of Women's disciplinary
action. *Mummy's* disciplinary action. Anabara moved swiftly
to safer subjects.

The Master of Stacks, said Rodania, was an obnoxious power-crazed creep, who unfortunately had to be tolerated because he was so efficient that Chapter could not afford to get rid of him. He was appointed thirty-five years ago, and under his rule the Stacks had gone from a chaotic shambles and drain on University money to a slick outfit that ran like clockwork.

No, Rodania had never been down there. Nobody had, just the Stackmaster and his team of assistants. You ordered a book and it was hauled up the chute to the Round Room. Of course nobody had done a stock check recently! Did Anabara have any idea how many books were down there? Millions! Larridy University Library had a copy of every book ever published, both here and on the Mainland! Yes, Rodania would put her mind to it and see if she could come up with a way of getting past the Sentinel charm, although that was highly illegal and flew in the face of umpteen University regulations.

They were perilously close to a discussion of *other* regulations that one or two individuals had flouted. Anabara thanked her cousin and left before she slapped her silly.

But meanwhile, there had to be another entrance to the Stacks, or how had the pillock, sorry, Zaarzuk got in? Down the book chute? He was too big for that. No chance of questioning him—he'd be off hauling mule carts up Skuller, or whatever punishment the Master had seen fit to dish out. Anabara cringed to think she'd landed Yanni in such a position. She sped back over the roofs to the Round Room to distract herself by looking for the mimic charm. This time the beadle bowed her through the doors.

There were three reading levels above the main floor, circular galleries reached by spiral staircases. At the very top was the stained glass cupola. From the third level balustrade it was a quick spurt up to the narrow ledge that ran round inside the dome. She heard gasps from down below. Don't panic, citizens. The girl can fly.

As she edged past the windows, clinging to the mullions—the tinkle of glass. She froze. Don't say Paran really had restored them. My God, he had! The entire window was alive. Horses fidgeted, hooves clinked on pavements, and look! even the standards were rippling in the breeze, supple as fish scales. She edged further. And these must be the ones he hadn't got to yet—rigid in their lead confines, only their eyes moving. She inched back to study the repaired windows. An angel yawned, spread its wings like a peacock tail, then folded them again, snick-snick-snick. For several minutes she was lost in amazement.

Right. Let's find that mimic charm. She checked all the nooks and crevices of the tracery. Somewhere there would be a little carved artifact or some kind. Aha! There it was, wedged in that spandrel. A wooden troll, grinning over its shoulder, mooning. Very classy. She reached up. Her fingers almost brushed it when— Shit! A rap on the other side of the glass almost sent her tumbling off the ledge. Her pulse skittered. Paran. Shaking his head.

What? she mouthed.

'It's jinxed,' she heard him say. 'Leave it to me. I have plans for it.'

Booby-trapped. Should have thought of that. Probably set to bawl obscenities if you tried to move it. Maybe fitted with a cocklebur jinx as well. God, she certainly didn't want *that* stuck to her hand, effing and blinding all the way to the Infirmary Charms Unit.

Well, there were books to retrieve, if nothing else. She and Loxi could divide up the list until she figured out a way of getting into the Stacks. She set off and met him coming back into the Precincts, carrying yet more volumes. His hair was hazed with fine rain. My God, he was *so* ridiculously gorgeous. Why the hell didn't she fancy him?

'Hey, Nan. I hear the Guard took you last night. What's going on?'

Looked like he was the only person on the Mount who hadn't got wind of her indiscretion. She was not about to fill him in. 'Long story. Let's get out of the rain, eh, then I'll tell you.'

They walked to Larridy's most famous chocolate house; made out of a gigantic wine tun, snugly housed in an archway under the Precincts' fortifications. One hundred and thirty oak trees had been felled to make it, and the guidebooks boasted it once held 60,000 gallons of the Prince Patriarch's wine. These days it mostly contained tourists. A waitress brought them gingered hot chocolate. Anabara recounted last night's adventure to Loxi and gave him Butros's message.

'So keep quiet till he's instructed you what to do. Don't go confiding in Enobar. Even if he swears on his mother's— *Shit*, Loxi. What have you told him?'

He blushed. 'Nothing!'

'I warned you, moron!' She grabbed his shirt front and pulled him nose-to-nose. 'And another thing! What the hell am I going to tell your mum? "Why'd you let my boy live up there with the mollies?" Eh?'

'Tell her from me I'm seventeen. I make my own decisions. Want to hear the big secret I told Enobar?' Woo! He was actually angry! 'I'm sick of pretending! I hate fighting.

I hate hunting. I hate the whole big macho Gull warrior thing. I want to go to university.'

'University? Seriously? Hey, good for you.' She let go. Smoothed his shirt for him. Paused in shock. 'Is this *silk*? Did Enobar give it you? Aw, Loxi, you realise what your folks are going to think?'

'Well, they've been thinking it for years, so who gives a shit?'

'But they'll beat you up, babe.' She rubbed his arm. 'Get yourself into the sparring room, eh. Get Yanni to teach you some self-defence.'

'Tscha!' He gave a jeering laugh. 'Check the face out. You think I'd still be this *pretty* if I couldn't look after myself?'

She pictured the other young Gulls she knew. The busted noses, chipped teeth, deformed knuckles. 'Fair point.'

She hadn't the heart to tell him. Loxi, you're only pretty because you always run away.

A dreary afternoon trudging the streets. Book collecting wasn't as easy as she'd thought. Snooty former students kept her waiting on their doorsteps in the rain, and her patience wore as thin as a pawnbroker's smile.

It was getting dark. Time to call it a day. Tscha! look at that—some families already had Wolf Tide jack-o-lanterns in their windows. There'd be kids out raking the streets tonight: *Knock-a-door, knock-a-door, Wolf Tide's come. Give us a sweet or get kicked up the bum!* Back in my day— Anabara caught herself. Sounding like an old Gullmother! Before she knew it she'd be chewing on liquorice twigs and wearing her legs thick-end down.

But it was true: back in her day Wolf Tide was just apples on strings, lanterns, and a trip to the river to watch the tidal bore—not this over-commercialised two day piss-up. Come tomorrow night, Larridy would be heaving with Offcomers. Pillocks in wolf masks. It was only called Wolf Tide from *wofe* tide, the old Galen word for the lunar high tide; but everyone was convinced it was about full moons and ancient pre-Way wolfman myths.

When she got in, Paran was sitting cross-legged in a chair by the hearth, filing his fangs with a sliver of blue whetstone. So that's how come their teeth were pointy. Yeesh. But she was determined to be up-beat.

'Evening! I take back what I said—those windows are incredible!' She put down the books and sat in the other chair. 'The scholasticus is literally weeping with joy. And, yeah, sorry about that bog scum comment.'

He paused his filing to stare. Then resumed. Rasp, rasp.

'So, good work.'

Stare.

'Did you talk to Butros?'

Nod.

'And? What did he say?' Rasp, rasp. 'I hope you told him the truth.'

Pause. 'Absolutely.'

She narrowed her eyes, but let it go. And now a whole cozy evening with him by the fireside lay ahead. Maybe she should read one of the books? *Blah Theory. Applied Blah. The Complete Blahs of Professor Boring.* Loxi was welcome to it.

Her mind wandered back to the Stacks again. Why was the scholasticus so twitchy? How was she going to get past that sentinel charm? She racked her brains. All the time the rasp-rasp-rasp of the file. Her own teeth winced at the noise. Do you *have* to do that? she wanted to yell.

The Fairy cocked his head. 'Well, well. Here comes your horseboy.'

'Don't be ridiculous.' She blushed scarlet. 'He'll be locked up in a penitent's cell. And I've told you—we call them Zaarzuks.'

He tucked the whetstone away and watched her. All she could hear was the rain. And kids out scrounging for Wolf Tide. Then boots. Striding. Her heart began to canter.

Knock-knock!

She sped to the door and opened it a crack. Sure enough, it was Dal Ramek. He'd ditched his robes. 'Are you mad? What are you doing here?'

To his credit, he looked chastened. 'I come to grovel at your feet. Forgive me.'

'I'll think about it. Now get back, you idiot, before someone realises you've gone.' She started to shut the door.

'No! Wait! I come to tell you things,' he whispered. 'Important things about the Stacks. I risk everything!'

She opened the door again. 'Quickly then. Tell me how to get in.'

'Ssh! There is an alley near the slums. You know it?'

'By the Slackey, yes.'

'Here there is a drinking trough, with a carved Zaarzuk chieftain. Charmed. I talk horseflesh and he lets me pass, yes?' He glanced left and right. 'There's more, but I dare not tell you here, standing in the road like this. Let me in.'

She opened the door for him. A yellow flash!—the Zaarzuk was flung sprawling across the street.

'Oh my God! Are you all right?' She blinked. The stench of sulphur filled her nostrils. 'Oi, Paran! This charm of yours is acting up.'

He came and studied the threshold. 'The viper jinx has been triggered. Interesting.'

The Zaarzuk picked himself up and limped back, eyes glinting in the daylamp.

'Ah yes, I see what the problem is,' said Paran.

'Well?' demanded Anabara.

'He's lying.'

'You call me a liar, Fay-dog?' Dal Ramek put up his fists. 'Disarm this door and face me, coward!'

Paran bared his fangs.

'Stop that!' cried Anabara. 'He just wants to tell me about the Stacks, for God's sake!'

'Not so,' Paran hissed. 'The horseboy has a piece of unfinished business. Which chafes him, somewhat. He means to bed you, whether you will or no. Ah, you'd deny it, would you? Then come on in, horseboy. Cross the threshold and prove me wrong.'

The Zaarzuk replied in his own language. Then spat at the Fairy's feet. His spittle sizzled on the threshold, vaporised by the charm. Anabara watched opened-mouthed as he strode off, boots kicking sparks off the cobbles as he went.

'It's a brave tongue for cursing in, is it not?' observed the Fairy. 'He vows he will not stay to be insulted by a spavined knave and whoreson cock-sucking defiler of grandmothers and young boys such as myself; whose pox-raddled member, he prays God, will presently be struck by glanders and drop off.'

The footsteps dwindled into the distance. Silence. Just the rain. I don't believe it!—he snuck down here, bent on getting me into bed? Even if I said No?

'A rough wooing would mend his manners,' whispered Paran. His tongue flicked round his fangs. 'Shall I go after him and pay him in his own coin?'

Anabara banged the door shut in horror. 'No!'

'No? It would be a sweet chore. But as you wish.' He cocked his head again. 'You have another visitor. I will make myself scarce.' He darted up the stairs in his nasty spider-ish way.

Great. Now what? Anabara closed her eyes and waited for the footsteps. Well, whoever it was, she was safe. A *viper* jinx? Good God. So that's what he meant by 'nothing can enter here with ill intent'. She'd heard about them: the more evil the intent, the worse the whiplash of the jinx. Paran's notion of justice in a nutshell.

There was a tappity-tap.

She opened the door a crack.

A big spoon-faced figure loomed in the daylamp. 'Can we talk?'

Heh, heh, heh. Anabara held the door wide. 'By all means, Detective. Won't you come in?'

But instead of knocking her on to her fat arse, the charm let Mooby through unscathed.

CHAPTER THIRTEEN

'Whoa!' said Mooby. '*That* I was not expecting.'

Bloody hell! thought Anabara. Nor was I. She gawped at the great brick-built woman filling her room. Looked like Butros was right: Mooby *was* on the level. Nothing for it but to play host. 'Um, have a seat. Drink?'

'Not for me, thanks.' Mooby sat. Anabara sat.

Mooby cleared her throat. Her hair was matted to her scalp like bleached bladderwrack. Out of uniform she looked as naked as a snail out of its shell. Rain dripped from her navy blue old lady coat. Her brown trousers were too short. Three inches of downy shin on display. And the blouse. Candy pink. With a pie-crust frill collar. This wasn't a fashion statement, it was a distress flare. *Someone take me to the seamstress! Please!* Anabara bit her lips hard.

They both said, 'So'. Then, 'No, you.' Lord, it was like a blind date.

Mooby took the bull abruptly by the horns. 'Right. Owe you an apology. Bang out of order, treating you like that. Unprofessional. Let my frustrations get the better of me. Ponce says you're considering pressing charges.'

Ponce! Anabara bit her lips even harder. What to do? This was a different Mooby from the one who'd slapped her about in the cells. What the hell was going on? She decided to trust the charm. 'Actually, I'm not pressing charges.'

Mooby drew a long deep breath, let it out again. Ran a finger round the pie-crust. 'Cheers. Appreciate that.' There was another toe-curling silence. They shifted in their chairs. 'Look, I'm off the case,' Mooby said. 'Sidelined, pending disciplinary hearing. Pressure from the top.'

Chief Dhalafan, thought Anabara. Obeying grandmama's orders. 'I see.'

Another silence. Then: 'God, I hate this place,' Mooby burst out. 'Old boy networks, everyone's someone's relative. Undermining me, going behind my back, blocking me at every turn. This is the most sexist, racist outfit I've ever worked in—and I'm from Bogganland! And another thing—so much for the legendary Larridy hospitality! Know something? I've been here six months—*six months!*—and you're the first person that's ever asked me in and offered me a drink. *Ever.*'

There was a long silence. She didn't mean to let all that out, thought Anabara. A flush crept up from the frilly collar and covered Mooby's face like a stain. And suddenly she wasn't just some ball-breaking bullying Offcomer. She was a real woman. A large unhappy one, a long way from home. Overbalanced by an act of welcome—which Anabara hadn't even intended to offer.

'Look, detective,' she said, guiltily. 'I'll put in writing to the Chief that I have no complaint.'

'Cheers, but no way will Murder Squad hand the baby back now. Bastards. Right. Enough bitching.' She cleared her throat again, slapped her thighs with a pair of vast knobble-knuckled hands and got a grip of herself. 'Thought I owed you an explanation: your business card was found on one of the stiffs.'

Anabara went cold. Yes—she'd dropped one, hadn't she, that night. Saw it flutter to the ground. 'Half Larridy's got my card! You hauled me in for *that?*'

'That, and a hunch. What do you know about slave trafficking?'

Anabara's heart thumped. 'Not a lot. What everyone knows.'

'Here's my thoughts,' she leant forward. 'Some nice Larridy folks are up to their nice Larridy ears in trafficking. Right! here!' Mooby stabbed the chair arm with a finger. 'And at least one of them is in the Guard. I get the psychs to seal up one illegal Thin Place, bang, another one opens. Trade coming through the whole time, always one jump ahead. It's totally doing my head in. So when I hear about a nice Larridy girl who has dodgy business interests in the Slackey—with the same father-and-son Tressy duo who promptly turn up dead—well. Let's shake her down, I think. Poke the hive, see what big important Larridy bees come buzzing out. Your card's my excuse. Care to comment?'

'Ponce told me not to.'

'PAH-HA-HA!'

Anabara jumped. God, that sounded like a demon-possessed fog-horn!

'Anyway,' Mooby was abruptly serious again, 'turns out I was wrong about you.' She scanned the room, glanced up at the ceiling. 'The Fairy in?'

'Nope.'

'Tell me about him. Like, name, where he's from, so on.'

'Paran a'Menehaïn. Freeman, artisan class. Came over looking for work at the last Crossing Time. I hired him when my former associate disappeared.'

'Yeah, Thwyn Brakstone. Know where he is?'

'Went home, I guess.'

Mooby gave her a long disbelieving stare, but didn't press it. 'Reason I know I was wrong about you, I had a report come in this morning. From one of my undercover guys working the rivers.'

The wind rushed outside. 'And?'

'Well, apparently, some mad bird—little Galen-Gull demy—turns up at Saturday's slave auction, claiming her uncle is the Patriarch and demanding to buy a slave. And because he has a sick twisted sense of humour, old Boagle-eyes Golar—the slavers' boss—sells her the ship's Fay. Know what that is?'

'The old "fairies can't drown" superstition?' Anabara tried. 'Keep one on board to prevent shipwreck?'

'Afraid not, lovey. Your ship's Fay's the one they keep for long voyages. For when there's no women handy, get my drift. Last decades in their little cages, some of them.'

Anabara's hand flew to her mouth. Loxi hadn't mentioned *that*.

'Yeah,' said Mooby. 'My feelings entirely. Now, mad demy bird was never meant to keep him, you understand. It was a spot of cat-and-mouse. Let her get home, then go after her. Teach her a lesson, fetch the Fay back, stick the poor bastard in his cage again. Only something went wrong. Any idea what?'

She was trembling. 'Nope.'

'Well, according to my guy, the skiff comes floating back down river next morning with two corpses in. Tongues cut out. And each one has a nasty big spiky manacle rammed down his throat. Still no comment?'

Anabara shook her head again. Wrapped her arms tight round herself to stop the shaking. He killed them. Paran killed them after all.

'But by the time the bodies had been dumped where the mud-lark found them, no manacles. Straightforward tribal punishment killing, which the Murder Squad aren't going to lose sleep over—apart from your card. Someone's trying to tie you into this.'

Golar, thought Anabara. Her spirit quailed. Those moonstone eyes. He hadn't forgotten that mad demy bird and his lost ship's Fay. And now he'd lost two crew members as well. Oh dear God. What was she going to do? How far was Mooby to be trusted?

The detective fixed her with a bulging watery gaze. 'Now then. Apropos of nothing at all, Murder Squad are a bunch of macho tossers. They have one brain cell which they pass round in an emergency; rest of the time they think with their dicks. Still, I took the precaution of accidentally misfiling that undercover report when I handed the case over this morning.'

'Thanks,' whispered Anabara.

'Pleasure. So only ATU know about it. My squad,' she explained. 'Anti-Trafficking Unit. All the same, if you do happen to have any heavy-duty cutting tools lying about the place,' her gaze zapped to corner where the bolt-cutters were propped, 'you might want to lose them before Murder Squad call. Which they will—redoing my work in case the stupid *Bog-whacker* missed something. Another thing, hope your Fairy's papers are in order.' She slapped her mighty thighs again and got to her feet. 'Right. I'll be making tracks.'

Anabara stood. Steadied herself on the central mast timber. 'Thanks, detective.'

'You, my little demy friend, are as mad as a bag of grasshoppers. But you're on the side of life. Afraid I hadn't clocked who your parents were. Heroes of mine, Nolio and Bharossa, to tell the truth. Read all about their work. Anyway, I salute you. Shake?' She stuck out a hand.

Anabara shook it. 'Um, anonymous tip-off? The shack those Tressies lived in—it used to be Brakstone's. You might want to dig up the floor.'

Mooby gave a her a crushing grip. Nodded. 'I'm all over it. Take care, now. And, um, cheers. Might take you up on that drink some time.' Throat clear. 'If you... Whenever, obviously.' With another hand-crush she was gone.

Anabara stumbled back to her chair. The door closed. Mooby's light tread faded. Rain came in gusts. Some trick of the wind kept hurling drops at her windows like handfuls of shingle. The storm hunted round the city and the flutes howled like wolves. He's going to come for me, she thought. He's biding his time, but he'll come. The horrors of that night surged up again, along with a host of new fears. Out they burst from the cellar of her mind, gibbering like a pack of goblins.

Pelago, help me, protect me! Her hand clutched the amulet. What could she do? Move in with grandmama till it was all over! But when would it be over? It wouldn't be over till that monster had killed her! Every fresh burst of rain became Tressy fingernails clattering on her windows, clawing for purchase. I wish I wasn't so alone! I wish my Linna was still living here. I just need someone to be with. She tried to stifle her sobs so the Fairy wouldn't hear. So the *killer* wouldn't hear!

Too late—he was coming back down the stairs. She rubbed a sleeve over her face, snatched up the nearest book and pretended to study. *...thus we may see that a particle of psycho-matter traveling backwards in time, or rather, forward in* *reverse time...* He was watching her. She read on. But then a movement caught her eye. A tiny blue humming bird darted across the room and hovered in front of her! It glowed as if lit from within. She cried out in delight.

'Oh, where did you come from?' She reached out a finger. The bird landed on it. Again the wings whirred. Mauve light scattered like dust over her hand. 'What *are* you?'

'It's a sleep charm,' said the Fairy. 'Hush, all is well.'

Her mind surfed for a moment on a velvet wave. She had just long enough to think, *Bugger, I remember this from last time,* then she tumbled down, down, down into blackness.

She woke next morning with a lurch. Rain against the port-hole window. Not yet dawn. There it was again: a hammer-ing at the door. That's what had woken her. She reached for the lamp switch and pushed back the quilt. What on earth— Why was she still dressed? Hammer-hammer. Yes, I'm coming.

She stuck her feet in her boots and clomped down the stairs. The lamps were all on. Just a moment—that fecker charmed me again! Paran stood in front of the door. He raised a finger to his lips before she could yell at him.

'It's the Murder Squad. They have a search warrant.'

'What? At *this* hour?' Shit! The cutters. They were still standing propped in the corner. 'Hide them!' she mouthed.

Bang bang. 'Ms Nolio, open up. It's the Guard.'

'Will the charm let them past?' she whispered.

'If they are honest men doing their duty, yes.'

Her hands shook as she opened the door. Four of them. They bundled past her into the room. The first was dark and simian, the second was a Gull. She recognised him. Benny Macko.

A red-haired officer dangled a warrant in front of her, then flipped his ID open. She didn't have to look: it was Lieutenant Jack Gannerby. Larridy born and bred. Three of them grinned. The fourth stood silent with his arms folded. All in black, eyes hidden behind dark glasses. Feck. Psych Unit.

'Who's this?' she asked.

'Him? Oh, he's just along to learn,' said Gannerby. 'Take no notice.' He put his badge away. 'Well, aren't *you* a naughty little minx. Not co-operating with Guard enquiries? What's all that about?'

'Nah, Lefty, man,' said Macko. 'She wasn't co-operating with Bog-whackers. She'll cooperate with us, eh, won't you Nan?'

'We can come back in blond wigs and boots,' suggested the monkeylike one, waggling his eyebrows. Eyebrow. 'Interrogate you in the bathhouse, maybe?'

Time for the spoilt Galen princess act. Anabara stamped her foot. 'Shut *up*, you fat ape!' In the corner of her eye she could see Paran. Had he hidden the cutters? The three men snickered. The psych was silent.

'Yes, Doogie! Shut UP!' warbled Gannerby. 'Bit of respect, for Dhalafan's favourite private eye. Sorry to drag you out of bed, Ms Nolio. We need to take a quick look round. Just a formality.'

Looked like the Lieutenant had commandeered the squad brain cell this morning. She folded her arms and jutted out her lip. 'Fine. But don't you dare mess up my stuff.'

'And we need to see the Fay's ID,' he said.

'The *Fairy's* name is Paran a'Menehaïn, Lieutenant. He's standing right there. Ask him yourself.'

He barely glanced. Just clicked his fingers. Paran produced his Freeman Pass. The Lieutenant handed it to the psych, who flipped through, then pocketed it, face inscrutable behind his shades. Had the charm-sensitive lenses picked anything up?

Anabara snuck a look at the cutters. They were still there, in plain view! Quick, a distraction.

'Hey! He can't just take that!' she squeaked. 'How's my associate meant to manage without ID? I'm going to complain to Uncle Hector about you!'

'Calm down, Ms Nolio,' said Gannerby. 'Psych Unit needs to run some tests on it. I'm taking the Fay in for questioning, too.'

'What, now? You can't. He's got work to do.'

'This very moment, sweet cheeks. You'll just have to muddle through without him.'

Shit. Not good, not good.

The two other guards had started their search, opening drawers, pulling books off shelves, riffling through the old case files in the cupboard. Macko flipped back the hearth rug, indicated the floor safe. She sprang the charm for him, trying not to let her eyes flick towards the cutters. Why was Paran just standing there? The psych paid him no attention, just prowled and scanned with his bug-eyed glasses, like a wolf mantis looking for breakfast.

'I demand a receipt for his Pass. The Larridy Citizens' Charter says—'

'Macksy, write the Fay a receipt,' sighed Gannerby.

Doogie and the psych started up the stairs. Doogie paused for another eyebrow waggle. 'We're just off to rummage through your drawers. Want to come? Check we don't try on your panties?'

'Aw, leave it out, Doogie, eh,' protested Macko, busy writing.

Let them paw her things. A bigger fear clutched her—
what would they find in Paran's room? She thrust the grisly
images from her mind. How come they hadn't spotted the
cutters yet? Sweat trickled down her back.

The Lieutenant was watching her. 'Getting antsy? Why?
What do you reckon we're going to find?'

She flounced. 'Actually, Lieutenant, I have no idea what
you're looking for.'

'You have no idea, full stop,' he replied. 'When are you
going to stop playing detective? that's what we're all wondering. Not till granny stops bankrolling you, is my guess.'

Suddenly it was not difficult to achieve the Princess
pout. 'She does *not* bankroll me!'

He shook his head at her. 'Listen, Peaches, why don't
you go back to finding lost pussycats, and leave the real work
to the pros? That way we'll all rub along nicely. If you play
with the big boys, you're going to get hurt.'

'That cat was a pedigree Candacian blue, and it was
stolen!' Another foot stamp. 'I'm putting your patronizing
remarks in my report to Uncle Hector! Plus I'm going to
say you used racist language about a resident alien, and
that the officer upstairs insinuated things! And I'm telling your Mum, Benny Macko!' On and on she whinged.
Paran stood motionless in the shadows. Oh God, let it be
over.

At last it was. The ape came back downstairs. 'Clean as a
whistle, Lefty.'

The psych nodded.

'This place got a cellar?' Gannerby asked. She shook her
head. 'Well, that's us done then. Pleasure working with a
fellow professional, Ms Nolio. You have a nice day now. Give
Uncle a big spitty kiss from us.'

Macko handed her the receipt for Paran's Pass, and the three officers trouped out of the house, all grins and silly salutes. The psych followed. Anabara closed the door. Leant against it. Shut her eyes.

Dear God! They'd forgotten to arrest Paran! And how had they missed the cutters? The Fairy was staring at her. She went cold. Oh no. 'Please tell me you didn't just charm them? Shit, Paran, I *told* you perception work's illegal!'

'You said hide the cutters. I hid them.' He twitched the receipt from her fingers balled it up and tossed it in the grate.

'But you need that! What if—' She gasped.

He flipped the Freeman Pass in his fingers, then palmed it away like a conjurer.

'But, but— They took that away! You just charmed the *Guard*!' she squeaked. 'My God, you charmed a fecking *psych*! That was a *psych*, you moron, that one in dark glasses!'

'Was he now?' said the Fairy. 'Well, he was along to learn. We must hope he does so speedily, if he is the best the Guard have to offer.'

He was putting on his grey cloak. 'Don't you get how serious this is?' she shouted. 'Five years without parole! They'll work out what you did! They'll be back!'

'Oh, I daresay they'll forget me. I am not memorable.'

'Paran, stop.' He paused, hand on the latch. 'It's true, isn't it? You did kill those rivermen.'

'Indeed I did.' She saw the reptilian eyelids flicker. 'Eventually. But rest assured: I left no evidence. What was it you feared just now—that the Guard would find their tongues nailed to my chamber wall?'

'No,' she lied.

'We keep no trophies. You are forgetting the old tales.'

She covered her mouth. Gagged. 'I don't believe you'd do that.'

'Ah, do you not? But consider: a year and a half I was caged and used on board that ship. And in all that time, one act of kindness. One.'

'Loxi?' she whispered.

'Yes. And for that single mouthful of water, he has earned my kindness in return. It is our habit to deal back what's dealt to us. Trust me: I always repay in the end.'

'Always? That's so cold!' she protested. 'Don't you ever forgive anyone?'

But he just stared. 'I have no time for that foolishness.'

'You're scaring me.'

'Yes? Then perhaps I needn't describe what happened to the last person who called me a moron. At present your credit runs high with me, Anabara Nolio,' he said. 'But you're squandering it with lies and insults. And your tiresome pleas for me to have mercy on those who don't deserve it.'

The door swung shut. He was gone.

CHAPTER FOURTEEN

She felt like a wet shirt on wash day. Mangled to within an inch of her life. He was a total monster! Half snake, half machine, head full of balance sheets, brain like an abacus, click-click-click, forever totting up who owed this, who deserved that. He was not... Well, of course he wasn't *human*. Why was she still looking for humanity in him?

More footsteps. She was seized by dread it was the Guard again, that Paran was wrong and Gannerby knew he'd been charmed. Now she'd be done for aiding and abetting a psych crime! Sure enough, a knock.

But it was only a town messenger. There was a message from Linna, ordering her to be in at ten o'clock. *There's something we need to talk about.* Uh-oh. That didn't sound good. There was also a sealed note. *'Meet me in the Town Bathhouse ASAP. Dt Mooby.'*

She got there first, so she steamed her worries away, dashed them away in the cold plunge pool, had them smoothed away on the massage slab. Still no Mooby. But who should be in the lounging room, skiving off her washer-work, but Jennet Pettyfrock. Anabara did a quick mental check: have I moved on and matured since school days? Nope. Still hate

her. Purring like the cat with the cream jug all to herself!
Anabara went and lay on the couch furthest away.

'Ooh, hoity-toity!' cooed Jennet. She came across the
room and perched at Anabara's feet. Her robe slipped from
her shoulders, oops! to display her latest hickey collection.
Looked like a bad case of marsh pox. 'It's all true, what they
say about them.'

Anabara closed her eyes. But the Gullmothers were
wrong: if you just ignored them, they didn't stop doing it.

'About the gold rings.' Anabara stiffened. 'Yes—thought
you'd be curious. Even if you *are* a frigid little tease whose
britches are made of iron. La, don't glare at *me*, Nan Nolio.
I'm just saying what *he* said.' She paused for a reaction.

Anabara stomped down hard on the surge of fury.
Closed her eyes again.

'Pity the beadles dragged him away. Hammering on the
alehouse door: *Mr Dal Ramek, we know you're in there!* Bursting
in! La, Mopsy and me didn't know where to put ourselves!
And the *language!* Pillows flying, feathers everywhere—
What are *you* staring at, bugger-lugs?'

Anabara's eyes flew open. It was Mooby. She jerked a
thumb. 'Out, scrubber. Guard business.'

Off flounced the girl.

'Sorry, got held up.' She was back in uniform, thank
God, but barefoot in deference to bathhouse rules, trousers rolled halfway up her fuzzy shins. 'Got herself boffed
by Dal Ramek? Silly mare. He's just using her to get himself
expelled.'

Anabara sat up. 'You know him?'

'Oh God yes. Record as long as your arm over in
Bogganland. Zaarzuk territory borders on ours.'

'No! Like what?'

Mooby waved a hand. 'The usual mindless Zaarzuk hell-raising—horse theft, arson, public drunkenness and indecency. Last ditch attempt to keep the boy out of gaol, the novice thing. Chieftain's firstborn, or he'd've been banged up long since.'

'You're kidding!' A Zaarzuk prince!

Mooby nailed her with a bulging-eyed stare. 'Steer clear of him, lovey. Zaarzuks only know three types of women: virgins, wives and whores.' She crossed to the music charm and set the madrigals playing loud. Then she sat, knees spread like a bloke. 'Right. More important things. We've got trouble.'

'I know. I had a dawn visit from Murder Squad. They've obviously got more than my business card to go on, because—' Mooby had a finger to her lips. 'Sorry. Because they came to arrest Paran and they brought a psych with them,' she whispered. 'You think there are listening charms in here?'

'Probably not. Precaution. Take it they found nothing? Plus they didn't arrest him. Hmm. Then either the psych's a complete tool, or your Fairy's packing some serious charm-craft. Bear that in mind.'

'I am doing, believe me.'

'Yeah, well he's in my pending tray. But at the moment he seems to be in my tent pissing out, which is where I want him.' Thigh slap. 'Anyhow, trouble. Thought I could stake my life on my squad's loyalty. Breaks my heart to say this, but someone's talking.'

'Who?'

Palms up. 'No idea. Thought about hauling all four in front of the psychs and making them re-swear their Fidelity Oath. But suddenly I'm thinking, what if it's the psychs who are bent? I'm getting my man off the boats as a matter of urgency. Lord, this whole thing's making me paranoid.' She shook her head. 'Thoughts?'

'Listening charm in the squad room?' suggested Anabara.

'Already occurred to me. Had the top psych in to check. He's given it the all clear. Yeah, I know—what if he's bent? That's why we're here now, not at the Station. Look, you're a sensible woman—well, you're not, you're barking—I've no wish to scare you, but it's nearly Wolf Tide, and we've got God knows how many Tressy barges bringing the tourists in. All perfectly legit. But my sources think something big's going down, so we'll probably have old Boagle-eyes on the loose in Larridy. Stick close to a'Menehaïn, that's my advice. Don't know what his game is, but he'll look out for you. Very loyal, your Fairies, if you've done them a favour.'

Anabara nodded. Her head whirled. She clutched the sides of the couch. 'What kind of big thing?'

'Well, we've never traced the Breaking Camp. The slaves we've interviewed have all had their memory doctored. Place might as well be in Tara-doodle for all the joy we've had. But my theory is it's right here, and they'll be bringing in a new shipment at Wolf Tide—while we're busy arresting drunken prats in wolf gear.'

'What's the Breaking Camp?'

'Back in the day, that's where they broke in any condemned Fairy criminals transported here. All perfectly legal and above board.' Mooby sneered. 'Anyone with the cash could pop to town and buy themselves a slave. Pricey up front, but economical to run. Hardly have to feed them, last decades without ageing, work hard, phenomenally strong.'

Anabara shook with rage. 'It's a total obscenity. They taught us so much, and we repay them like this!'

'Tell me about it. Illegal migrants get what they pay for, generally: crossing, false papers, and so on. But the unlucky ones—the friendless, powerless ones—they pay up, then get double-crossed. Hence the need for a Breaking Camp. Do *not* ask me to describe the enslavement process. Not if you want to sleep at night.'

There are ghosts down there. Ghosts of Fays. I have seen their lights. A trickle of icy water ran down her heart. She thought of the creepy Master of Stacks. And the secret entrance, right by the Slackey.

'Ring a bell?'

'Maybe.' She shook herself. 'I need to check something out.'

The sea gooseberry eyes were on her again. 'Leave me word about any daft stunts you're planning, in case you need back up.'

'Certainly will.' No way. What if her suspicions were groundless? Expose the University to unnecessary Guard investigations? She was too dutiful a Galen girl for that. Well, she was too scared of Aunt Léanora, anyway.

'Yeah, sure you will.' Mooby sighed and stood. She did a sweep of the lounging room. Took in the smoking censers, lingered on the pink marble caryatids. 'You'd think they'd give us statues of naked blokes to look at, wouldn't you?' Eye roll. 'Yeah, right. That would be the men's quarters. Tell me something: are there any straight guys round here? That aren't total plonkers?'

'I live in hope.' Whoa! Got that one wrong.

Mooby gave a wonky smile. 'Thought I spun widder-shins? Yeah, everyone does. But I'm just your average big homely gal, looking for Prince Charming.'

'Aren't we all?' Anabara thought about the pink frilly blouse. Cringed with pity it would be impossible to express. She stared down at Mooby's feet in embarrassment. Toes crooked from old breaks. Gnarly as the hands. 'You're a fighter.'

'You betcha. Boggan wrestling. Be glad to give you a bout sometime. See how I match up against the legendary Galen art.'

'Hey, more than happy. Come up to the...' Bugger. 'Um. There's kind of an issue with my Precincts membership right now.'

'Yeah, so I heard. None of my business, but I'm really hoping that's not Dal Ramek's picture you've got in there.' She nodded at the amulet.

'No! Of course not.' Her fingers closed round it. 'This was my mother's.'

'Well, keep me posted. I'm off for a spot of digging in the Slackey.' Mooby padded from the room.

Anabara frowned down at the amulet. Why did everyone think it was a locket? Another icy trickle. Paran. He'd hidden the amulet, like he hid those cutters. Which meant she was walking about with a perception charm dangling round her neck. Feck, that was six months, even for a first offence! What the hell *was* this thing? Something so dangerous, the penalty for being caught with a reality-altered artifact was piddling in comparison?

Deep breath. Stay calm. She cast her mind back to the moment when Uncle Téador had given her the necklace. He had hoped it might protect her on her dangerous mission. *It doesn't feel evil. No, not evil.* He believed it had 'something of the soul' embedded in it. But whose soul? And what did that soul want to do? Terrible deeds?

For sure. That was why Paran would sooner cut off his right ear than tell her what the amulet was. Yet she couldn't square that with her uncle's belief that the thing wasn't evil—and the fact that her mother had worn it. Unless, of course, the amulet was only dangerous in the twisted mind of the Fairy. A creature who never forgave. Who ate the tongues of his enemies. She gagged again. Don't think about it.

She left the bathhouse and hurried back down the hill to fetch the library books she'd collected the previous afternoon, and to pick up her tiny pocket daylamp. The rain had stopped. Rags of blue appeared between the clouds that raced overhead. Mule carts laden with pale yellow pumpkins were winding up Skuller to market. Overhead the red and black Larridy bunting fluttered. In every crooked corner and arch a stall selling roast chestnuts and sweetmeats had popped up. The air was sugared with their wares. She bought a poke of candied chestnuts. Wolf masks grinned like necklaces of severed heads. Suddenly dread was on every side again. She began to hurry, glancing down each alley she passed. The market teemed with potential assassins. Stay alert, don't make yourself an easy target!

She emerged breathless into St Pelago Plaza. The sight of the Gatehouse flooded her with relief. It was always like coming safe home, like nothing bad could get you here. Maybe everyone felt that way. The Temple Mount had offered sanctuary for over a thousand years. Even to murderers, clinging with bloody hands to the ancient sanctuary knocker. Huh, Paran could learn a thing or two from studying this doorway, thought Anabara.

She went through the great stone arch to the library to offload the books. It was quiet. The students were at Morning Prayers. Or in bed. God only knew where His Royal

Highness Dal Ramek was. In the beadles' cellar strung up by his thumbs, she hoped. Better still, by his nuts. A frigid little tease whose britches are made of iron! She sprang up on to the high perimeter wall. Not a chance Jennet had made that up—the insult had his grubby Zaarzuk thumbprints all over it.

Yep, it was all true, what they said about them. Filthy liars and braggarts. Charming when they got their way, rough when they didn't. Hadn't the Gullmothers always warned her there wasn't a word for 'No' in Zaarzuk? Not exactly a big surprise, was it, that he'd been busted in the alehouse in a drunken threesome. Obviously the bastard had a talent for persuading a girl she was the special one. Embarrassing to have fallen for it even slightly. A knock to the pride, but no harm done. Let the washer-wenches line up for the hon-our of becoming notches in his bedpost. As far as Anabara was concerned, Dal Ramek was history.

But oh, oh, oh, the man knew how to kiss!

She batted the thought away and strode along the para-pet. Every forty cubits it was guarded by a stone warrior. Or had been, a thousand years back when the wall was built. These days only blackened stumps remained, like rotted teeth; but she could still feel the faint thrum of their force-field as she stepped over them. Even Paran wasn't going to be able to restore these. The sandstone had long since been weathered away, washed down Skuller, back to the sea it had come from. Gone, gone forever. Curse those generations of Chapter who'd let it happen. She fluttered down to the alley below.

Her nose told her she was getting close. An upset pail of dog-turds in the street. There was a crowd, a commotion. Crime scene ribbon across the Slackey entrance. Mooby and the ATU, digging for Thwyn's body. She slipped past the gawpers and down the narrow alley that hugged the ancient fortifications of the Precincts. The noise faded as she rounded a corner.

There—that must be it. Well, she'd been past that trough any number of times without so much as a glance. Yes, it was a Zaarzuk all right. The fur hat, the flowing hair. His right hand gripped a scimitar. It looked like he was standing in a deep archway, but when you peered closely, there was no back wall—he was guarding the entrance to a tunnel. A small person could just slip through past him.

No, a small person could not. The charm was a dense as a ten inch thick velvet curtain. 'Let me pass,' she urged. 'I am a favourite of the Chieftain's son. Tadzar Dal Ramek is my friend.' Not a flicker. 'I am a servant of the Way. My uncle is the Patriarch. Let me pass.' Nothing. Maybe the stone warrior couldn't understand Commons? What had Dal Ramek told her? *I talk horseflesh and he lets me pass.* That was a non-starter: the only thing Anabara knew about horses was that they had a biting end and a kicking end, and a bit in the middle you sat on if you were a complete lunatic.

Perhaps an appeal to the statue's macho Zaarzuk pride? 'You are so strong! Please rescue me!' she begged. Nope. Dammit, she was going to have to find Dal Ramek and persuade him to take her in. And frankly, the last thing she needed right now was to find herself trapped in a dark tunnel with a horny...

Now there's a thought. She hesitated. Well, it was worth a try. She stepped in close, pressed herself against the statue, put her lips to his ear. 'If you let me pass, I'll show you my titties.'

The charm melted, the statue swiveled on his pivot and she slipped through and scampered up the tunnel. Sucker. The air smelt of old stone. She felt for her little dayl-amp, gave it a twist. Low tunnel walls appeared in its faint glow. Hewn out of the rock of Larridy. You could still see the rough pickaxe marks. How far she was from the Stacks themselves was impossible to tell. She tried to picture the Precincts. Quarter of a mile?

A map. Yeah, that would have been a smart idea. If one existed. Fingers crossed, the Stacks were laid out in a sim-ple grid pattern. What had Dal Ramek told her? A maze of tunnels. That sounded like a labyrinth, maybe charmed to incorporate extra dimensions and maximize the space. A wave of fear. There was a real danger of getting trapped in some other fold of reality and never getting out again. Nobody knew where she was. Why, oh why hadn't she told Mooby what she was doing?

She squared her shoulders. Come on, how complicated could it be, if dick-brain Dal Ramek had managed not to get himself lost down here? Just keep your head, and every-thing will be fine. The tunnel took long zigzags down. No other tunnels branched off. So far so good. Down, zig, down again, zag. On and on. The air was getting warmer all the time. And then as she zagged again—light. She'd reached the Stacks.

There was no sound. She edged closer. The last twenty yards of tunnel were paved, the walls smooth. A narrow archway opened on to a corridor. She stuck her head out, right, left. Nobody. Just a long vista of dressed stone arches curving away out of sight, uphill to the right, downhill to the left. Lit at regular intervals by old-fashioned flame torches, Fairy-engineered to burn without flickering.

Suddenly she understood: it was a small scale replica
of the City Isle. This corridor was an underground Skuller.
Anabara smiled. Not so hard for a Larridy lass to navigate
her way about. The only crucial thing was to remember
where the escape entrance was. The arch she was standing
in was identical to its countless neighbours. You would never
spot the tunnel. Hmm, a clever person would have planned
ahead and brought a stick of chalk.

She put the daylamp away and searched her pockets in
vain for something to scratch with. A fragment of stone? She
glanced down. Tscha, look at that—a horseshoe chalked on
the floor. Dal Ramek. Not such a dick-brain after all. The
only question now was which way had he turned to find
those lights, those Fairy ghosts: uphill or down?

As she stood weighing her options, a flickering movement. In the corner of her eye. Like something she might
have imagined. Her heart boomed in the silence. Only one
thing moved like that: a Fairy. She waited. Nothing stirred.
Maybe she had imagined it.

'Paran?' she whispered. 'Is that you?'

A grey figure peeled away from the stone. Yes, it was
him, the sneaky creepy bugger.

'For God's sake! You scared the life out of me! What are
you doing down here?'

He came towards her, steps dragging. Was he injured?
Now he was close she could see his eyes were dead and blank.

'What's wrong with you?'

He curled back his lips and hissed at her. The canine
fang sockets were empty.

Oh dear God!

It was not Paran at all. It was a slave. And in his hand was
a long-bladed hunting knife.

CHAPTER FIFTEEN

Her hand clutched the amulet. 'Stop!'

The creature paused. Light glanced off the blade. 'Don't kill me!'

For an endless moment they stood frozen like that. Anabara's legs quaked. Yanni. She was going to die without being reconciled to him. The black pebble eyes, they were locked on her right hand. The amulet! Some power in it the creature sensed? She unclenched her fist to reveal the stone.

A tremor rippled through the Fairy. It fell to its knees. Turned the knife hilt towards her.

She stared in disbelief. What did it think she was? Some powerful warrior queen? Quickly, before it realised its mistake.

'How dare you threaten me! Drop the knife!' It fell with a clank on to the stone. 'You're a slave?' Nod. 'Whose slave? Why are you here?' Nothing. 'Do you understand Galen?' Nod. 'I command you to speak! Why don't you answer me?'

The creature opened his mouth. She peered, then flinched back. Nothing but a stump! Oh God, they really did do that to them. 'Show me your hands.'

He held them out. The flesh had covered the manacles completely. All she could see was a ridge, like a fat worm under the skin. 'You've been a slave a long time?'

He nodded. Raised both hands, fingers splayed.

'Ten years!'

He held them up again. Twenty. No! Thirty. Then three. '*Thirty three years!*' Nod. 'That's terrible! Why are you down here? What do they make you do?'

He mimed opening a book. Then pointed upwards.

'You work for the *library*? Impossible! The university doesn't own slaves!' It couldn't be true. Let it not be true! But she knew it must be. That's why the scholasticus wouldn't let her down here. His darting eyes, his panic.

'How many slaves work here?' He held up a hand. 'Five! Who is your master—the scholasticus? No? The Master of Stacks?' A nod. 'Does he... does he treat you well?'

He made a hissing sound in the back of his throat.

'I'm sorry. I'm so sorry.' The slave watched as if tears were the weather. A squall that would blow over. She wiped her eyes on her sleeve. 'Does he at least feed you properly?'

Another hiss.

That the university was embroiled in this! Unbearable. And there was nothing she could do for him. She had no cutters to liberate him, nothing to ease his suffering. Wait— the chestnuts. Did they eat sweetmeats? She pulled out the crumpled paper poke.

'Here. Have them. It's all I've got. I'm sorry.'

The creature snatched. She turned away, revolted. He ate like a cat, choking and bolting the chestnuts down.

What was she going to do? Could she take him back out with her? No, they'd realise the truth had been discovered and kill the other slaves to cover their tracks. How high up the university hierarchy did this go? The scholasticus knew, that was for sure. What about the rest of Chapter? How many people that she loved and respected were turning a blind eye? Thirty-three years—it had been going on in her parents' time! Dear God, did grandmama know?

Suddenly she remembered Mooby's theory about the Breaking Camp. She looked back at the kneeling slave. He'd finished eating. Ah, his eyes were brighter now! A memory broke the surface: that's what had happened to Paran that first night, after she'd given him milk to drink.

'Tell me—is this where they bring Fairies to enslave them?' she asked. 'Is this where the Breaking Camp is?' Please say no. Don't let it be true.

But the Fairy nodded. He mimed a long spiral, down, down.

'They come in through this tunnel?' Nod. 'Does the Master of Stacks run the camp?'

He shook his head, then rubbed his thumb over first and second fingers.

'They pay him? Who? The Tressy slavers? Golar?' Nod. 'Are there any slaves there now? No? But more are coming?'

Yes. He held up a finger.

In one day's time. At Wolf Tide, just as Mooby had predicted. What to do, what to do? She'd found out enough. She should get out now while she could, and report back to Mooby. But she couldn't bear just to leave him like this.

'Listen, I'm going to put a stop to what's happening here.' The slave clenched a fist and punched the air. Her heart lurched. Be careful what you promise him—you don't want to end up foresworn. He began gesturing urgently. 'What is it?'

He was pointing to her, to himself, then upwards. He hissed and drew a finger across his throat. Now he was imploring her with clasped hands. What did he want? He repeated the sequence. Suddenly she saw: command me to kill the Master of Stacks!

CATHERINE FOX

'No! I want him brought to justice.' He nodded, bared his zigzag teeth. Was that meant to be a grin? What had she said? Justice. He thought she intended to kill him herself! Better to let him think it. Wait, should she permit self-defence? Or would he just twist that to his own ends? I can't handle this! she thought. This terrifying responsibility. One false move— But she had to. Think. Think like a Fairy. What did they understand? Vengeance.

'I have a score to settle. My parents were murdered. You must save the Stack-master for me,' she said. 'Unless he tries to kill you. You may strike back to save your own life. Do you understand?'

He nodded.

But what if he was lying? Instinct told her he was not. Somehow—who knew how?—by possessing the amulet, she had usurped the role of slave-master. Her authority now trumped the Master's—or the slave would have killed her for sure. She should go. But was she forgetting something? Was there a loose end, some glaring omission that would cost lives in the future? The Fairy watched her, waited.

'Stand up.' He gestured to the knife. 'Yes, you can keep it.' He got to his feet and stood, knife in hand. 'Help will come,' she told him. 'The Guard will come. Don't kill any members of the Guard. They are my friends.' Again she wavered—what if they were collaborators? Pelago, guide me, I'm doing my best. 'I must go. Tell me—are there any more ways in and out?'

He nodded. Three more. He pointed to the arch, then held up seven fingers. Then again, seven.

'Fourteen? No?' Maybe he meant seven times seven. 'Forty-nine? Every forty-nine arches, there is a tunnel out into the City?' Nod. 'Where in the City do they come out?

What are the passwords?' But he did not know. He'd probably never seen the City. '*Farewell, friend,*' she said in Fairy.

He fell to his knees again, pressed his forehead against her feet. 'Don't do that. Get up!'

He stood and raised a hand.

Five? 'Five what?'

He held the knife against his throat. His eyes beseeched her. He made choking sounds. A lurch of horror: he was trying to speak. But she couldn't make out the mangled words. Then her blood ran cold. *Release me.* If no help came in five days, he was begging for permission to kill himself. 'No, I can't let you do that!'

He clutched her hand. Then froze. Cocked his head, just as she'd seen Paran do. Someone was coming. Fear seized her. She tore herself from his grip, started to run, then at the last moment, turned back.

'Yes,' she sobbed. 'I grant you my permission.'

Up the stone passage she fled. Zig, zag. Zig, zag. Her daylamp bobbed in the dark. Its glow was getting fainter with every passing moment. Now and then she paused, stifled her ragged gasps and listened. No pursuers. Higher, higher. Surely she was almost there? Another turn, and yes, a gleam. She stopped a few yards from the exit and caught her breath. Light filtered in round the stone Zaarzuk. It was a one-way charm, thank God, only armed to block intruders. She leant on his right shoulder and he pivoted silently. She stumbled back into the alley. The statue slid back into place behind her and resumed his guard.

My beautiful home city. She blinked in the brightness. A perfect golden apple—but its core was heaving with maggots. She sat down on the edge of the trough and put her head between her knees. What was she going to do? She tried to quell the mounting panic. Mooby would be tied up in the Slackey all morning. Who else could she turn to? The Vice Chancellor? The Dean?

She knew how it would go: they'd close ranks and protect the university's reputation at all costs. They'd keep the Guard out of it, conduct an internal enquiry, sweep it all under the carpet. There would be no justice for the poor Fairies. The Master of Stacks would 'retire' with a fat fee to ease his going. The Breaking Camp would vanish and reappear who knew where. The library slaves would be handed over to Border Control and replaced by human assistants.

Well, that's not how it was going to happen. She was not going to be party to this. So what to do? Mooby she trusted, but what if the traitor in Mooby's squad found out? If word of this new discovery was leaked, how long before some tragic accident happened to her? Then a worse thought occurred: supposing the slave was forced to betray her, now she'd vanished with her powerful amulet? What if the Master of Stacks already knew, and was at this very moment sending word to Golar? Fears burst out like a jabbering pack of goblins again. Butros. He would be able to advise her. Please God, he'd be in his Chambers and not in Court!

She took a series of cuts through narrow alleys. Pigeons burst clapping from alcoves. Footsteps. Someone was after her! The rooftops would be safer than the crowded marketplace. She was about to spring up on to a convenient wall when someone called her name.

Linna.

'Hey! Slow down.' Her cousin was panting as she hugged her. 'Been chasing you, girl. Didn't you get my note? Got the devil on your tail, or something?'

'Work. Something urgent's come up, eh. Need to get hold of Butros.'

Linna looked steadily into her eyes. 'I'll walk with you. Got something to say.' Linna linked her arm through Anabara's. No, definitely not good. Linna wasn't going to let her escape. 'About Loxi.'

'Aw God. It's not my fault!' wailed Anabara. 'I'm not the boss of him. He's seventeen. He can live where he wants, eh. Can I stop him?'

'Na, ah. Save the wheedling for Auntie Laitolo, you,' said Linna. 'So it's true then? Wearing silk shirts and hanging out in molly bars with the Galen girlyboys?'

Shit. Molly bars? 'Tscha, it's nothing. Probably Enobar dragging him out for a drink, that's all. You know what he's like with anything cute in trousers.'

'Uh huh. Right.'

'I swear! Here's the thing: Loxi wants to go to university. That's what this is all about, eh. *Of course* he's hanging out with Galens. Discussing ideas. Philosophy and stuff.'

'Philosophy, my arse.'

'Look, Linna, it's a different world up here, you *know* that, you've lived here. Tell Auntie it's all fine, eh? Please, I haven't got time for this now!' She tried to pull her arm away, but Linna was a big powerful Gull lass.

'Na, ah. Look at me.' Anabara obeyed. 'What are you mixed up in, girl? Down in the village there's rumours of slaving and Tressy traders. Murder. Yeah, yeah, I'm not working for you any more. Plus I'm pregnant, so you can't tell me nasty scary stuff because I'm supposed to be all booties and bonnets. Hello? I still have a brain. I can still think, eh.' She gave her a shake. 'Talk to me.'

'Linna, I *can't.*'

Another long searching stare. 'All right. But remember this: you ever need a place to hide, we'll hide you. You're one of us, don't you forget it. Your own folk will look out for you, eh. Always. No matter what.'

Tears surged up. 'Thanks, Linna.'

'Mother says you're to spend Wolf Tide with the family. Ah, ah! Just passing on the message. I'm up here now to buy firecrackers and toffee apples for the kids. Auntie Laitolo isn't far behind me, so consider yourself warned. Go, go.' She planted a kiss on Anabara's cheek and shoved her off in the direction of the legal quarters. 'Kick Butros's arse for me.'

A lackey showed her into Butros's chambers. She waited in a leather armchair. Ebony shelves floor to ceiling, rank upon rank of calf-bound legal volumes. Document pouches with purple silk tassels, brass-trimmed dispatch boxes. She felt too sick to snoop, even. Not that there'd be any point—it would all be charmed to within an inch of its life. A gilt clock ticked, measuring the time in gilders per second. Butros was in some top-secret high-powered legal consultation. Would he interrupt it for her?

The door opened. A swirl of red silk, a breath of chypre.

'You have five minutes.' Butros sat. 'And if this "desperately important matter" turns out to be your St Dalfinia bathhouse membership, I'm going to put you across my knee and spank you.'

'Well, it's not, you pervert.' She told him what she'd just discovered.

He was silent. She watched his fingers drum on the chair arms. 'This suggests a long-standing criminal conspiracy of frightening proportions. What makes you certain the alleged slave wasn't lying?'

She pointed to the amulet. 'This. He could sense its power. He thought I was a warrior queen, or something.'

'Of course he did! Because warrior queens all wear tacky silver lockets. That's how they recognise one another at queening conferences.'

'Only it's not a locket, it's an ancient Fairy artifact.' She came close. 'Look.'

He raised an eyebrow. 'Is this some kind of joke?'

'Feel.'

He took the stone in his long fingers. Froze. 'Shit. That's a perception charm! Where the hell did you get this?'

She sat back down. 'Uncle Téador gave it me. It was my mother's. But I think Paran charmed it.'

'Oh, please.'

'Butros, I'm sure you're wrong about him. No way is he just a lowbred worker. He's mended the library's ancient stained glass charms. He has! Go and look. Plus he charmed the Guard when they came and searched my house.'

'Stop! Back up a bit. The Guard searched your house? You let them in without sending for me to bounce them? Isn't that—I speak purely theoretically, you understand—what you *pay* me for?'

'Yes, all right, I'm on to it. Anyway, they had a warrant. It was the Murder Squad.' She told him about the search, and last night's conversation with Mooby, the leaked report. And Paran's admission.

'You're saying the Fay *did* kill—No! Do *not* answer that, just thinking out loud. Shit. I'm really not liking this. What was Murder Squad looking for?'

'Bolt cutters. And an illegally freed slave, I guess, who's a murder suspect. The cutters were blatantly propped in the corner, but even the psych didn't see them. And then they "forgot" to arrest Paran. I'm telling you, Butros, you're wrong about him.'

'Then he must be using a military-grade cloaking charm.' There was another long silence. Butros narrowed his eyes. 'Right. That does it. Nobody mind-fucks *me* and gets away with it. Tell that little bog-sucking shite-weasel of yours I want to see him again. I have contacts who'll strip his filthy brain to shreds and find out what his game is, never fear.'

'*Mercenaries?* No. Butros, you can't!'

'They prefer the term "ex-military freelance psychic consultants"—and yes I can. Make an appointment with the lackey. Until then, I suggest you forget anything "Paran" has alleged and/or implied as regards the murders.'

'I'll try.'

'Hah!' Furious finger fandango. 'Well, if he duped me, he'll dupe the world at large, which is a comfort, I suppose. But just between ourselves, I'm a tiny bit pissed off about this.'

'You're a bad loser, that's why.'

'I'm a quite *staggeringly* bad loser,' he agreed. 'But I will set those feelings aside.' He glanced at the clock. 'Briefly, this is clear cut and unambiguous, Anabara. Slave ownership is a criminal offence. The Guard must be informed, regardless of any repercussions for our beloved University. Who's involved and how long it's been going on, we don't know—though the timings suggest it began with the current Stack-master. Don't confide in any member of staff, even Yannick. They'll need to preserve deniability. Finally, there's the matter of the alleged Breaking Camp. Since we have no idea who's colluding, either in the University or the Guard, I advise you to speak *only* to Mooby, then leave it with her, and disappear.'

'But—'

'Ssh! Your role ends when you've reported this. Apart from any testifying in Court, of course, for which I'll coach you. The Guard will set the appropriate wheels in motion and wrap this up. *The Guard*, not Anabara Nolio—got that? No more amateur heroics, please.'

She nodded. Took a deep breath. The weight was beginning to slide from her shoulders. 'Butros, grandmama doesn't know about it, does she?'

'You're suggesting she knows, yet she's managed to keep it secret for thirty years? Much though I esteem your grandmother, that's about as plausible as Enobar biting his tongue for thirty seconds.' He leant back and laced his fingers behind his head. The amber-green eyes glinted and a rare smile dawned. 'Well, well, well. There's going to be one almighty shit-storm when *this* comes out. As an alumnus of St Pelago's, obviously I'm devastated. But as a greedy amoral snake, I smell a lot of money in legal fees. Nice work, girl detective. Keep your head below the parapet over Wolf Tide. Got anywhere to hide out?'

'I could go to the village.'

'Do that. Which reminds me: Mr Laitolo. I've advised him to make a statement to Mooby. He should probably keep a low profile as well for a couple of days.'

'I'll take him to the village with me.'

'Good. Alternatively, he *is* rather cute, so maybe I'll invite him to stay in my apartment'—Butros thrust his face into hers—'and show him my *mirrored ceilings.*'

'You have mirrored ceilings?' She gave him a wide-eyed innocent look. 'Goodness, I have no recollection of that.'

'Very droll. I'll send an updated bill.' He got to his feet. 'Endeavour to pay it. You don't want to stray on to the list of people who've pissed me off, I'm sure.' With another swirl of silk, he was gone.

Well, the sun seemed to shine more brightly now. Her tread was lighter. Anabara took a deep breath. She'd report to Mooby, then get herself down to the Gull village tomorrow till it had all blown over. She caught sight of Chief Dhalafan, coming out of the High Court. He spotted her and beckoned.

They met under a plane tree. Vast paw-shaped golden leaves whispered across Palatine Square.

'Anabara, my dear,' he kissed her cheek. 'I hear we entertained you in our VIP suite. Was the accommodation to your liking?'

She smiled. 'No complaints, Chief. It was a misunderstanding. Detective Mooby has apologised.'

'Has she, indeed. Well, we'll file it under "a clash of cultures" then. I daresay our Larridy ways seem quaint to Offcomers. You had a visit from Lieutenant Gannerby and his men this morning?'

She nodded.

'I'm sure you're sensible enough to realise I cannot intervene here?' he said. 'Good. I know your dear grandmama expects everyone to shield you from this world's nastiness, but you're a grown woman, and this is your chosen profession. It will inevitably mean your investigations intersect with those of the Guard occasionally.'

'Of course.' God, it was good to talk to someone who didn't patronize her. Girl detective. Go back to finding pussycats. 'They have to follow up all the leads they have. I understand that, unc— Chief.' Her conscience smote her about the slaves and the Breaking Camp. She shouldn't be holding out on him like this.

'Good. I have six months till I retire. I really think at this stage I should be allowed to put my feet up on my desk, and drink contraband brandy at eleven in the morning, not chase round on Dame Bharossa's orders. So another time, *please* don't set her on me.'

She put a guilty hand over her mouth. 'Sorry. She likes to help.'

'You don't need her help, Anabara.' He gave her another peck on the cheek. 'You're forgiven. Stay out of trouble. It's so awkward having the Patriarch's niece in my cells. Everyone tells me off.'

She felt a secret glow as she headed to the Precincts. *You don't need her help, Anabara.* The man worked a magic, that was for sure. He was witty, urbane. But with that force-field of power that made you want to impress him. Even now she had to battle the urge to run after him and boast about her brilliant detective work, put him in the picture, hear his praise. It was the old father-figure thing, sure it was.

Yeah, said her conscience, and the old Larridy thing as well—going behind the Offcomer's back. She had a sudden vivid image of Mooby in her pink frilly shirt, saying *God, I hate this place.* And she was right. It stank of corruption. Slaves. In the very heart of the Precincts. Not that Dhalafan would be party to a cover-up, even if the University's reputation was a stake. Would he? Anyway, it was Mooby's job to put Dhalafan in the picture, not Anabara's.

The triple domes rose above it all. They had witnessed worse than this. On impulse she slipped into the chapel dedicated to her parents. The familiar smell of lilies and polished wood greeted her. She made the threefold sign and curled up in her old corner, gazing up at their frescoed faces. Their names glowed in gold. Entwined. *Kharis Bharossa* in Galen. *Danilo Nolio* in Gull. It was a funny place. She liked it, even though snobs like Butros called it 'an evenly-matched brawl between Gull and Galen taste.' The spare elegant lines of the building were clogged with pink and green Candacian marble. Above the fresco—supported by cute little flying Gull children—was a gilt scroll in High Galen: *The Way is still the Way, though all forsake it.*

Was that true? Was it? Tears began to roll down her cheeks as she gazed up at her parents. Everything you stood for, all your work for Fairy rights—it's been made a complete mockery of! Under your very feet new slaves were being broken in all the time. And all your scholarship, all the research you did—you must have used books brought from the Stacks by the slaves you were trying to defend! Anabara thought of her own school history book. A potted guide to how human nature betrayed the Way. All those wars in the name of religion. The twilight of the prince Patriarchs, with its mind-boggling levels of corruption and decadence. Nothing changed, did it? We never get any wiser or better. But this shit-storm would pass, too. The sun would still rise.

And now, at last, she'd played her part. Done something real that her parents might have been proud of. Would they say, *Well done?* She ached to hear those words, listened, listened for them, like the chapel was a giant shell that still held a whisper of the sea.

But there was something niggling at her. Something she'd forgotten. Had Paran been tinkering with her memory again? No, it was about the slave, she thought suddenly. If his job was to fetch library books, why on earth was he armed? Was he guarding something?

Oh God. She leapt to her feet. The Zaarzuk's visit had been detected. Terror shrilled through her veins. She'd forbidden the slave to kill the Master of the Stacks. She'd forbidden him to kill the Guard. But if Dal Ramek set foot in the Stacks again, there was nothing to stop the Fairy from cutting his throat.

CHAPTER SIXTEEN

She set off at a run towards the Novice Quarters. Please don't let him have gone back to the Stacks already. Don't let him be dead. She tried to fend off visions of him sprawled with his throat slashed, his heart cut out; but she was half sobbing with fear as she rounded the last corner— and ran straight into her brother's arms.

'Oh God, Yanni—Dal Ramek!'

She felt a jolt go through him. 'What's he done to you?'

'No, no. Nothing. Oh God, where is he? I've got to find him,' she gabbled.

'Stop. Focus.' She took a deep breath. 'Now tell me what's going on.'

Forget Butros and his deniability. She explained in a few quick sentences.

'I'll take you to him.' He set off. 'Then afterwards you and I need to talk.'

She trotted to keep up. 'Yanni, I'm sorry about… the bathhouse thing. It was just kissing. Honestly. Please don't be mad any more.'

'All forgiven.'

'When I thought the slave was going to kill me,' she said, 'all I could think was, I'm going to die without ever making up with Yanni.'

'Don't! Don't torment yourself.' He put his arm round her shoulders, rested his head on hers. 'You really think there is anything you could do that would stop me loving you?'

'But you were so angry.'

'You bet I was.' He stopped by a small penitential shrine. 'Wait here.' She watched him duck under the low archway. A moment later he emerged with the Zaarzuk, who gave her a stony stare.

'My sister has something to tell you,' said Yanni.

Dal Ramek's eyes widened. 'Your sister? She is your *sister?*'

'Certainly.'

'And this is my punishment?' He gestured to the shrine. 'To meditate?' Yanni inclined his head. 'Then I tell you to your face, Master, you disgrace the name of brother. If some cur dishonours *my* sister—God forbid!—I take my whip to him, I drag him by his heels behind my horse!'

There was a long silence. The Zaarzuk seemed to hear what he'd just said. Colour mounted in his cheeks.

'Food for your mediation, brother,' said Yanni. 'I'll wait over there.'

Anabara turned to the Zaarzuk. He was already beating his breast. 'Ms Nolio, I know it—I am that cur I spoke of! I deserve—'

'Shut up,' she said. 'I want you to do something for me.'

'Name it, and I will do it. Word of a Zaarzuk.' He made the threefold sign.

'I want you to promise me that you'll stay out of the Stacks.'

Silence. 'Why you ask this?'

'Never mind. Just promise me.' Panic welled up. 'Please! You gave your word!'

'True. So: I promise.' Again the three-fold sign. 'But why? Some great danger? I see it in your eyes. You've been down there? Why you won't tell me, hey? Then maybe I go to the Vice Chancellor. Maybe I ask him, does he know about the Fays in his library?'

'Don't!' She grabbed his arm. 'Oh God—have you spoken to anyone about this?'

He shook his head. 'Only you. So tell me.' His hand covered hers. 'I keep it secret. I swear.'

Lord, she'd end up telling half the world! But he was so stubborn there was no alternative.

'So!' His eyes flashed when she'd finished her hurried explanation. 'He lies in wait for me! Very good. I will take his knife from him and slit his treacherous Fay throat!'

She gave him a shake. 'No! He'd kill you before you'd even seen him! My God, they taught the Galens how to fight—even Yanni couldn't defend himself against a Fairy. And you promised me!'

'Hah!' The Zaarzuk folded his arms and scowled. 'But you, will you go down there, while I must stand idle?'

'No. I'll leave it to the Guard. What's the matter with you? Don't you care what's going on? I want the slaves freed, not killed!'

A glowering silence. Then, 'Who is this Yanni? Your lover?'

'Oh for God's sake.' She pointed across to where he brother was pacing. 'That's Yanni. Go back to your prayers.' She turned, but he caught her arm.

'Ms Nolio.' He glanced across at the Master, dropped his voice. 'Anabara. I curse myself for this. I think you maybe hear… certain rumours?'

'A frigid little tease with iron britches—that rumour?' Damn, I was *not* going to say that.

'Ach!' He winced. 'This is bad! What can I say? Last night I am very very angry. Your Fay—Fairy—he taunts me. So in my rage I say things I do not mean. I drink, I go with harlots. But my heart is yours. Believe it.'

'Sorry—not interested.'

'You are angry. I deserve this. But…' He glanced across at Yanni again. 'You like me, I think?'

'Yes, I like you,' she replied. 'But I don't respect you.'

Again the colour mounted in his cheeks. He let go of her arm. Lifted his chin. 'Then Tadzar Dal Ramek will earn your respect.' He turned and ducked back into the shrine, clouting his head on the arch. He cursed in Zaarzuk, then vanished from her sight.

'Well,' said Yanni as they walked back towards the Novice Quarters, 'do I need to lock him up, or will he stay out of the Stacks?'

'I think he will. He gave his word,' said Anabara. 'Is it true he's trying to get himself expelled?'

He gave her a sorrowing glance. Ah, he looked like Uncle Téador. She blushed. No gossip. They walked on in silence. Then Yanni asked, 'Have you eaten today?'

She cast her mind back through the blur of hours. 'No. I'm not hungry.'

But he made her eat a bowl of broth in the student buttery. Afterwards he lead her back out to the big plaza in front of the temple. In the open, she realised, where nobody could eavesdrop. They sat cross legged on a stone bench. If only she could be as serene as Yanni. But probably the very architecture of his brain was different from hers. Contoured by years of meditation.

'I don't understand,' he began. 'If an armed slave was guarding the Stacks, why didn't he kill you?'

She pointed to the amulet. 'This.' And she told him about it, and about the two Fairies who had brought the *paran* to the Patriarch after their parents' murder.

'Our mother wore this? I don't recognise it,' he said.

'It's got a perception charm on it. Feel.'

He reached out and took it in his hand. 'A creature, carved in green stone?' She nodded. 'Yes, I wondered what happened to that. But why is it charmed? Why did uncle give it to you?'

She told him everything. By the end she could feel his anger blazing red like a forge. 'It's not my fault! I told Uncle Téador I was going to the auction,' she cried. 'He said he sensed I had to do this. He let me go, Yanni!'

He raised a hand to halt her defensive blurting. She watched his face. He was tapping his reserves of calm. She knew she had to wait. Don't be mad at me, don't be mad at me. I can't bear it. The wind sang in the flutes, infinitely sad.

'Ana,' he said, 'if it would keep you safe, I'd cut open my heart and hide you in here, where nothing could ever harm you.'

'I know, I know. I'm sorry Yanni. I've just got to report to Mooby, then I'm out of this. I promise.'

'Thank you.' He seemed to be watching the flight of a gull, as it hung and wheeled on the wind.

He knows what it is to lose the ones he loves, she thought. I was too young when they died.

'I wonder,' he said at last, 'if there's something deeper at work. If the Patriarch has discerned an echo of it. Some ripple from our parents' death finally reaching us. Who is this "Paran" and why is he here?'

Her heart pounded. Was Yanni right? 'Maybe it's the blood debt? "If it takes a thousand generations they will

carry on trying to honour it,"' she quoted. 'That's what
Uncle Téador said. Yanni, do you think he's here to protect
us?'

'That depends whose side he's on, I'm afraid.'

'I could ask him,' she said. 'He has to tell me the truth.'
Except he'd probably just point to his right ear, and tell her
squat. 'I've never really got a handle on Fairy politics, to be
honest.'

Those warring dynasties with their unpronounceable
names, the shifting alliances, the endless stupid blood feuds.
All her life people had been lecturing Anabara on the ins
and outs of her parents' diplomatic missions, their selfless
efforts on behalf of lowbred refugees. It was a great wall of
blah-blah-blah, the backdrop to her childhood. She
wondered, suddenly, if she'd refused to understand out
of pure resentment. Why had Mum and Dad cared more
about a bunch of Fairies than their baby daughter, than *me*?

She was still wondering this when she saw the beadle
coming. He approached, bowed to the Master, then to her.
It was the same part-Gull who had escorted her out of the
library.

'Ms Nolio, sorry to interrupt. The Patriarch wishes to
speak with you.'

Yanni, hugged her tight, and murmured a blessing
in her ear. Then she set off with the beadle towards the
Patriarch's quarters.

'I saw you both from my balcony,' said the Patriarch. 'Come
and admire my view.'

His view? What was going on? He led her through his
apartment and opened the immense window on to the
Appearance balcony. This was where the Prince Patriarchs

had deigned to show themselves to the crowds on feast days, and scatter their commemorative pennies and lordly blessings.

Anabara looked out across the empty square. There was Yanni, still sitting on the stone bench. He looked tiny and lost. Behind him rose the temple with its onion domes.

'He's the best brother in the world,' she whispered.

'Yes. But in the end, even the most careful of brothers can't keep his sister safe,' said the Patriarch. 'He knows he can't keep her locked in a silver cage like a finch. Yet if something happens to her, he will always reproach himself.'

He was talking about himself and her mother. Was he afraid that history was about to repeat itself? She opened her mouth to tell him everything, but he shook his head slightly. Then glanced towards the carved balustrade. It was a riot of fanciful masonry—vines and fruit and tiny birds. Listening charms? Her eyes widened.

'This place embodies the pinnacle of the High Galen decorative art. Not a single square inch without its little embellishment. Utterly charming!' Her heart jolted. 'This happy thought struck me afresh since we last spoke together.'

Her mind raced. Their last conversation had been monitored? He'd brought her out on to the balcony for a reason. Another jolt—vigilance charms inside? Well of course there were. Security for the Patriarch was always tight.

'Charming, but a nightmare to dust it all,' she said to fill the silence.

'But I have lackeys for that!' he laughed. 'Why, I am surrounded by attentive staff!'

Spied on by attentive staff. Carramans, she thought suddenly. It was only the library contract they'd lost. They still did all the maintenance work on the Patriarch's Palace charms. Had they been listening in on her conversations with her uncle? She went cold. Quickly, sound relaxed: 'Ha, ha! Lucky you, waited on hand and foot!'

'Yes, what a lucky fellow I am!' He hugged her close. She felt him slip something into her pocket. 'Ah well! There are times when we must *only receive.*'

'Only receive?'

'Only receive and remain silent, as the Saint himself taught us. Learn from others, my child, even if their ways are at present hidden from you.' He was acting like a caricature of a pious old fool.

She nodded earnestly. 'I will try to master this, uncle.' Her hand crept into her pocket. A little book? No, it was glass. Suddenly she knew: it was that spooky writing tablet.

'Few have this gift!' he sighed. 'But I suspect you will encounter one or two close to hand. Completely unexpectedly. Even the wise cannot say for sure who they are. So be alert, keep watch, pray. But come!' He clapped his hands. 'Enough sermonizing! Let's take some tea and have a nice cozy chat.'

It was several hours before she had chance to examine the strange writing tablet. Finally she was alone and safe, back in her house. She'd reported to Mooby, who, like the slave, had clenched a fist and punched the air. A detachment of Mainland Guards would be poised in the alley to intercept the next shipment of future slaves as they entered the Stacks at Wolf Tide. A raid on the Library would be timed to coincide with it. Thwyn's body had been dug up and formally identified, some Tressy men and women from the Slackey had been taken in for questioning. Warrants for Golar's arrest were being sought on the basis of Anabara's and Loxi's information. And now her role was over.

Except it didn't feel like that. That conversation with the Patriarch had shaken her. He'd been so unlike himself, so cautious and tricksy with his pompous old ass act, she didn't know what to make of it. She'd pottered about the marketplace 'acting normal' as Mooby had recommended. She'd bought sweetmeats to take to her little cousins tomorrow. She'd handled a request for work from a wine merchant who suspected someone was pilfering from his cellar. But did he really want a fancy new charm on his cellar door, or had he been hired to lure Paran into a dark corner where he could be seized again? As she walked home down Skuller, every statue and bit of tracery concealed a vigilance charm, every friendly passerby was a double agent, every archway the mouth of a hidden tunnel.

I can't live like this, she thought. It's like the worst of the Palatinate era. Poisoned rings, fratricide. The charms in her uncle's apartment had been there ever since those treacherous times. Her suspicions about Carraman reared up again. Damn, she'd forgotten to mention them to Mooby. Maybe it was nothing. There was hardly a pie in Larridy that Carraman didn't have five fingers in. Yet *something* had happened to trouble Uncle Téador, that was certain. The tablet?

She put her shopping in the pantry, sat cross-legged in a chair and took out the curious slab. Only receive. Stay silent. Don't attempt to send a message. That's what he'd meant. Her breath misted the black glass. One or two people close at hand also had 'this gift'. Presumably the prototypes which kept going missing from the University of Galencia. It struck her suddenly how useful this device would be to the criminal world. Her uncle must have been examining his when he stumbled upon some alarming exchange of messages.

Messages about her? Had to be. Why else had he given her
the tablet?

There was nothing on the glassy surface now. She turned
it over and looked at the back. It appeared to be some form
of slate. The edges were bound in white steel. What was
inside? Some densely compacted charmwork, thin as vel-
lum. Rodania might know. She peered closely. Her breath
misted the glass again. She wiped it with her sleeve, and as
she did so, the tablet grew lighter, started to glow, almost
as if it had woken up. Aha! Now what? She didn't dare use
the white-steel pen. Instead she ran her finger over it. And
there! A message in Commons. It read: *Good. C.* Her fingers
tingled. An answer to an earlier message she'd missed. But
what? Who from? Who was this 'C'?

Carraman!

Business links with Golar, access to the Patriarch's private conversations—*that* was how he knew about her contract with the Library. Not Enobar blabbing to Toby Buttery
after all. No, hang on. The break-in had happened before
she'd told the Patriarch about the contract. She frowned.
But Carraman could have heard her telling Uncle Téador
she was going to buy a slave, though! Which meant there
might not be traitor in Mooby's squad after all. She rubbed
the glass again. The word faded. Dammit, there must be
some trick to it. But try as she might, the tablet wouldn't
yield up its secrets. After quarter of an hour she had to put
the thing away before she started banging it on the table
and screaming at it.

But what if the message on the tablet was a ruse? After
all, she knew nothing about how the thing worked or who
might be manipulating it, planting false clues. If there was a
traitor in the Guard—especially if it was a psych—what was

to say he or she wasn't trying to create a smoke screen? 'C' wasn't much to go on, was it? Slow down, Ana. Leaping to conclusions here. If only she could get the device working properly.

Paran would know how it operated. She felt a surge of fear and revulsion at the thought of him. What *was* his game, why was he here? Which side was he on? Damn, if only she'd paid attention in Fairy History. It was way too embarrassing to own up that she didn't actually have a clue what her parents had given their lives for. Other than it was something to do with promoting amnesty, which was meant to be a way to break the political deadlock and stop centuries of vendettas. Anabara had forgotten which Fairy dynasties had favoured the idea, and which had hated it. Hated it so much they'd assassinated the human messengers.

She had a vivid flashback to that history lesson. The mistress explaining how Uncle Téador had narrowly prevented the vendetta spilling over into the human realm. 'By his Refusal to Exact Reprisals, boys and girls. Who knows what that means? Yes—forgiving people when they do something bad to us. I want you to remember *that* (eyeballing Anabara) next time you're fighting in the playground!' All the other kids had turned and stared at her. That was right after Uncle had been made Patriarch, so she'd have been about 6. She wondered again if Yanni was right and a ripple from history was reaching them at last. Was there some master-plan afoot?

Yeah, right—one which involved Paran being enslaved. Some master-plan. What had Mooby said? 'The unlucky ones, the friendless, powerless ones'—those were the ones who ended up enslaved. If he'd really was an elite mind warrior come to Larridy to protect her and Yanni and repay the debt, was it likely he'd end up as a ship's Fay?

He was probably upstairs now, perceiving her thoughts. God, was she destined to spend the rest of her life with a mind-reading murderer in her spare room? And all the time her credit would be sinking like sand in an hourglass—until finally it was all gone and he was permitted to turn on her.

Outside the wind had picked up. The flutes howled at the waxing moon. One more night and it would be full. And this year, the astronomers were saying, the moon was closer to the earth than it had been for three hundred years. So this Wolf Tide would be the most spectacular in living memory, especially if the wind stayed in the same quarter and swelled the flood. The Gull communities were already tethering their boats firmly, and getting the saltings sheep up on to higher ground.

She put the tablet back in her pocket and went to fetch herself some bread and cheese and milk. She'd just sat down again and started to eat, when a tremendous thump against the door startled her. Milk went everywhere. Fecking kids, playing Knock-a-door! There was a lull in the wind. Silence. She mopped up the milk. Then another sound made her pause. A tiny whimper. Like a kitten. There it was again.

Curiosity got the better of her. If it was kids, they were going to get their backsides well and truly kicked. She opened the top half of the door and looked out on the street. It was deserted.

Then she looked down. Oh dear God! A man, naked. Covered in blood. She wrenched the door fully open, fell to her knees and rolled him over. Face was battered, eyes swollen shut. Blood spilled from his mouth. No! Someone had taken a knife and carved on his chest: *Molly*.

It was Loxi.

CHAPTER SEVENTEEN

The wind blew. Leaves scuttled over the cobbles. Someone was wailing, *Loxi, Loxi, don't die!* It's me, she realised. I'm howling. Then Paran was there. He scooped Loxi up and brought him inside.

'Close the door,' he said. 'Quickly. And the shutters.'

'Oh, God save us!' She fumbled them all shut. He'd laid Loxi on the hearth rug. 'Is he alive? The Infirmary, we must get him to the— ' Flames were snaking round the Fairy's head. She cringed back. 'What's happening to you?'

'Hold your tongue. Ask me nothing.' His eyes glowed like coals in a grate. 'I can call your cousin back and mend him—but I need your help. Don't open the doors to anyone. Don't break my concentration. Nod, if you understand.'

She nodded. Fire writhed under his skin, dripped in runnels down him.

'Afterwards my strength will be spent. You must give me food, or I will die. Will you do this, no matter what?'

She nodded. Her teeth chattered. *Fire*, said her uncle's voice. *A pure-bred fire lord. These creatures are all fire.* That's it— *that's* what I saw that night when we made the deal. Fire.

'If you fail, you are foresworn. I repeat: do not ask me anything. There is no point, I will only wipe your memory.'

Again she nodded.

'Good. Sit at his feet, don't move, watch for us both.'

She obeyed.

Paran knelt and took Loxi's head on his lap. He raised his left hand. A slit of light appeared in the air in front of him, as if a thick curtain had been sliced. He slid his hand through and withdrew something. It glinted blinding white. She screamed in terror. A *paran*!

'You're an assassin!' she cried. 'Who's your target?'

'Don't ask, you fool!'

'Tell me! Why are you here? Who have you come here for?'

Fire dripped like blood from his fangs. 'The Patriarch.'

'No! You can't—'

A spark leapt from the blade and snapped on her lips. She opened her mouth. No sound came.

'You're wasting time!' hissed the Fairy. 'If you love your cousin, watch and pray.'

She closed her eyes. He's going to kill my uncle! Oh what have I done? I wish I'd never freed him, never seen him! An after-image of the *paran* blazed, like the sun off glass. She could hear the Fairy murmuring. Everything was shrinking. Or ballooning out. The room was vast as a temple. No, she was a giant, a giant crammed into a doll's house. Her head throbbed until she thought it would burst. Don't let me throw up. Sweat trickled down her face. Fever. That's what they all said it was like, going into Fairy. Few humans could endure it. The air reeked of gunpowder, of storms—the stench of deep charm-work.

All the time the wind blew outside; the flutes howled. Feet passed the door. Shouts, in another kingdom far away. The Fairy's murmuring rose and fell. Loxi's body convulsed. She opened her eyes. The room was keeling and rolling like a ship in a gale. She saw the blade deep in Loxi's stomach. The Fairy drew it slowly to the throat. He pulled the rib cage apart like a clam. And reached inside.

His heart! He was going to eat his heart! She tried to scream.

Paran raised his head, stared. Not human. Why had she ever trusted him? 'Pray, you simpleton!'

She shut her eyes again. Gabbled prayers. Pelago, don't let him kill Loxi. Oh God, please, I'll do anything you want. I'm sorry for everything. Don't let him kill uncle. Save us, save us! Her body was drenched with sweat. But it was icy in here. Funeral drums boomed in her head. Agony. Round and round keeled the room. Her stomach heaved.

What was he doing to him? She had to look. The yawning chest was closed. Paran slid the flat of the blade along the wound, wiping it out, vanishing it. As if time was running backwards and the evil was being unravelled. But Loxi still lay lifeless. Waxen. Tears ran down her cheeks.

Now Paran bent his head towards the dead face. She watched him fasten his mouth on to Loxi's, and exhale. The mended chest rose. Fell with a sigh. The Fairy breathed into him again. Again his chest rose. Fell. But now the livid flesh was tinged with colour. A third breath. And suddenly his heart stuttered awake.

He was alive! Fresh tears poured from her eyes. She clutched Loxi's ankles, pressed her face against his feet and wept on them. Thank you, thank you!

When she looked up again Paran was sliding the blade over the hacked letters on Loxi's chest. Erasing them one by one. M. O. The two L's. The Y. Loxi moaned.

His face, mend his poor face, begged Anabara.

The Fairy nodded, set to work. The split lip, the fractured jaw. The swollen eyes— But then the blade winked out like a snuffed candle, vanished.

'I'm done,' he gasped. 'Remember your promise.' He sagged, then slumped unconscious.

The room righted itself. Her head stopped pounding. Loxi moaned again. Suddenly it was real: her cousin, naked, bloody, on her hearth. Do something. She lurched to her feet, snatched up a blanket and covered him. Found a cushion. She stroked his head. They'd hacked his hair off, his beautiful hair.

Beside him lay the Fairy. His eyes stared at the ceiling. As she watched, a haze crept over them, like the bloom on a black plum. *Remember your promise.* But he should remember *his* promise—not to harm any member of her family! She wrung her bloodstained hands. What should I do, saints in heaven, what should I do? I can't fail him. He just saved Loxi, poured out his life force to save him. But if she revived him now, he would assassinate the Patriarch—and that would surely mean war. Let the creature die, said a voice, just let it die! Terror each way she turned: if she let him die, she'd be foresworn. Some other fire assassin would hunt her down and kill her in retribution. Coward. Did she not have the courage to lay down her own life? For the sake of her uncle, for the sake of Larridy?

Back and forth swerved her mind. She couldn't understand. Paran *knew* the Patriarch was her kinsman. Then she saw: his orders from Fairy were in conflict with her own deal. He was in a double-bind. There would be another default penalty. Not a cut-off ear this time, but a death penalty. He would he assassinate the Patriarch, then come to her afterwards and offer her his *paran*. Like the two messengers had done all those years ago. He'd expect her to kill him, to right the balance.

Then kill him *now!* urged the voice in her mind. Kill him now, and save your uncle, save Larridy from a war it cannot win! It was not just Larridy: if the Patriarch was assassinated the entire Mainland Federation would be sucked in. She saw the States, like beads on a string, slipping one after another over an abyss. Relentless, inevitable destruction. Then the Fays would break through and colonise our world, just like the racists always said they would.

Look at him—for all his terrifying power, just lying there. It would be the work of a moment. Didn't she know a dozen locks to break a neck, a score of strangles? Hell, she could probably stamp him to pieces like a dead spider, sweep the fragments out into the gutter. Or do nothing. Hide his empty shell in her cupboard and seal the door. Forget him.

But she knew she was incapable of it. She wept in despair. This snarled-up tangle of obligations, there was no unpicking it. Where had it begun? With a wet rag pushed through the bars of a cage. A mouthful of water, a single act of kindness. How could she possibly end it now with an act of betrayal? Oh, but it shouldn't be like this, the cost of kindness shouldn't be this high. Uncle, I'm sorry. Whatever I choose—do this, do that, do nothing—it's wrong. Everything's wrong. I won't even be able to warn you, because he'll wipe away my memory.

Unless...

She leapt to her feet. The room rolled for a moment, steadied itself. She'd send a message. She rummaged in her desk for a scrap of parchment, took up a quill and scrawled her message. Quickly she read it over. It would have to do. She took a fresh sheet of blotting paper and pressed it to the ink, then folded the parchment. The sealing wax dripped like blood. She pressed her signet into it. Her mother's. Galen 'K' for Kharis. Is this the right thing? Is this what you'd have done? Mum, help me. Please.

Her hands were scabbed with blood, like she was already a murderer. Blood everywhere. Too much blood. A smear on the parchment. She wrote her uncle's name and direction over the stain. Added '*urgent*'. Underlined it. There. She put the letter in her pocket. Later I'll be sure to find you, she thought. I won't remember what you contain, but I will send you.

Loxi stirred and whimpered in his sleep. The Fairy lay motionless, his fire all ashes. Anabara reeled to the pantry and fetched a jar of honey. She knelt beside him. One last moment to reconsider. The wind racketed down the street. It shook the houses, snatched slates off roofs. *Knock-a-door, knock-a-door, Wolf Tide's come!* Where would this act lead? But you could never know for sure where any act would lead. You could only ever do the next thing. The act of kindness that lay to hand. And trust it was the right thing. Please let it be the right thing.

She slid her arm under his neck and raised his head. It made her flinch, although she'd been expecting it, that sensation of lifting an empty husk. His mouth was smeared with Loxi's blood. It gaped open. The fangs glistened red. She picked up the spoon and dipped it in the honey. Saw the slow amber drip down on to his tongue. A memory of the village: feeding baby cousins. Cradling them. She was appalled by a rush of tenderness for this thing in her arms. Then the haze over his eyes melted like frost on a sunny window. He reared up, like last time. Seized the spoon, devoured the honey. Set the jar aside.

Then he turned his gaze on her. And smiled.

Oh! What was happening? New shoes! My birthday! Waking gloomy, then remembering, *Yay—holidays!* Everything was fresh baked honeycakes and larks singing over the salt flats, and flying, flying up into an endless summer sky.

'See?' he said. 'All is well. Your cousin lives. I tell you again: you need have no fear of me.'

Yet there was something. Something terrible. Her mind groped towards it. She tried to speak but no sound came.

'Ah yes, forgive me.' He stretched out a finger towards her and she felt the charm click off her tongue. 'You were saying?'

Again, a memory—half a memory—of terror. And fire! 'Oh God, you're a…' But what was he? 'Paran, you mustn't do it.'

'Do what?'

It was gone. She stared at him. Looked round the room. Loxi, sleeping on her hearth under a blanket. That's right, he'd been beaten up. Blood everywhere. 'What happened?' she asked. 'Wait, you healed him! But he was… wasn't he dead?'

'Maybe his injuries weren't as grave as you feared,' suggested the Fairy. 'Head wounds bleed freely. As to the rest, don't worry—there'll be no scars. We Fairy artisans are all skilled in leech-craft and herb-lore. What is an artisan, after all, but a maker and mender?'

She frowned. 'But I thought… I'm confused.'

'The shock, no doubt.'

'Yes, the shock. Thank you for what you did.' She looked again at her sleeping cousin. 'Oh, Loxi. I warned him they'd beat him up. But I can't *believe* they'd… mutilate him like that.' She choked on a sob. 'You're sure there'll be no scars?'

'No scars. But this isn't Gull work. Would a Gull use Commons? It's a decoy. Did your cousin talk to the Guard?' She nodded. 'Ah, then I fear that someone in the Guard has betrayed him to the rivermen.'

'What? But who's talked? Butros told him to report only to Mooby!' Not Carraman. The Guard. Then she saw why she'd been desperate to believe it was Carraman— because otherwise it had to be someone she knew. Knew and liked. At this, she was stepping into nothingness. Stomach in free fall. 'No! Is it Mooby? Is Mooby the traitor?'

'No. She passed my door charm.'

'Then who did he talk to, the idiot?'

'I don't know. But this was a punishment beating. And a warning to you. That's why they dumped him here.' He reached out and stroked the hair back from Loxi's brow. The intricate Gull tattoo was bleared by blood. He murmured in Fairy. *My poor* something. Anabara felt a squirm of revulsion. The Fairy sensed it. Withdrew his hand.

Quickly she asked, 'How do you know all this?'

'I surmise it. Some of it I saw, in the last remnant of his thought. I saw him enticed into an alley and set upon. His attackers were three old crew mates.' He hissed. 'I recognised their faces, oh yes.'

'Then they're here in Larridy already!' Fear shuddered through her. 'Is Golar here too?'

'That remains to be seen.' He stared at her, blank-faced as ever. 'I imagine by now your cousin's attackers are drunk in some tavern. They will be easy enough to find. I won't "go about killing people". You don't favour that, I know. But perhaps if you are agreeable, I might select one of the three, and coax him to confide in me?'

'Coax—? No! Don't tell me!' He waited. 'Look, couldn't you just read his mind and find out that way?'

'I could, of course. But where's the pleasure in that?' He stood. 'Come. We need to clean the place up. I'll fetch water.'

Loxi was sleeping near the fire on her reclining couch. They had bathed him and made him comfortable. She grieved for his hair, a warrior's pride and joy. But that was ridiculous. He was alive, for God's sake! What was a bad haircut? It would grow back. She should be singing hymns of gratitude. So why did spasms of dread keep clutching her stomach?

I'm forgetting something, she thought as she mopped the last patch of floor. I'm forgetting something really important. It was like going upstairs and standing there thinking, what have I come up here for? It was definitely something to do with Paran. Was there something she was supposed to warn him about? She leant on the mop and racked her brains. The slaves in the library? Golar? Or Butros and his vengeful plans to get the truth? Maybe that was it.

'My counsel wants to see you again,' she said. 'He's pretty pissed off. Look, I shouldn't tell you this, but he's going to hire some nasty ass mercenaries and find out—'

'Stop. I know all this. Your thoughts chirp like a tree full of crickets. Spare me the chore of listening twice.'

'Huh.' She glared at him. 'If you're so clever, maybe you can tell me what I've forgotten. It's scaring me. Like something bad's going to happen and it'll be my fault.'

He was beside her in a heartbeat, staring deep into her eyes. After a moment he took the mop from her hands, 'Leave this work, I'll finish for you. You've had a lot to bear, these last days. And now, on top of everything, your cousin's been attacked. Small wonder you're scared. Why not stay by him tonight? You can keep an eye on him and nurse him if he wakes. Come, sit here beside him.' She sank on to the couch. Her eyelids began to droop. 'These are dark times. Though for all that, I think you'll both sleep soundly.'

'Whoa!' She put up a hand. 'Stop that right there, mister. Don't fecking sleep-charm *me*.'

'But sleep is a great healer.' He tilted his head. 'No? Don't be afraid. You'll be safe here while I'm gone. Nothing can enter here with ill intent, remember. I have deeds to do. Come, rest here by your cousin. Sleep well.' She began to sway where she sat. 'Enobar,' he whispered. 'You still love him?'

She snapped awake. 'What? Of course I do! Why?'

'Oh, just checking. His folly led your cousin into danger. He got him drunk, then abandoned him for a pretty stranger. But you are inclined as ever to mercy, I dare say?'

'Paran, don't you dare lay a finger on him! Enobar counts as family! You can't harm my family, remember?' As she said this, the thing she couldn't recall hovered again, just out of reach. What *was* it?

He peered into her eyes again. Then he hissed. 'Well, well. Clever!'

'What?'

'You fear for your uncle, the Patriarch. You have a message for him. In your pocket.'

'Really?' She rummaged and pulled out a sealed letter. It was smeared with blood. Another surge of panic. 'What? When did I write that?'

'See here?' He pointed to the underlined word. 'It's urgent. Why don't you give it to me, and I will deal with it at once?'

No, no! screamed a voice in her head. She hesitated. 'Thanks, but I'll deliver it myself.'

'As you wish.' He tilted his head again, placed a finger against his lips. 'Curious. Your mind starts aside like a warped bow. There's a kink of resistance in you, and it grows stronger all the time.' He tapped the finger against his mouth. 'You have no Fairy blood in your veins, I suppose?'

'Don't be ridiculous! Why do you ask that?'

'No matter.' He blew softly in her face. 'Sleep now.'

Oh, feck it. Here comes the velvet wave. The last thing she knew was the Fairy plucking the parchment from her slack fingers as she toppled over on to the couch beside Loxi.

CHAPTER EIGHTEEN

S he was woken the following morning by a rapping at her door. Grey clouds scudded past her porthole window. The bossy knocking continued. I bet it's Rodania, she thought. But what on earth's brought her down here?

Her next thought was: What the FECK? She was in bed with Loxi.

'Anabara!' Tap-tap-tap. 'Are you in?'

She lay frozen like gull chick who's spotted a sea eagle overhead. *Loxi*?! Did we—? She peeped under the quilt. Naked! But no—*she* was dressed. She fell back with a moan of relief. Auntie Laitolo would not be banging their heads together and dragging them by their ears to the altar.

Something had happened, though, hadn't it? Why couldn't she remember? Deep sigh. Paran again. He'd presumably charmed them halfway to Tara-doodle, then brought them both up here for reasons best known to himself. This was getting beyond a joke.

She slid out from under her covers. Loxi looked pale and ill. He'd cut his hair off! With a breadknife, it looked like. Woo, was that boy drunk last night or what. Auntie was going to marmalise him. Memories flickered like a deck of ruffled cards. No time for that now. She hurried downstairs to let Rodania in.

'Weren't you awake?' Her cousin bustled in with a bake-house bag. A waft of hot honeycake. 'Honestly. It's gone nine, Anabara. Some of us have— Oh dear Lord! Is that blood?'

Anabara looked down at her clothes. 'Oh God!'

Back it all came. There was Loxi, bleeding on her hearth, Paran tending him. Herb-lore? Fairy artisans were skilled in leech-craft and herb-lore? No, that didn't seem right. There were gaps in her memory, like pictures missing from a wall. She slumped into a chair.

'Eat.' A honeycake was put into her hand. 'Now then,' said Rodania after Anabara had finished. 'Do you need a doctor? Where are you injured?'

'It's not my blood.' She drank some hot chocolate. 'Loxi was beaten up last night.'

Rodania's hand flew to her heart. 'Is he all right? Where is he?'

'Upstairs.' She frowned. 'He's fine. Head wounds bleed freely. Maybe his injuries weren't as bad as I feared?'

'Thank God for that! Enobar was convinced some students had jumped him.'

'Students? Why would—'

'*However*, we made enquiries, and heard that a pair of Gull bruisers were searching the bars for him—which was even worse, as you can imagine! So Grandmama informed the Guard and sent to the Infirmary, but— Well, thank Pelago he wasn't badly hurt.'

'Yes, thank Pelago.' But suddenly an image unfurled: Loxi, with bloody letters hacked on his chest. 'No, it *was* bad! My God, he was half dead! Beaten up and... and muti-lated. Not by Gulls, by old shipmates. And then... I *think* Paran healed him.'

'Hmmph! *How*, exactly? Incantations? Did he have any high-tech paraphernalia? A *paran*, for example?'

'Y—no.' Something blinding white? 'Not sure. He's been messing with my memory.'

'You do realise that's extremely complex charmwork? To say nothing of illegal. Frankly, I don't like the sound of this, Ana. What *is* he?'

'No idea. Butros thinks he's using a cloaking charm.'

'What? *That's* illegal too! It's your duty to report him. Where is he now?'

'Who knows. Off murdering Tressy boatmen? It's his hobby. He likes to eat their tongues.' She gave a bright smile. 'I've got a confession to make: he was a slave till I freed him. I bought him on the market like a sack of potatoes.'

'Ana, you're raving.' Rodania got up and edged towards the door. 'I think I'd better send for a doctor.'

'No, wait.' Anabara pulled out the glass tablet and flourished it. 'Look!' That did the trick. Back across the room, like a cat after a bobbin. 'Sit. I'll explain what's going on, then you can play with this little dwidget.'

'*Dwidget?* That's not some *dwidget*, you looby, it's a psychtab!' She bounced up and down in her chair. 'I've read scientific papers about them! How did you get it?'

Anabara fended her off. 'Uncle Téador gave it me.'

'That's *so* not fair!' squeaked Rodania. 'Why didn't he give *me* one? *I'm* the scientist! *Plus* I'm six months older than you!' Then she caught herself, recalled she was a grown up.

Anabara told her tale. There was a long silence when she'd finished.

'Slaves?' whispered Rodania. 'In our library?' Tears gathered in her eyes. 'And a Breaking Camp? No. Such things can't still exist. Not in this day and age. They just *can't!*'

Anabara watched her cousin try to take it in. Everything she'd believed to be honorable, pure, noble—built on a lie. 'I'm sorry, Rodi.'

'No, you did the right thing. It can't be hushed up. It *mustn't* be.' Rodania got out a hanky and pressed it to her eyes. She always had a hanky, never had to use her sleeve like Anabara.

'But after this is over, you *have* to report that Fairy, Ana.' Rodania tucked the handkerchief back into her cuff. 'You simply can't let him rampage about Larridy wielding perception charms! I know you meant well freeing him, but this is precisely why slaves have to be handed over to Border Control.'

Time to play her ace: 'Uncle Téador knew what I was planning, and he approved.'

After a brief inner struggle, Rodania sniffed. 'Fine. Well, I came down here to tell you I've got the override password for the Stacks. Totally redundant now, but you may as well still have it, I suppose.' She handed Anabara a slip of parchment with a string of numbers and letters on it. Anabara pocketed it. 'I had to dis-encrypt the security charm vault to access it.'

'But that's illegal!' gasped Anabara. 'I may have to report you.'

'I *know* it's illegal!' Rodania clenched her teeth. 'But *you* seemed to think it was important!'

'Kidding.' She gave her a hug. 'Thank you. You're a star.'

Rodania nodded and jiggled in her chair like she needed to be excused. '*Now* can I look at the psych-tab? Please?'

Anabara warned her of the dangers, then left her to it while she took some breakfast upstairs to Loxi. He was still asleep. His right hand rested on the quilt. Bruised knuckles. He'd tried to defend himself, then. Landed a couple of punishing punches. That was something his pride could cling on to.

He woke when she sat on the bed edge. Gave her a sweet sleepy smile. Then he stretched and ran his hands through his hair. Felt the hacked off ends. Froze. She saw the truth drench him like a bucket of water. He pushed back the quilt in horror and squinted down at himself. Froze again.

'No way!' He rubbed his hand over his chest. Disbelief, panic. 'But they held me down and cut me!'

'I know. Babe, it's all right. Paran fixed you, good as new.' She patted his leg. 'It's going to be fine, eh. No scars. Here, I brought you breakfast.'

But Loxi lay back with an arm over his eyes. She watched a tear trickle out. His lips moved. She leant close. 'Didn't catch that.'

'But it's still true, eh? I still am one,' he sobbed. 'It's never going to be fine, Nan. Never.'

Ah shit. SHIT. Aw, Loxi. No more kidding herself he was just the sensitive type, interested in Galen philosophy. She rocked him while he wept. Crushed his head against her chest. Ground her teeth. She could stomp up to heaven right now, like some whopping Gullmother, and smack God's chops. What the FECK were you playing at, making him this way? You must have known he'd never fit in, never be happy. Why this pointless fecking waste of a life? She was crying too. She wiped her eyes. Well, I'm not standing for it.

'Listen, you.' She shook him. 'We're going to *make* it fine. You hear me?' She gave him another shake. 'Look at me.'

He raised his head.

'You're still you, eh. You're still a man.' She raked his raggedy hair, pushed it out of his eyes. 'And I still love you.'

He nodded, but his face twisted in grief. 'Thanks, Nan.'

'At least it wasn't our own folks who beat up on you.'

'Yeah. This time.'

'There won't *be* a next time. Not if you get yourself into that combat room and learn to fight,' she cuffed him, 'like I *told* you.'

His gaze slid away from hers. 'Yeah, I should probably do that, eh.'

Now what was eating him? She decided not to press it. Things were bad enough as it was. 'You went to the Guard, like Butros said?' He nodded. 'Someone's stitched you up. Who did you talk to?'

He hesitated. 'Nan, don't be mad, you. I know Butros said talk to Mooby, but she was busy, and I just wanted to get it over with, eh, so I found Charlie. I thought, he's on Anti-Trafficking. Man, he's one of us...'

Her head jerked, like someone had slapped her. Charlie Rondo. Please no. Not a fellow Gull. Back, you stupid tears. But it had to be true. The message on the psych-tab. Not from Carraman—from Charlie. 'Aw, Loxi, what have you done? It's him. Charlie's the traitor.'

'Nah, he can't be. Charlie? Charlie taught me to whistle. We played hooley together.' His voice rose in panic. 'Man, he's married to my second cousin!'

'Did you talk to anyone else? Then face it, you. Charlie sold you out to the Tressies.' He'd turned white. 'How much did you tell him?'

'Everything I knew,' he whispered. 'Like Butros said.'

'Oh dear God.' It was like plunging through a rotten floor. Only to plunge through the one below. 'Our own folks! Then we can't hide out in the village tonight.'

'Golar,' he choked. 'He's coming, isn't he?'

They stared at one another in terror. 'Paran will protect us.' She clung to Loxi's arm. 'We'll stick close to him and it will be all right. We can stay here. Nothing evil can get past his charms.' It was true. Why did it feel like clutching at straws? 'No worries, eh. This time tomorrow it'll all be over.'

'This is all my fault, Nan. I'm sorry.'

'No.' She shook her head. 'It's mine. I should never have gone to the slave market. Why did I go and get involved?' she wailed. Instantly she was ashamed. She stood up, squared her shoulders.

'Well,' she said, 'if you can't undo it, you got to go through it.' It was an old Gull saying. 'Eat your breakfast. I'll get Enobar to bring you some clothes down. Make the bugger earn his wage for once, eh. Then I'd better warn Mooby about Charlie.' Ah, you stupid tears. 'Hey. It's going to be fine. Promise.'

As the morning wore on Anabara got her terror back down to manageable proportions. Like the wind—which was still hunting round Larridy in great whoops and shrieks—it didn't seem so bad in broad daylight. It was still a nightmare, but she and Loxi would be safe in her house. After all, they were protected by psychotic levels of security. My God, even Butros didn't resort to viper jinxes!

No, they had nothing to fear with Paran around. How many times did the Fairy need to repeat that, before she believed him? When had he ever let her down? He was bound by his solemn oath. Her credit ran high with him. And creepy though the thought was, he seemed to have... She wanted to say *feelings* for Loxi, stroking his hair like that. Tscha, she was doing it again: projecting human emotions on to him. Fairies *had* no emotions. She thunked her forehead. They are incapable of empathy, remember? Even that monster Golar had warned her not to make the mistake of thinking him human.

Rodania had gone, taking the psych-tab with her. Then Mooby came. 'Charlie? Ah, dammit. I liked that boy. I thought I was a good judge of people. *Dammit.*' But the planned raids had not been jeopardized. Loxi hadn't known about the slaves in the library, or the Breaking Camp, thank God; and Mooby had been keeping her squad in the dark since her suspicions had first been aroused.

'Shite feck bollocks. Charlie. God-DAMMIT. And now I've got to worry about the pair of you, as well. Right. We'll get you up the Precincts. You'll be safe there. I'll arrange an escort.'

'We'll probably be safer here, detective. The door's armed with a viper jinx. So are the windows.'

'La la la. I did *not* hear that. I *so* did not hear that. All righty. Change of plan. Stay here, don't even stick your nose out of the door till I give you the all clear. Got that? Good. I'm off.'

After Mooby left the street got steadily busier. Anabara sat at the little window on the landing, waiting for Enobar. Where the hell was he? A minstrel troupe tramped by, bells jingling. A creaking mule-cart laden with ale barrels. Chairmen carrying fares too idle or hungover to haul themselves up Skuller. The statutory pillocks in wolf masks. A fire-juggler, gangs of over-excited kids with a day's holiday. Three Gulls, each with a saltings sheep carcass slung over his shoulder.

Come *on* Enobar. But most of the traffic was heading up the Mount. Precincts curfew would be early tonight. The big gate would be shut and bolted against non-residents before the worst of the roistering got underway.

It was getting dark when Enobar finally showed up with a big basket. She opened the top half of the door first to check he was alone, then let him in. 'What took you so long?'

'I was in an urgent meeting, and—Ow!' He yelped as he crossed the threshold. Stared in shock. 'Oh my God! Your charm just... *snapped* me!' He dumped the basket and rubbed his backside. '*Ow!* That really hurts. Like a wet towel!'

'Well, it's never done *that* before,' said Anabara, as if it was a pet dog. Urgent meeting, my arse.

'So, yes. I brought the clothes, I brought the wine, I brought the food, I brought the sweetmeats, I brought the firecrackers. Rodi says you're spending Wolf Tide here. But we are *so* going to have a good time!' He started unpacking the basket. 'How's Loxi doing? Your Fairy healed him?'

'Yes.'

'Thank God, thank God. Tell him I kiss his hands and his feet. Swear to God, my life's blood is his, my beating heart is his.' He reeled off a few more empty Candacian vows, committing his family for five generations to a life of willing slavery. 'So. He's an artisan herbalist? Reckon he does love potions? When can I meet him? Is he in?'

'No. Be very grateful.' She folded her arms, nailed him with a glare. 'He blames you for this.'

'Wha-a-at, *me?*' Eyes wide. Hand on chest. Enobar would lie if you asked him what he'd had for lunch. Couldn't help himself. And now he was about to tell her crock of shit about what had happened last night. 'He blames *me?* Oh my God! I was distraught! It wasn't—'

'Let's cut the crap about how it's not your fault.' He squeaked. 'Let's focus on the future instead. Loxi needs looking after. Promise me you'll get him into the combat room every day until—'

'Are you *kidding* me?' he cut in. 'Your cousin is *lethal!* He put two students in the Infirmary yesterday! Bit one guy's ear half off. Swear to God, it took four beadles to drag him away!'

'*No!* Loxi? Get out of here!'

'Seriously, I would rather go one-on-one with a shark in a plunge-pool. He's *insane.* Does this insane scary war cry? Is that a Gull thing? Anyway,' he went back to unpacking the basket, 'I couldn't train him up if I wanted to. He's banned from University premises for six months. He'll have to move in with you. Oh, don't worry, the vampire's all over it. It'll be fine. Vampire says "race discrimination", Chapter freaks out, the ban disappears, vampire sends her ladyship a bill for 800 gilders. Ba-ba-boom. Where do you want the wine?'

Anabara was still standing open-mouthed. 'Loxi? Fighting?'

'Oh God yes. Believe it. They called you a slut. Made horse jokes?' He clapped a hand over his mouth. 'Damn! I promised not to tell you. Don't let on, will you?'

Her face burnt. Me. He was defending *me?*

'Yes, so, I'll just take him his things.' Enobar eyed her, and got out of range. 'Then maybe we can open a bottle? Come on, lighten up. It's Wolf Tide! Oh, there's a message from Rodania somewhere in there.' He scampered up the stairs, anklets tinkling, with a pile of clothes.

Anabara rummaged in the basket, half-blind with fury and mortification. If there had been a single person left in Larridy who hadn't heard about the bathhouse incident, there surely wasn't now. *Ear-biting?* Oh my God! Talk about magnifying her folly!

There was the letter. Uh-oh. Not good. Rodania's impeccable handwriting was a scrawl. *URGENT* underlined three times.

Her heart was already thumping as she broke the seal.

Have cracked it. Disaster. Guard plans leaked to enemy network. Stackmaster in contact with G (?Semmayit Golar) and a Guard, C (?Charlie Rondo). Slaves to be killed before raid can take place, camp to be broken up. Warn Dt Mooby. Take utmost care. Do not go to village, they are lying in wait for you. Trust no-one. Send reply please. Rodania.

The letter had been written at four o'clock. It was now nearly nine. She was already too late.

CHAPTER NINETEEN

S he left by her back door, made her way across rooftops, up the Mount towards the Precincts. The orange Wolf Tide full moon bulged up above the horizon, vast, terrifying as Judgment Day. Far below the streets thronged. A procession of ants wended down Skuller towards the Docks, to watch the Wolf Tide tear up the river.

The sky had cleared. A million stars glinted, but the wind still blew, punching her off course, snatching her breath. Too late, I'm too late. But she had to try. She'd promised the slave: *Help will come.* Please, let me not be too late. Each leap took her closer. The flutes howled. Leaves and rubbish scoured the chimney pots. Someone's hat hurtled by. Then a vicious gust slammed her into a wall. She scrabbled for a handhold, a foothold, fell somersaulting, righted herself, grabbed the nearest gable. A tile whirled past her head and exploded against a turret.

Let Loxi be safe. Let him not come after me. She'd left a note, but would he listen? Thank God the rivermen couldn't hunt her up here. A Gull might pursue her, but surely Charlie's best flying days were behind him? He was too big, too earthbound. She set off again. There were the Precinct walls. *Boom!* sang the mighty bass flute. The ancient cedars groaned and cracked. She got in by the old grain barns, past the crumbled dragon man and headed for the Round Room. It was dark. Shut. But she'd be able to sneak in from the Cloister side. Sweet-talk an old gargoyle, force a downstairs window.

She was about to jump down into the courtyard when it struck her: the stained glass charms. Dear God, they were fully armed again. The moment she set foot in the Library they'd come out of their lead-work and slice her to shreds. A sob shuddered through her. Too late, too late. The Minstery bell struck nine, each chime buffeted this way and that. Only two hours left till high tide. It's all my fault! Pelago, help me, what should I do, what should I do?

The moon nudged up over the buildings. Too huge, too close. It cast a fiery light on the ancient stone.

Talk to the charms. Explain. Maybe they'd let her through when they heard her tale? She wrung her hands. Then froze. Her palms—what was wrong with them? No! Her heart contracted. A trick of the moonlight. They looked like they were on fire. Fire tattoos. Not possible. She spat and rubbed them on her clothes, shook them. The moon inched higher. Her palms glowed brighter. Oh dear God, what's happening to me?

A hand seized her arm. She screamed.

It was Paran. His eyes, his clothes, his hair were all on fire.

'It's the moon!' she gabbled, 'You're burning! The moon's doing it!'

'You told me you had no Fairy blood in your veins!' He forced both her palms upward. Fire squirmed like maggots under the skin. His hands were hot on her wrists. Dry, like a burning snake. 'Then what's *this*, you liar?'

'But I don't understand!' she cried. 'I'm pure human. Why—?' Suddenly she saw. That night she freed him. His blood pouring over her hands. Into the open blisters. 'No!'

Understanding hit him in the same instant. He recoiled. They stared at one another in revulsion and fear.

'It must be *your* blood!' she gasped. 'Oh God! What will it do to me?'

'Who cares? You fool, you treacherous fool! It's what your blood has done to *me*!' He let out a long wailing cry. Rage. Despair. Whipped away by the storm. 'A lifetime of training, wasted!' Fiery tears seemed to pour from his eyes. 'This explains everything. My weakness, my wavering. You've infected me!'

'I didn't mean to,' she sobbed. 'I didn't know!'

'Believe me, that does not absolve you.' The wind grabbed handfuls of flame off him and tossed them into the night.

'But it can only have been a drop. A tiny speck.'

'That's all it takes. There's no cure. I'm ruined!'

'But I didn't know! I'm sorry.'

'Sorry? Sorry?' he hissed. 'Don't let yourself hope I'll forgive you. I'm not that far gone. This crime of yours wipes out my debt. From now on, I owe you nothing.' He raised his right hand. It flamed like a torch. 'Anabara Nolio, our deal is void. I hereby rescind and cancel it.'

'No! You can't! I need your help, Paran.'

He bared his fangs. 'Don't use that name! Go and thank your Saint that I'm now so riddled with mercy, I cannot bear to kill you.'

There was another savage gust, then a flash like red lightning. His imprint lingered on the air.

'No!' she shouted. 'Come back! Come back!'

But he'd vanished.

She blundered across the rooftops, hunting for him. The bass flute roared like an ogre. A flicker of fire—there he was! But it was only the moon's reflection. Another flash—no, just the moon. He's gone, he's abandoned you. St Pelago's flag snapped, its ropes whined. The clock chimed quarter past. The slaves! You can't give up on them, there may still be a chance.

With another sob she set off for the Round Room. Battled the wind till she was up there, clinging to the cupola. Larridy was spread out like a map. The docklands were on fire! No, it was bonfires, mutton roasts. Crowds with lanterns. Braziers along the banks. To the west, a necklace of fire—the Gull Islands strung out into the distance, beacons blazing. Fireworks ripped into the night. Far off on the Mainland rockets winked and scribbled trails.

She turned to the window. Moonlight gleamed on the dark glass. A warrior saint. A knight on horseback. 'Will you let me pass?' The wind snatched her words away. She couldn't hear a thing. Were they awake even?

'There are Fairy slaves down in the Library Stacks,' she shouted. 'They're about to be killed. Please let me pass.' But the force of the charm was unrelenting. 'Please! You *know* me. I'm employed by the scholasticus, my uncle is the Patriarch. It was my associate who restored you.'

Still nothing. She rattled the window catch. The charm-field swelled, thrusting her towards the edge. If she tried again it would hurl her off. Passwords. There must be passwords. Locked up in the security charm vault. Rodi! But it would take her hours to dis-encrypt them. Anabara sagged in despair. It was hopeless. Like on that black night out on the salt flats when her courage broke. I've failed. I have nothing left.

The moon broke free from the rooftops. Her palms writhed with fire. 'Look!' She turned her hands one at a time to the stained glass. 'I have Fairy blood in my veins. You *must* let me past to save my kindred!' But a gust sent her tumbling; slammed her on a flat leaded roof below.

She lay winded. The moon looked down. And suddenly rage coursed through her. Feck this. Feck you all. She got to her feet. I'm going in. Come after me and do your worst!

The downstairs windows were guarded by weathered caryatids. Too dozy to put up a fight. She sprang up on to the stone sill and kicked in the lower pane. Glass tinkled on to the marble floor inside. She knocked out the fragments, then squeezed through.

Silence. Apart from the wind outside, smacking the buildings about. Orange moonlight on the checkered floor. She leapt down and tip-toed into the room. Ranks of shelves. Desks. The levels rising above her, one, two, three. Then the cupola. She watched for movement. All was still. Maybe they'd believed her? Or maybe all Paran's work had unraveled now he'd cancelled their deal. A new terror reared up: the house charms. Was Loxi safe? Nothing she could do. She began to creep towards the Stacks.

Then she heard it. Behind her. Another tinkle of glass. She whipped round. Her heart boomed. Idiot, it was just the last pieces falling out. She set off again. Had she still got the password? She felt in her pocket for the scrap of parchment. Too dark to read.

Halfway down the corridor she paused under a small round window, and tried to memorise the numbers and letters in the faint light of the moon. There it was again. A tinkle of glass. Her pulse began to gallop. And again. Closer.

And now an eerie light gathered at the corridor mouth. Jingle, jingle. Wind-chimes in a breeze.

Oh dear God. An angel. I'm trapped. It's over. Snick-snick-snick, the peacock wings unfolded. It filled the archway. A sword in its hand. No escape. She backed away. It advanced. She stopped. It stopped. She could hear herself whimpering, couldn't help herself. She cringed away again, it came on. And now her back was against the door of the Stacks. Still it advanced. All lit up as if by sunshine. A dozen colours spilled on to the walls and floor.

Then it gestured her aside. She staggered out of the way. It touched the door handle with its sword tip. A cascade of clicks. The door swung open. The angel gestured her through.

'Oh dear God, oh dear God! I thought you were going to kill me!' she gibbered as she stumbled into the Stacks.

The stained glass angel stared. Then unmistakably, rolled its eyes.

'Thank you.' She turned and fled down the tunnel. When she glanced back the angel had taken up guard in the doorway. Well, no rivermen were going to get past *that*.

The tunnel emerged into the same arcaded road she'd seen the day before. The top. Only one way to turn: left, down the hill. She stood still and listened. Not a sound. The storm was raging, but down here it was like a tomb. Oh, let it not be a tomb. The thought propelled her feet off down the hill. It would be simple to retrace her steps. She wouldn't get lost.

The way was lit as before by old-fashioned torches. She followed the slow curve. A maze of tunnels. But where? Then she came to a taller wider arch. Set in the stone portals were letters: *Aa*. A tunnel, an echo of the side streets off Skuller.

She ventured in. Yes, it seemed to spread out into a maze of alleys. Little higgledy-piggledy houses. She peered through a window. Filled with shelves. *Anatomy. Areapogitucus His Booke. Animals of Southern Galencia.* She retraced her steps back on to the main street. Further down hill, another larger arch, this time labeled *Bb.* So the Stacks were still alphabetical, not by subject. Small wonder it took a Fairy to find anything down here. She pressed on. *Cc. Dd.*

Where, in all this network of sub-mazes, would she find the slaves, the Master of Stacks? Surely there had to be some kind of central office? The logical place would be at the top, in the underground equivalent of the Precincts. Had she missed it, passed it already? Panic surged again. Too late, too late. She began to trot. Was she even going in the right direction? Where were they? Housed in *Ff* for Fairy? *Ss* for slave? She was losing it.

Stop. She took some deep breaths. Use your brain, she told herself. There was clearly a system of parallels going on down here. What was the nerve centre of Larridy, the seat of power? It was Palatine Square. *That's* where she'd find the Master of Stacks. Somewhere about halfway down.

Sure enough, in another few minutes just past *Mm,* she came to a portico. Above the arch was the City motto: *Blessed are Those Who Walk in the Way.* She made the triple sign. Groped for childhood prayers. Pelago, let my feet walk in the way. Let no ill befall me. Make my path smooth, O light in darkness, life in death. Let nothing evil walk here.

She took a deep breath and entered. The light changed. Like sunlight. For a wild moment she thought it was open to the sky, that she'd somehow strayed outside again. But of course it was night outside. She ventured further, and gasped. Impossible to take in!—the breathtaking beauty of the place. There was the law court, the city hall! Above was a charmed mosaic ceiling, blue sky, a cloud drifting, a gull. Stone trees grew up from the floor. Candacian planes, their leaves green in a permanent underground summer. She'd heard of such charm-work, but thought it had long since vanished from Larridy.

She had not gone ten paces into the square, though, when she saw her prayers would not be granted. There was evil prowling here. Silver drops on the cobbles. Fairy blood. She stifled a scream. A long smear where something had been dragged. She followed it. No, no. Don't let it be true. But it was. A body. A slave. His throat cut from ear to ear. Too late, too late. She bent over him. Someone had folded his hands across his breast. Laid him out. She glanced up. He'd been placed beneath the statue of the south-facing Fairy warrior. Like one of the four that guarded the corners of Palatine Square.

Heedless now, she ran to the western corner. Ah God. Another slave. Throat cut, hands folded. The Square wavered through her tears. She ran to the north, knowing what she'd find. And to the east. Dead, all of them dead! Why? Pelago, why did you let this happen? But perhaps *she* had let it happen. There was a strange pain in her chest. Like something had snapped in two. It really is like that, she thought, your heart can break like a stick of kindling.

She knelt by the fourth slave and wept. I'm so sorry. His eyes were dull. Was this the one she'd met? Impossible to say. They all looked the same, that's what the breaking process did to them. Was he free now? Had his soul gone home? She thought of how he had begged leave to kill himself. The Stackmaster must have ordered them all to commit suicide. Perhaps they'd been grateful. At least they'd been laid out respectfully, not dumped like rubbish. I did what I could. I tried my best. Gave him permission to strike back if his life was threatened. I'm so sorry. I thought it would be enough.

Wait.

Her heart hammered. An image flashed into her head. The slave holding up his hand. *Five* slaves. It *had* been enough. He'd escaped! He'd laid his kindred out and escaped. Which meant...

She scrambled up. Stumbled to the centre of the Square, where a charmed fountain played. Something crunched underfoot. Fragments of black glass—a broken psych-tab! Her eyes darted round. Oh, sweet saints in heaven! There. Impaled on the Law Court railings, splayed out like a scientific specimen. She gagged. The Stackmaster. Naked. Emasculated. Tongue and heart cut out. Her lips babbled. Help me, saints, get me out of this, I didn't mean this to happen, save us, save us!

And then a fresh wave of horror hit her. *You may strike back to save your own life*—she'd forgotten to limit his self-defence to the Stackmaster. Save us! What had she done? Somewhere out there, free to roam Larridy, and free— thanks to her foolish permission—to kill anyone he thought threatened him, was the fifth slave. A mindless automaton, answerable to no-one.

But before she could decide what to do, footsteps.

She whirled round. Another set of steps. And another. Then a giggle. A Tressy riverman stepped out from behind a plane tree, knife in hand.

'Come! Come to me, pretty lady.' He made a kissing sound, like he was calling a cat. 'Here, pussy-pussy!'

She turned to run. Another stepped out. Another. Five, six. All round the Square. Each way she turned, her way was blocked. Knives. Crossbows. One pulled out a psych-tab. He smirked. The silver pen glinted as he wrote. Of course—they'd been frantically destroying all evidence of the Breaking Camp. She must have tripped some ancient alarm when she entered.

They giggled as they closed in. 'Puss-puss! Here!'

Choose. Quickly. Her gaze raked round, seeking the weak link. That one. The insane Gull war cry echoed round the Square as she flew at him. Down he went, like a skittle. She'd barely touched him. Now she was back on Skuller. A crossbow bolt whistled past her, sparked off the archway. Down, down she ran, with the pack baying after her. God, show me the way out. Forty-nine. Every forty-nine arches there's a way out. She raced on, eyes hunting for the scribbled horseshoe on the floor.

The stampeding feet were gaining. There! A chalk smudge. One, two, three. She counted as she ran. Nine, ten, eleven. But her pursuers were fast, impossibly fast. Fly? Too low for that. They'd catch her! Fifteen, sixteen, seventeen. Speed my steps! Pelago, help me. Twenty six, twenty-seven.

Then a scream behind her. She stumbled, went head-long. At the last moment she rolled and curled in the near-est arch. Let them not see me! They hurtled past. Then came a sound like a thousand mirrors falling. An explosion of jagged light filled the tunnel. The charms! More screams. They echoed. On and on. Anabara stopped up her ears. But she could still hear them.

Finally it was over. Jangling filled the tunnel. She opened her eyes. A procession was going by back up the hill. Glass hooves chinked. Armour chimed. Coloured light slid over her. The last knight raised his visor and stared down at her. Then he spurred his glass horse on up the hill, and they were gone.

The last faint tinkle dwindled. Silence. Then a sob. A voice keening. She got to her feet. Crept towards the sound. Nothing could have prepared her for this. A single blood-splashed riverman sat rocking himself in the butcher's yard the charms had left in their wake.

Anabara doubled over and vomited. The man keened on. She managed to straighten up and look at him. It was the weak link, the one she'd kicked. He swayed on his knees. Was he praying? Maybe he'd lost his mind. Why had he been spared? Suddenly it fell into place: he was a double agent. She picked her way through the carnage towards him. Her foot skidded. She retched again. The air was rank with blood and ruptured guts.

He saw her, raised his hands. His eyes were starting in his head.

'You're Mooby's man?' she whispered.

He nodded.

'That's why you let me escape back there?'

He nodded again. Made the triple sign. 'I saw you. At the slave auction. You are very brave.'

'I wish I was.' She shuddered and retched again, but there was nothing left. 'Get up. We've got to find Mooby and warn her. The enemy knows everything. They can communicate secretly. With those psych-tabs.'

'Yes. Fay-glass. Just now even, my captain sends a message.'

'I saw him.'

'You are betrayed, lady.' He trembled. 'He sends to Golar. Golar will come for you. Run! The cause is lost. The evil will escape.' He looked around him. 'Except these ones. My countrymen. God have mercy! What were those... *things*, those men of glass?'

'Charms, ancient stained glass charms.' She took his arm. 'Come away. There's nothing you can do. We must try and get out. Somewhere near here there's a tunnel. Come on.'

Their footsteps squished. Paran, Paran, please come back. Sweeten my memory. Wipe these sights from my eyes. The riverman followed her like he was drugged. She'd long since lost count of the archways. Nothing for it but to search each one till she located the forty-ninth. At last she found it. They tacked up the long weary zigzags. On and on. Pitch blackness, feet stumbling, fingers tracing the walls.

Finally, noise. Muffled footsteps above. Voices. Where in the city would they come out? She'd lost all sense of direction.

'I'll go first,' she whispered.

'Save yourself. Give no thought for me,' he said. 'May the Lord of Light guide you.'

They fumbled hands together, shook. 'And you. Go well.'

She leant on the stone door. It swiveled, and tumbled her into a small room. St Pelago stared with mad little eyes. A shrine! The very one she'd sat in that first morning after the auction. Crowds were still thronging the street. She stumbled out.

And there was Chief Dhalafan. She sobbed in relief. 'Uncle Hector!'

'Thank God!' He took her in his arms. 'You're safe!'

'There's a plot!' she gibbered. 'Slavers! The Stackmaster's dead!'

'Hush hush. I know. It's all right now.'

'But you don't understand! Golar—'

He shushed her again. 'I think you're forgetting I'm Chief of the City Guard, my dear. Mooby reports to me.

I thought you were safely at home, not careering about Larridy risking your life. We've got the situation under control, but I do *not* want to be worrying about you.' He took her arm and led her through the crowds. 'Now, I don't want any arguing, please. I've got a secure litter here. It will carry you to a safe house, where you'll be taken care of.'

'But—'

'No. Leave it to the professionals this time, Anabara.' He opened the litter door. 'Hop in.'

The fight went out of her. 'Thanks.'

He bent and dropped a kiss on her head. 'I'm so sorry you got caught up in this, my dear.'

Tears rolled down her cheeks as the litter bumped and jostled through the streets. I did what I could. It's over. I failed. I'm too small, too young to fight this battle. Who was I kidding? Yes, much better to leave it to the professionals. And now, at last, a safe house. Thank God for a safe house. And for Uncle Hector, lifting the burden from her. Like the father she'd never known.

The litter turned off Skuller into some quieter alley. A few more twists and turns, then it came to rest. She heard the bearers' footsteps recede. A metal gate clanged shut. Well, this must be the safe house. Would there be someone here to greet her? She opened the litter door and clambered out. A small enclosed courtyard. Unlit. The moon stared down. Through what looked like a net. Could it be a bird-net, stretched overhead? Was this a fowler's yard, maybe?

Suddenly, dogs. Everywhere. Slavering, snarling. She sprang with a cry up on to the litter roof. Dogs! The yard boiled with them like a cauldron. They leapt and snapped. They could smell the blood on her boots. One got its paws on the roof. She kicked its head. Behind her another gnashed at her ankles. And above, the net! She was trapped.

Then—oh, thank God—a tall man approached.

'Call them off, call them off!' she screamed.

The dogs cringed back from him, parted to let him through. A flickering torch lit up his face. Pale moonstone eyes. Eyes like the Boagle-man. He smiled.

'Welcome to your safe house, my lady. My dogs and I will be taking care of you.'

CHAPTER TWENTY

'Get back, scum!' She aimed a kick at his face. 'The Chief of the City Guard knows I'm here!'

'Yes, my lady, he does. He sent you to me.'

'Liar! He rescued me! And when he hears of this—'

'He already knows.' Golar raised a hand, cutting her off. 'My captain sent me a message from the Stacks. We had men waiting at all the exits with orders to capture you. No, Dhalafan did not rescue you—he sent you here, my lady. To me.' The dogs snarled. Golar snapped an order. They fell silent. But their panting silence was even worse.

'No! He wouldn't do that!'

'It's a shock, I know,' Golar said. 'But the Chief and I have had an understanding for many years. He looks away while I ply my trade. I make it worth his while. He keeps me informed of Guard activity.' He took out a psych-tab and held it up. For a second the moon winked off it. 'You see? Your beloved *Uncle Hector* has betrayed you, demy.'

Her legs shook under her. The whole world was shaking. Nothing was true anymore. Nothing was good. *C* stood for *Chief*, not *Carraman*, not *Charlie*. Chief Dhalafan.

'It grieved him,' went on Golar, 'but he is a professional. He saw that you had to be silenced. He begged only that I would make it quick. But that is not my way.'

'Paran!' screamed Anabara. 'Paran help me!'

'Are you are calling for the Fay?' Golar shook his head. 'I warned you not to make the mistake of thinking him human. He is treacherous. They all are. He will not come.'

'He will!' she cried. 'We have a deal! He'll protect me.'

'Then by all means let us wait for him,' said Golar. 'And while we wait, I will tell you what I have planned for you.'

All around the dogs panted. Their hot stench filled her nostrils. Above, the orange moon stared down through the net. How strong was it? Could she rip through?

'It's razor-web. Carraman's best, my lady,' he whispered. 'You will not be flying away tonight. Conserve your strength. You will need it. So. Here is how matters stand: you have robbed me of my Ship's Fay.'

She tried to spit at him, but her mouth was dry. 'I bought him fair and square! Two hundred gilders!'

'Grant that the Fay is yours, then. He killed two of my men. *You* are responsible for his actions. Therefore you owe me two lives.'

'I owe you nothing!'

'Two lives, I say. But more grave than that, you have been making a fool of me. You are an incompetent bungling time-waster, yet somehow you have managed to escape my snares and stumble upon the truth. And suddenly, a trade that has been quietly prospering these thirty years is jeopardised. By you, a stupid filthy little demy *bitch*.'

A quiver went through the dog pack. They slavered. One raised its head and bayed.

Her legs quaked beneath her. Pelago, save me.

'You have no love of dogs, I see. Excellent.' Golar's dead fish eyes feasted on her terror. 'Well, the matter of the Ship's Fay is soon settled. I have not forgotten your Gull kinsman.

He's a pretty little slut and well-trained. He mollied for me eagerly enough, once I'd broken him. My men are lying in wait for him outside your house.'

'They won't get him. He's protected, you sick Tressy gob-shite.' Her voice rose shrill with panic. 'My whole family is protected!'

'By the Fay? But where is he? What can be keeping him? Call him again, my lady!' He smiled his gentle smile. 'Has it not occurred to you yet that the Fay does *my* bidding? You may have cut off the irons, but his soul is still mine.'

'Liar!' Her hand clutched the talisman. But was it true? Did that explain everything? 'You'd better escape while you can, arsehole. He's going to rip out your heart and eat it.'

'Brave words! But again I must ask: where is this loyal Fay of yours? Why does he not come when you call—in your hour of peril?' He shrugged and looked about the dog-packed courtyard, and up at the razor-web, that little smile playing on his lips all the time. 'Well, I fear we must press on without him. I am a merciful man, and so I will give you a choice.'

Terror twanged through every sinew. A choice. Like the one he gave Loxi. 'Feck you! You're a dead man, Golar.'

'So brave! Let us see how far your bravery goes. You love your kinsman, yes? Then perhaps you would like the chance to prove it. Why not offer to take his place in that cage? Agree to this, and in exchange I will not set my hounds on you.' He snapped his fingers. The pack surged forward.

'No! You won't get away with this! Mooby knows everything. She'll catch you!' she gibbered. 'She's on her way now!'

'Of course she is. Just like the Fay. So there is your choice: save your cousin, or take your chances with the pack. They are Tressy wolf-baiters, my lady, trained to sport with their prey. But don't worry. If you are still alive by dawn, I will dispatch you.' Another sweet smile. 'The choice is yours. Take your time.'

The dogs began to leap and snarl. Their claws clattered on the litter roof. One leapt up behind her. The big pack-leader. Slaver swung in strands from its jaws. She lashed out. It snapped. Her left hand still gripped the amulet.

'Paran! Help me!' Golar was right. He wasn't coming. In desperation she screamed in Fairy: '*Paran, come to my aid!*'

At these words the stone writhed in her hand. A blinding slit of white. A *paran*. She was holding a *paran*!

In horror she tried to fling it away. But it was welded to her hand. Some other will greater than her own by-passed her control. It slashed at the hound. The blade passed clean through its neck. As if through air. For a second nothing seemed to happen. Then the creature's head toppled. Blood spurted. The carcass slumped off the litter and the pack fell snarling on it.

Monstrous strength surged through her. The world slowed. She sprang from the litter roof, hung on the air like a feather. Everything was lit up, every charm glowed: the web above, the gate, the ancient gargoyle jutting from the roof edge. Slowly the hounds came at her. The blade melted through them, left, right. They fell butchered like chunks of meat.

It was a dream. Of course! She was dreaming. Just dreaming. She saw Golar reach out to catch hold of her, watched the knife pass through his wrist, saw the hand tumble like a white crab to the cobbles. A dog seized it, infinitely... slowly... and made off. She watched the black hole of Golar's mouth scream, and the blood spool out from the stump in a lazy necklace.

Then she was bounding, bounding, each bound a league long, across the yard. The iron gate was a cobweb to the *paran*. She was through and in the alley. On and on she sprang. Skuller Road. The cobbles shone with charms. One skull-stone for each firstborn male Gull who had been spared. Charms everywhere! Silver-white, shimmering. She had not realised how full of charms her city was.

But now there were people and she must be careful. Must not harm them, the crowds, pushing downhill. Drunks. Little children. Folk in wolf masks. She held the blade high. Like a blazing torch.

'*Stand back!*' She was speaking Fairy. '*Stand back, o people!*'

They parted to let her through. In her dream she could hear their thoughts, the jumbled needs, fears, spasms of joy. The masks hid nothing. She could see the real wolfmen, with the moon mark on their foreheads. And there were ghosts. The dead were walking. Walking as they'd walked in life, up Skuller, down Skuller, going about their business. The living passed through them unaware.

Then behind her she heard the hounds. They were coming for her.

Yanni. She must get up to the Precincts to Yanni. Then she'd be safe. But the crowds were all surging downhill. *Knock-a-door, knock-a-door, Wolf Tide's come!* chanted the children. Mind the knife, mind the knife! She mustn't kill anyone.

The rooftops. It would be quicker. And the dogs wouldn't be able to hunt her up there. But as she tensed to spring, the blade winked out and vanished.

She collapsed.

Not a dream. The cobbles under hands and knees were real. So were the drunken crowds, tripping over her, cursing. She tried to haul herself up, but her strength was gone. 'Help me!' Her whisper went unheard.

Baying. Getting closer. No-one would help her. Thought she was drunk. She dragged herself through the thicket of legs to the road edge. A boot trod on her left hand. She felt the fingers snap. Pain knifed up her arm. Get up, she had to get to her feet. But a weight was pressing down on her. Like gravity had been turned up.

Oh God, the hounds. Squirming towards her through the crowds. No escape. They knew her scent. Somehow she hauled herself upright. Clutched at doorposts, windowsills, clawed her way uphill, away from the pursuing dogs. Where was she? Her bearings had gone. An alley opened to her left. She staggered into it. Climb. Get up higher. But there were no footholds low enough. On, on she stumbled, legs dragging like she was wading through water.

Too late. Snarling behind her. The pack erupted into the alley. She hammered on doors. Let me in, let me in! Nobody answered. All gone down to the river. Statue, up there in a niche. Last chance. She made a leap. Grabbed. But her injured hand couldn't haul her on to the ledge. She tumbled back down.

The *paran*. Summon the *paran*! She gripped the amulet. Called in Fairy. Nothing. Wrong words? What words had she used before? The dogs circled. Wary. They remembered the weapon. No, wrong *hand*! It has to be your left hand! But her broken fingers wouldn't make a fist.

'Pelago, help me!' she whimpered.

With a snarl the dogs fell on her. She fought them. Kicked. Snapped a punch. But there were too many. Her strength was spent. *Stay on your feet!* she heard Yanni's voice urging. *Keep your head, stay on your feet!* Nothing left. Darkness closing in.

In the last moment before she passed out, she saw a big man. He waded towards her through the pack. Cursing. Kicking them aside. The dogs obeyed him. Golar. It was over.

Someone was saying her name. He shook her. Patted her cheek. Then he raised her head and shoulders. Picked her up in strong arms.

'Ms Nolio? Anabara! What happened? Are you bitten? Speak to me! Speak!'

The Zaarzuk.

'Ach, God's love! You are so cold! Some witchcraft! Are you hurt?'

'Yanni,' she mouthed. 'Take me to Yanni.'

'Of course! I will do this. But the crowds, curse these crowds.' He hugged her close, hesitating. 'I have it. I will hide you here, and steal me a horse. My kinsman, he will guard you.'

The moon. The moon swung round and round the sky like an apple on a string. Then she was slumped over his shoulder like a sack. He was climbing a wall, trying not to jolt her. She heard him talk to someone in his own tongue.

'Here,' he said. 'I lay you down. And the Chieftain, he will guard you, yes?' Her head rolled. He shook her. 'Anabara? Do you understand me? If the hounds return, the statue will protect you. He is charmed. Look!'

Her eyelids fluttered open. She was lying high up in an embrasure. Stone Zaarzuk. Like the one by the Slackey. He spoke to it again. A grind of stone: the statue drew its scimitar.

'See? He will not fail you. Now I go for a horse. Down to the Causeway. Many, many fine horses, all Zaarzuk-trained. I talk with them this afternoon. Here, my cloak.'

She felt him spreading it over her, tucking her in. Tried to speak. To say, horses banned. Find Mooby, warn… Dhalafan… Golar… Loxi…

'Do not fear, I will return. Word of a Zaarzuk.' A kiss on her forehead. He was gone.

Far off the Minstery bell chimed. Chimed again. She tried to count, lost track. Howling. The flutes. Everything tilted. A moon rolled up the sky. Then another moon. And another. Then nothing.

'Ms Nolio? Anabara!' She opened her eyes.

A whinny. Jingling. Hooves skittered on stone. She heard the Zaarzuk speak to the horse. It minced closer, tossed its head. Stamped. Waited. The Zaarzuk raised himself in the stirrups, reached up a hand.

'Come to me! I will catch you. Trust me!'

But she couldn't move. Pressed down under a quilt of stone. Tears seeped from her eyes. Move, move! But her limbs would not obey.

Again he spoke to the horse. Next thing she knew, he was standing on the saddle. She was in his arms. The world reeled. Blackness.

'Hah! It's a brave horse! A fine horse!' He clicked his tongue. 'I have you safe, Anabara. Come, to the Precincts! I will take you to your brother!' He spurred the horse, and they were away.

The world flicked on and off. Buildings. Blackness. The moon. She was jolting and lolling in front of him like a raggedy doll. His arm held her fast. Skuller was empty. Wolf Tide. Must be time. Clatter of hooves on cobbles. On, on.

Then a pounding behind them. More horses. And hounds at bay.

'So! The filthy rivermen hunt me.' The Zaarzuk laughed. Urged the horse on, sang to it. Zaarzuk war songs. Then came the whine of a crossbow bolt. Spark on stone. 'Very good! We go the quick way. Let them follow if they are men!'

The world tipped up. She was falling. But he had her safe. Steep, steep. The horse turned. Turned again. Again. He spoke to it, yipped, whistled. It obeyed. Zig. Zag. The Fairy Teeth. He's riding us up the Fairy Teeth. Blackness again.

'Hah! Brave horse, brave horse!' He patted its neck. 'Nearly there, Ms Nolio. Now for it!'

Bloodcurdling Zaarzuk yell. The horse spurted forward. Galloping across St Pelago Plaza. Under the threshing chestnut trees. Leaves slapped their faces. The gatehouse was in sight.

Then more horses, coming from the right. Crossbow bolts sang. The Zaarzuk cursed.

'Tss!' He clapped a hand to his shoulder. 'I'm hit. On, on!'

They passed under the arch. Safe! Oh dear God, safe! He reined the horse in.

But the door. The great door was shut. Locked, barred. Too late! Behind them came their pursuers. The dogs bellowed.

'Sanctuary! Hold your fire!' The Zaarzuk's cry rang round the Precincts. 'I am Tadzar dal Ramek, and I claim sanctuary!' His bloodied hand gripped the great sanctuary knocker. 'I claim the protection of St Pelago! Open up!'

Behind them the charmed portcullis clashed down. Anabara saw the Tressy hunters, thwarted behind the white-steel bars. The pluming breath of the horse.

Then the great door opening.

And light streaming through.

And Yanni, running towards her.

CHAPTER TWENTY-ONE

She was on a long dark desert road. The wind howled. A huge orange moon pursued her. She tried to run, but her legs didn't work. She wouldn't get there in time to warn them. It was all her fault. She'd done something terrible. But what? What?

Suddenly she remembered: *She had hidden some creature, some feral Fairy child, in her cellar and let it starve!* And the money. She'd forgotten to pay. Every day the debt doubled.

Or was it just a dream? It *had* to be a dream. There *was* no debt. There *was* no starving creature. She didn't even have a cellar, for God's sake! But no matter how she fought and fought, she couldn't wake up and escape.

She's suffered some major charm-related trauma, Master, a woman was saying. *All we can do is keep her quiet and comfortable, and let the body and mind heal themselves.*

How long will she be like this, doctor? Will there be any lasting damage?

It was Yanni! She tried to call out to him. But she was locked up inside her body.

Well, her condition is compatible with exposure to some powerful psychic device. But unless we locate the source, I hesitate to make any predictions.

Then find it! For the love of God, find it! She's my little sister.
Pause. *Forgive me, doctor.*
Yanni, Yanni, I'm awake, I'm fine!
Master, I know, I know. But she's young and strong. We're optimistic.
Is there nothing else you can do?
I'm so sorry. By all means sit with her. She is sedated. If she becomes distressed, summon the nurse to administer more mandragora.

Afterwards Anabara couldn't say how long she spent on that dark road, chased by a terrifying moon, drenched with dread, fighting to wake up. Each time she struggled close to consciousness, someone tipped another draught between her lips. Sometimes nurses forced a tube down her throat and fed her. She heard them gossip as they bathed her.
Still so cold, poor child! Doctor says she'd be dead if it wasn't for the Zaarzuk.
He's discharged himself.
No!
Yes. Says it's only a flesh wound.
Typical. Wouldn't mind giving him a bed-bath.
Doxy! Well, fingers crossed, he'll be back in with a fever by the end of the week.
Huh, he'll be back before then, trying to see this one. Matron's thrown him out I don't know how many times. Ssh, dragon alert! Morning, Matron!
Morning, Matron! Time for your medicine, lovey.
No! I'm awake! Anabara shouted. I can understand you! I'm awake!
That's it. There's a good girl.

And back on the dark road again. *Why* had she let it starve? *Why* hadn't she paid up?

There were times when she was aware of her brother sitting there. She tried to talk to him, but her lips wouldn't move. Once she heard the Zaarzuk outside her room, demanding to see her. They sent him away. Sometimes the Patriarch was by her bed, keeping vigil, saying Last Prayers.

Then one night she dreamt there was a tapping at the window. Her uncle was there again. He got up and opened the casement. *Well! Where have you come from?* she heard him ask. Something flew whirring round the room. It hovered over her face. She felt the draft of its wings.

Hush, all is well. You have no need to fear, whispered a voice in her ear. *Sleep is a great healer.*

Oh! Everything was new shoes, her birthday, fresh baked honeycakes! Larks sang over the salt flats in an endless summer sky. Yes, here it came, the black velvet wave. And finally, finally she was rocked to sleep in the arms of a gentle sea.

'Feck off!' She knocked the draught out of the nurse's hand. 'Feck off and get me some proper food. I'm fecking starving!'

'Aha!' The doctor loomed over her bed. 'The patient is awake. Fetch the Master. Get a message to the Patriarch. Quick!' She gripped Anabara's wrist and checked her pulse. Then she leant forward, pulled up her eyelids, examined the pupils. 'Do you know where you are? Can you tell me your name?'

'Take this fecking tube out,' croaked Anabara, 'and I'll tell you anything you want.'

The doctor smiled. 'Very well. Nurse?'

Anabara felt a horrible rubbery slither, gagged. Her throat was sore. 'My name is Anabara Nolio, and I'm in St Dalfinia Infirmary Charms Unit.'

Bare feet on tiles, robes swirling. Yanni. Ah, nobody could hug like Yanni. He rocked her. Pressed his face to hers. She felt his tears. Then he held her at arm's length and gazed into her eyes. Searching.

'I'm fine, Yanni,' she whispered.

He turned to the doctor. 'Is she?'

'Well, she's cursing and being uncooperative and demanding food, Master. I'd say the signs are good.'

'Yes, that sounds like my little sister.' He took her hands and kissed them. 'You had me worried, you,' he said in Gull. 'I'm going to tie a sheep bell round your neck, eh. Get the Gullmothers to butter your feet so you never run off again.'

'Master, if I may?' The stethoscope was cold on Anabara's chest. 'Breathe in. Good. And out. Excellent.'

'How long have I been here?' whispered Anabara.

'Three weeks,' replied the doctor. 'Do you remember anything of the night you were brought here?'

She groped in her memory. A desert. No, that was a dream. The moon was on fire. Of course! 'It was Wolf Tide. Dal Ramek... He stole a horse and brought me here. There were slavers after us.'

'Yes, very good. And before that?'

'Dogs. They were hunting me. Golar's dogs.'

'Anything else?'

The moon looking down through a net. Blood. A white hand tumbling to the floor. Panic welled up. Her fingers hunted round her throat. The amulet—where was it? 'I've lost Mum's necklace!' she sobbed.

'Ssh! I have it safe,' said Yanni. 'Doctor?'

'Loxi!' She struggled to sit up. 'Oh my God! Golar, he's going to get Loxi!'

'Loxi's fine.' Yanni gripped her hands. 'Don't be scared. Everyone you love is safe. Doctor!'

'But Paran's gone!' she wailed. 'He abandoned me. I called, but he never came. And the slaves were dead. They were all dead. Oh God, Yanni! It's my fault! Then the charms came and killed the Tressies— Mooby! I've got to warn Mooby it was Dhalafan all along. It wasn't Charlie—'

'Hush. Mooby knows,' soothed Yanni. 'It's all under control. Don't distress yourself.'

'No! I'm not drinking it! No!'

But the doctor tilted the potion down her throat. Yanni continued to hold her hands as sleep crept over her once more.

'Well, your sister is making a good recovery, Yannick.' Her uncle and brother were sitting at her bedside a week later. 'I believe it's time for us to allow visitors, and for you to resume your duties as Master of Novices.'

'No! No, my lord Patriarch. Not yet.'

'"No" and "my lord Patriarch"!' Her uncle laughed. 'Well! It's not often I hear *those* words together in the same sentence.'

Yanni bowed his head. 'Forgive me, but no. She's still too frail.'

'And forgive me, brother, but I was not making an observation. It was an order: return to your post. There are twenty-three novices who need your guidance. Anabara will be well looked after here.'

As clearly as if the letters were daubed a yard high, Anabara saw her brother think *Don't fecking tell ME what to do!*

But then he bowed his head again and made the three-fold sign. 'Very good, my lord Patriarch.' He kissed her brow and padded softly from her room.

The Patriarch beamed at her. 'He is the best of brothers. But I thought you needed a little breathing space, my dear.'

'Thanks, uncle.'

Her strength was returning little by little. Her left hand still throbbed, but the broken bones were mending. When she flexed them, the fingers nearly made a fist. She was able to eat, and get out of bed to sit in a chair by the window. Sleep was less harrowing now they'd stopped doping her with mandragora—why anyone took that stuff for kicks she had *no* idea—but she was still haunted by fears she didn't dare speak about.

'Is there a secret burdening your soul, my dear?'

So he'd spotted that there was something she wasn't saying. Her eyes searched round. Was it safe to talk? Lord, it would be a relief.

'As you know,' he said, 'I am spied upon and tracked wherever I go. My apartment bristles with vigilance devices— for my own protection, they assure me. But this room's clear. While you were still unconscious young Butros swept in with a couple of very fierce gentlemen in dark glasses who conducted exhaustive checks. You can speak without reserve.'

She allowed her mind to venture back to that night. Felt again that horrible squirm as the stone writhed in her fist. Her heart began to race. 'Look, if I get worked up, promise you won't let them drug me again?' He nodded. She took a deep breath. 'All right then. That amulet of Mum's—it's actually a *paran*.'

He leant back. 'Ah! Is it indeed.'

'I accidentally summoned it up. When Golar caught me. I was screaming for Paran—you know, my associate, the Fairy. Then this... thing, this white blade appeared in my hand. I couldn't get rid of it.' She was trembling. He touched her arm. 'Please don't get the nurse, uncle! I'll be fine.'

He waited.

She took another shaky breath. 'It kind of took me over. I did things. Killed some of the dogs. Then I cut off— Oh God. I cut off Golar's hand. He must have bled to death! Uncle, it slices through *everything*! And I could see all the charm-work. Like it was all visible. And I was super-strong. I thought I was dreaming. But suddenly the *paran* just vanished, and all my strength was totally used up. And then the dogs came. That's when Dal Ramek rescued me.'

'Ah, Dal Ramek.' The Patriarch smiled. 'I regret to say that in the course of rescuing you he committed seven offences indictable by City law, two of which—aggravated horse theft and common assault—carry a custodial sentence.'

'But he saved my life!'

'I know. He rode his stolen horse into the Precincts as bold as you please, and claimed sanctuary. Nobody has tried that for over two hundred years. So, an interesting legal conundrum has arisen. Technically, if he remains in the Precincts he's under the protection of St Pelago and immune from the law. At least, until his fate is determined. Traditionally that's the Patriarch's job.'

'Seriously? Then you've got to get him off, uncle!'

'I will urge clemency. I'm very glad my niece is alive and well.' He smiled again. 'Don't worry. I daresay there will be insufficient evidence to press charges. Larridy has always had a soft spot for an impudent rogue.'

'Thanks. Uncle, you won't tell Yanni about the necklace, will you?' she whispered. 'Or he'll never give it back to me.'

'Are you sure you wish to have it back?'

Was she? 'I don't know. Look, there's something else as well.' She told him about Paran breaking their deal, and the Fairy blood now coursing through her body. 'I should probably find out about the effects of Fairy blood.' She trembled again and hid her hands under the covers. She still hadn't dared to look closely at the palms. 'But I'm kind of scared to know.'

He sat silent for a long time.

'Paran said there's no cure!' she burst out.

'Perhaps he meant no cure for himself?' He stroked her hair. 'I wouldn't worry, my dear. In years gone by Fairy blood was used in quack remedies. Unscrupulous herbalists made all kinds of extravagant claims about its properties— but it was *always* deemed beneficial, not harmful. Of course, modern medicine dismisses it all as nonsense. Either way, I doubt you'll be suffering any ill effects. Why not ask the doctor? She'll be able to set your mind at rest.'

'Good idea.'

'To know the worst can be a blessing—and more often than not, the worst doesn't happen. They say ignorance is bliss, but in fact it tends to breed fear. Try not to fear. My heart tells me you haven't seen the last of your Fairy. If it was Paran who sent you that healing charm, he has not abandoned you completely.'

'That was real? I thought it was another dream.'

'No, it was like a tiny blue humming bird. Powerful magic indeed, but of a wholesome kind, I think.' He kissed her forehead. 'I must let you get some rest now. Brace yourself for all those visitors Yannick has been frightening off!'

The first of them was Mooby. She crushed Anabara's hand in a mighty paw.

'Good to see you, Ms Nolio. Your uncle wants me to get you up to speed. Thinks it'll assist your recovery to know what's going on. Ponce disagrees. But last time I looked Ponce was just a slimy little jumped-up counsel, not the Metropolitan of all Galencia.' She plonked herself on the chair by the bed. 'He says you're not to answer any questions, so obviously I won't be asking any. But if you want to comment on anything I tell you, that'll be peachy.'

Anabara nodded. Then frowned. Was that a waft of chypre? 'Butros?'

He stuck his head into the room. 'Never fear. Ponce is right outside this door, taking notes.'

'Hey!' said Anabara. 'That's kind of you to come.'

'PAH-HA-HA! Oh, sorry,' said Mooby. 'You just said "kind" in connection with a lawyer. Assumed it was a joke. Out you go, ponce. Matron says one visitor at a time.'

Butros smooched a depraved kiss at Mooby and retreated.

'All righty, then.' Mooby clapped her hands on her thighs. 'First off, you are a stark raving nutter of the first order. You're lucky to be alive. But well done—owe you a great deal. Can't say how much I... how relieved...' She cleared her throat like a tramp on a park bench. 'Well, never did have that drink, did we? Hate to think we'd missed the chance to spar as well. Not like I have many friends here.'

There was a stifled snort.

Mooby blushed, cast an evil look at the door and pulled herself together. 'Yes, so cracking good work there. Gave me a real scare when I got the heads-up from your Gull cousin. Right before Wolf Tide. Told me you'd headed for the Stacks.'

'Oh my God—Loxi went looking for you?'

'Yep. Him and the little demy. Took out a couple of Tressies who were lying in wait outside your door, apparently. Look, I know it's a time-honoured Gull tradition and everything, but you might just want to have a word with your cousin about the ear-biting thing some time.'

'*Alleged* ear-biting,' called Butros. 'No witnesses have come forward.'

Mooby sighed. 'Whatever. Anyway, your other cousin— what's her name, Galen bean-pole, slide-rule up her arse?— Rodania, thank you. She'd already got a message through to me. Salvaged the operation. We re-grouped, intercepted the shipment of slaves down at the docks, arrested the ringleaders—all except Golar, who's disappeared down some wormhole. Mainland Special Forces all over his palace like a rash. Nothing. Gone underground. Hey, don't worry, we'll get him.' She leant forward and gripped Anabara's arm. 'Doing all right there?'

'I'm fine,' she lied. Golar was still alive. Still waiting.

'My Tressy agent told me you'd been snatched. Led us to the "safe" house. Bloody knackers yard is what we found. Illegal razor-web. Chunks of doggie all over the show. Plus one chewed-up left hand, presumed to belong to Golar. Pause for you to comment...'

'No comment!' sang Butros.

'No comment,' repeated Anabara.

'Fair enough. By the way, she's one smart cookie, that Rodania. One ve-e-ery smart cookie. Be glad to make use of her expertise in the future. Accessed all the erased stuff on the psych-tab. Her testimony alone is probably enough to put them behind bars.'

God. Rodi was going to be insufferable from now on.

'We were wrong. It was Chief Dhalafan, not Charlie.'

'Yeah.' Mooby pursed her lips. 'Mainland Guard HQ had their suspicions but no proof. That's why I was brought in. Owe you a huge apology there. Put your life at risk. Wish I'd known you'd got a psych-tab and were intending to go haring off after the slaves.'

She swallowed. 'Has he... been arrested?'

There was a silence. Mooby glanced towards the open door again. 'All right, so you haven't heard. Dhalafan's dead. And his personal psych's gone AWOL, surprise, surprise.'

'Dead! How did he die?'

'Heart attack, it looks like. But I'm thinking more a whopping dose of digitalis, self-administered. Still doing tests on the brandy glass found beside him. All kinds of pressure being brought to bear to sweep the scandal under the carpet. But nuh-uh.' Mooby shook her head. 'Not going to happen. I'm going to bust this whole thing wide open. That includes the part played by the university.'

'Woo! You go, girl!' whooped Butros.

She rolled her eyes. 'Bloody lawyers. All wetting themselves about how much money they're going to make.' But there was a grin lurking. Looked like professional respect was now *almost* bordering on friendship between her and Butros. They were both doing their best to hide it, though. 'Where was I? Yeah, so we found the remains of the Breaking Camp, like you said. Down in the bowels of the library. Possibly the nastiest thing I've encountered in my entire career to date. And that includes wading through half a dozen Tressies after they'd had a run-in with a bacon-slicer.' She raised her eyebrows. 'Or whatever.'

'It was the ancient stained-glass charms. They've been reactivated.'

'Holy bollocks. That's the last time *I* have an over-due library book! Reactivated by a certain so-called Fairy artisan going under the name of Paran a'Menehaïn, I hear. Where's that little tinker wandered off to, I ask myself? He's wanted for questioning in connection with the mutilation and murder of the Stack-master.'

'But that—' She caught herself. It wasn't Paran. Her pulse began to race. The fifth slave! She'd forgotten about him. Still roaming about Larridy. A nasty possibility crossed her mind: was he technically *her* slave, now the Stack-master was dead?

'But that—? Know something about this?' Mooby was asking. 'What's wrong? Where's a'Menehaïn?'

There was a whoosh of red silk. 'My client is *not* answering questions. If you continue to harass her, I'll have you crated back to Bogganburg in a lard tub, Detective Ball-buster.'

'That's *Acting Chief* Ball-buster to you, tallywags!'

The noise brought Matron in, breathing fire. She threw the pair of them out.

Her next visitor came by night. She woke with a jolt. Something was trying to get in her window. The slave! He'd found her. She fumbled for the nightlight.

'Psst! Ms Nolio.'

Tscha! That idiot Zaarzuk. But she was smiling. She wrapped herself in a woolen robe and made her way shakily across the room and pulled back the curtain. There he was, on the narrow sill, clinging to the mullions.

'Let me in! Quick-quick, before I fall.'

She opened the casement. 'You shouldn't be here!'

He leapt in, grinning, dark eyes flashing. 'What is this? A bad girl, out of bed, hey? And now the horseman has caught her!'

'Ssh! Get off, you ape!'

'But I must do my duty!' He swept her up in his arms and carried her back to bed and tucked her in. 'Lie still and be good, or I will crawl under your covers and do my filthy Zaarzuk things.'

Instead he sat on the edge of the bed and took her hands. They searched one another's faces in the glow of the nightlight. She was trembling and smiling. Blinking away the tears. Tadzar, Tadzar. He was smiling back. His hair had grown. A ragged halo of gold. She started to say *thank you for everything*, but he laid his fingers on her lips.

'Hush. It is my honour to serve you. I would ride through seven seas of fire for you, Anabara Nolio. Truly, I would do this to earn your respect.'

Tears brimmed over. He stroked them away. God, she was still so stupidly weak, or his nonsense wouldn't get to her. She cleared her throat. 'So. Are you all right? Those Tressy pigs shot you.'

'Pff! Is nothing. A hornet sting. But you—you are so thin! Like a poor starving sparrow. They say you will be completely healed, yes?'

'That's what they think.'

'I thank God for it.' He made the triple sign. 'But... I fear there is something you should know.'

Her heart thumped. 'What?'

'I saved your life.'

'I know you did. And I'm truly—'

'Hush.' His fingers were on her lips again. 'In my country, I save a life, that person belongs to me.'

'Tscha! I don't belong to you, mister.'

He turned up his palms. 'What can I say? Is the rule. You are mine now.'

'But we're not in your country.'

'Then I take you to my country. I will steal me another horse and ride away with you and keep you forever—in my heart, in my life, in my bed. Word of a Zaarzuk.'

Footsteps. The main light snapped on. '*What* is the meaning of this?'

The Zaarzuk was on his feet, clutching his shoulder. 'Matron, it is my wound. It troubles me. I seek medicine, but then I see Ms Nolio's nightlight is on, so I—'

'Yes, I'm sure. Mr Dal Ramek, you must leave immediately, or the Master will be summoned.'

'I go, I go.' He bent swiftly and kissed Anabara.

'*Mr Dal Ramek!*'

'Remember,' he whispered. 'You are mine.'

The light snapped off and he was gone.

Clown. Impudent rogue. She tried in vain to scowl her smile away. The wind stirred the curtains. She heard the bell chime. As she drifted back to sleep she could still feel the imprint of his mouth on hers.

CHAPTER TWENTY-TWO

Waiting. Waiting, waiting, waiting.

Anabara was not good at waiting. A month passed and they finally let her out of the Infirmary. Not to go home and pick up the threads of her life, to see if she still had any tiny remnant of business left, any clients who hadn't given up on her and gone to Carramans. Oh dear me no. She was packed off to the Gull village to be fattened up by Aunt Malla's non-stop seafood-and-stodge-fest.

All the Gullmothers of the village joined forces to keep a sharp eye on her and congratulate themselves on being right all along. Hadn't they always said Nan Nolio was heading for trouble? Learnt her lesson now though, hadn't she, eh. High time they found her a husband and put a stop to her nonsense. Messages were sent out through all the Gull settlements near and far. But strangely enough, the young Gull men were not exactly falling over themselves for a bride who got herself mixed up with slavers and Zaarzuks.

She went out on the salt flats each morning to escape the lectures—and the *knitting lessons!* Baby booties, for God's sake! Linna was almost sick she was laughing so hard. Instead she started training. Ah, it was good to be flying again. It was late autumn now. The dragon fruit had been harvested and fermented into ale, or threaded on long strings to dry round every Gull hearth. The saltings boy lambs had been slaughtered, all apart from next year's lucky rams. There seemed to be a great aching emptiness everywhere.

Maybe that was just Anabara. Everyone kept telling her how lucky she was to be alive. But all she could think of was what she'd lost. In the end, the worst thing was losing your innocence. That's what turned you into a real grown up at last. She wasn't talking about some sweaty fumble under the quilt. It was coming to terms with the fact the world wasn't a safe shiny happy place—that's what lost innocence meant. A daft part of her kept on crying for Dhalafan. The Dhalafan she'd thought she'd known and loved all her life. The Dhalafan who had never really existed.

And Paran, for God's sake! Why the hell was she missing *that* bugger? Hadn't she got what she'd been praying for— release from their nightmare deal, and her little house all to herself again? But here she was, still looking out for him, still hoping that when they finally allowed her home he'd be there waiting for her. She clung on to the Patriarch's words: *he has not abandoned you completely.*

Nights were frosty now. All the great Galen divers had migrated south. But sometimes as she flew low over the salt flats she still thought she heard the last echo their call. *Come home to me, come ho-o-ome!* Linna, belly now the size of a small pumpkin, was reprieved from knitting and sent off with her each morning to supervise the training sessions. *Don't* let her overdo it. *Don't* let her fly too high. *Don't* let her get wet. Make sure she's back in time for lunch. Oh, and if you do happen to run across a boy who hasn't heard about her— knock him out, drag him home, and we'll get them married double quick before he comes round. The young Gull shepherds strode away as fast as their stilts would carry them whenever Anabara showed up. Woo, didn't want to make eye contact in case they ended up betrothed!

Only Loxi dared keep her company and fly with her. Loxi the mollygull. Live and let live, eh. That's what all the young Gull bruisers were saying these days. They defied the village elders and the Gullmothers. Refused point blank to try and teach Loxi a lesson and beat the perversion out of him. Nah, live and let live. His business if he cropped his hair short and dressed like a Galen. Let him wear them molly diamond ear studs, him, if that's what wanted. It was a free world, eh.

Well, nice to see that broad-mindedness and tolerance had arrived in Gull circles at last. Although Anabara *had* heard there was a rumour going round that Loxi's diamond studs were actually trophies: one for each ear he had bitten off. And that nobody was keen to see him add to his collection.

Slowly her body healed. Slowly her strength came back. Then one day Enobar sauntered down to the Gull village, sent by Grandmama to spar with her and hone her fighting skills again. Their bouts were watched with interest by the young Gull warriors. *His* type weren't normally welcome round here, but the policy of toleration seemed to include him. Sure, to the Gull eye he looked like a shrimpy little girlyboy. But another rumour was doing the rounds. Something about Tressy rivermen singing falsetto after finding themselves on the wrong end of one of those spinning back-kicks. Woo, that boy looked lethal. Nah, no business of theirs what another bloke did with his bits. So long as he didn't thrust it down their throats, eh. Live and let live.

Delays, setbacks, loopholes and endless frustrating adjournments. Waiting was the name of the game in the criminal justice system, too. Of course it was. Speed was never going to be a priority while top counsels charged fifty gilders an hour.

'Change of financial arrangements,' announced Butros one afternoon.

They were sitting on a windswept rock in the middle of a waste of salt furze, far from any snoop charms—unless someone had cunningly concealed one in the gannets that screeched overhead. Butros had exchanged his silk for cashmere and Candacian shearling, while Anabara was bundled up in an old shepherd's coat belonging to Linna's husband Matteo—which smelt of sheep and came down to her ankles—plus a few hundred scarves. She still shivered.

'From now on my work for you is pro bono.'

'Oh my God! It's a trick! You're not the real Butros Kaledh!'

'I think "thank you, Butros" is the phrase that's eluding you here,' he replied.

'Thank you Butros. Why are you being nice? It scares me.'

'Don't flatter yourself. I am merely bowing to the inevitable. You never pay me. This way I can offset you against tax.'

'Plus you're making obscene amounts of money defending the University.'

'I'm making *pornographically* obscene amounts of money,' he agreed. 'I need a bath after I've contemplated it. But that's enough about my erotic life. The reason I'm here is firstly because you're the prosecution's star witnesses. My esteemed colleague, Damora Lhossi, the counsel defending the Tressy scumbags—that's a technical legal definition—is a completely ruthless lowdown amoral bitch.'

'Duh, Butros. She's a lawyer.'

'And screw you too, darling. Unfortunately, she's also clever. Not as clever as *me*, but then, who is? All the same, she's going to try to rip your testimony to shreds and undermine your reputation in any way she can. I need to be sure you're prepared, so you don't balls up my case. Briefly, it hinges on the fact that the Stackmaster was a rogue agent acting by himself, and nobody else knew anything, your honour.'

'Bullshit! The scholasticus knew!'

'Did he *tell* you that? No, he did not. That remark was speculative, and if you repeat it, my client will sue for defamation. As will Carraman, by the way, if you allege anything about his involvement.'

'But I *know* he's involved!'

Butros sighed. 'You don't *know*, you *infer*. I am not defending any slander action pro bono, so behave yourself please. And secondly—now that *Acting Chief* Mooby is safely out of hearing—I need to locate that Fay of yours. I don't want the defence blindsiding me and producing him like a rabbit out of a hat. Where is he?'

'Disappeared.' She told him all about that terrible moment up on the rooftops under the Wolf Tide moon. 'That was over two months ago. He's not coming back.'

'Wrong. Let me spell out the legal ramifications here: your liberating him was conditional upon his agreeing to the terms of your deal. He can't rescind the deal without forfeiting his freedom.'

'But he did.'

'What, he chose to be enslaved again? Not a chance. He was lying.'

'Butros, watch my lips: He. Can't. Lie. To. Me. The deal specifically said—'

'Bullshit. He's been lying through his pointy little teeth from the word go. Tell me again *exactly* what you said when you made the deal.'

She thought long and hard. 'I said, "if I ask you something, you must always tell me the truth". Oh crap.'

Butros broke into sarcastic applause. 'And there we have it. You left yourself wide open. He only has to tell you the truth when you ask him a direct question. The rest of the time he's free to fib like a Candacian catamite.'

Her mind raced through the things Paran had told her. Lies, all of it! Or not. Just because he *could* lie to her didn't mean he automatically had done.

'Yes, but hang on,' she said. 'He rescinded the deal because I'd infected him. He said my crime wiped out the debt and he didn't owe me... Oh. Right. That was a lie.'

Butros patted her hand. 'Go home and write a hundred times *All Fays are lying filth and not to be trusted.* You haven't seen the last of your Mister Paran, believe me.' He got to his feet. 'Before I leave, is there any way in which I, your humble unpaid counsel, can serve you?'

'Yeah. Make them let me go. I want to go home, Butros.'

'Consider it done.' To her amazement he took out a psych-tab and made a note.

'My God—you've got one too!'

'Catch up, please. *Everyone's* got one.' He tucked it back in his pocket. 'Everyone important, that is.'

He was as good as his word. A couple of days later she was finally heading back along the river bank towards the Gullgate. Loxi had been sent along too. He was carrying enough food to last Anabara about a year. Or as Aunt Malla put it, 'A few bits and bobs to tide you over.'

A fine bright late autumn morning. Gulls wheeled and screamed in the blue round the Minstery towers. She could hear the wind flutes singing. It was high tide. Part of the flood plain was still submerged. Everywhere she could see signs of the wreckage left behind by the Wolf Tide. Broken branches, silt-covered rocks, an abandoned fishnet tangled in a tree top. But Larridy shimmered up from the water like a holy vision.

'I'm going to be fine, Loxi. You don't have to come with me.'

'Yeah, I do. Or auntie will skin me. Told her I'd see you safely in the door, eh.'

They walked on a bit in silence. Loxi kicked a skull stone that lay on the river path. The wind hissed in the blond rushes. She thought of Dal Ramek. Still confined to the Precincts under the protection of St Pelago. *Remember you are mine!* whispered the breeze. Tscha!

'Still want to work for me, you?' she asked Loxi. 'Fetch a few more library books?'

'If you need me.'

'Might be kind of tricky, though, eh.' She nailed him with the Gullmother ball-shrivelling glare. 'With you being banned from the university and everything.'

He blushed. 'Aw, Nan, man! You weren't meant to hear about that. Anyway, it's all sorted, eh. I'm allowed up there again.'

'All right. But no more ear-biting, you.'

He bared his teeth at her. 'Psycho Gull warrior. Scary, eh?'

Certainly was! Paran would be proud. She hoped to God Loxi hadn't eaten the ears he'd chomped. Better not to ask. Instead she said, 'Are they real diamonds?'

'Tscha!—like I could afford *that*!'

But he was blushing again. Woo, wealthy lover? Then her mouth dropped open. No! Not *Butros*?!

Better not ask *that* either.

They passed through the Gullgate. The air was full of the smell of starch and blueing. Sheets and bolster cases billowed on the lines. Her heart fluttered like a baby gull. Home. What was waiting for her in her little house?

'It's going to be weird without Paran, eh,' she said.

'Mmm. Who's going to do the security stuff?'

'No idea. Butros says he'll be back, because the deal's still valid. But God knows when. We've still got that bloody mimic charm to sort.'

'Nah, he did that, him,' said Loxi. 'Fixed it so it shouts "thief!" when you try and nick a book.'

She laughed. 'Seriously?'

'It yells your name, and what books you're trying to take. And if you don't hand them back in, it starts shouting out what you did last night. Woo! Sharp decline in unauthorised loans, you better believe it. Here we are.'

The familiar blue door. Paint still flaking. Must get on to that. She hesitated a moment. 'Well, here goes.'

Home. Everything was exactly the same. Hearthrug, table, chipped blue and white crockery on the dresser. The main mast pillar. But it looked strange, like she was watching someone else's dream. There was a vase of flowers on the table. Purple harvest daisies. And she could smell beeswax polish.

'Someone's been in,' she said.

'Eno and me. Tidied the place up, eh. Your granny sent us.'

She punched his arm. 'Hey, thanks.'

'Oh, and your brother sent your mum's locket.' Loxi handed her a small velvet pouch.

The amulet. Ba-boom! went her heart. 'Tell him thanks.' She fastened it round her neck. Felt again the cold of the stone against her breastbone. Instantly, a memory reared up: *the fifth slave!* She'd managed to banish him from her mind. Been telling herself he'd be long gone. Off to the Mainland to join the nomadic Fairy tribes. Come on, he'd have found her by now if he was going to. Surely. She hadn't got round to mentioning him to anyone. God, maybe she should tell Butros after all? Except he'd go *mental.* A survivor who could contradict the scholasticus's testimony? That would totally screw up his case.

Loxi was busy unpacking Aunt Malla's supplies. Anabara wandered up the stairs. The eighth step creaked, just like it always did. She opened her bedroom door. Another little vase of daisies on the window sill. The bed was made up with freshly laundered sheets, pillows plumped. Grandmama's linen. She could smell the lavender.

Her heart began to pound again. Do it. Check the spare room. She crossed the little landing and opened the other door. Empty. Of course it was empty. Bed stripped. Quilt neatly folded. Not a single sign that she'd ever had a Fairy guest. With a sigh she turned and went back down the stairs.

'All done,' said Loxi. 'Want me to stay for a bit?'

'I'll be fine.' A sob caught in her throat. She disguised it with a cough. 'Don't worry, you. Life goes on, eh. Got to pick up the pieces. Make some more money. I'm totally broke again.'

'Not going after the library for compensation, then?'

'Nah. There's too much grief going round the Precincts as it is. I'm not going to add to it.' She gave him a hug. 'Hey, thanks for everything, you. Love you lots.'

'Love you too, babe. I'll be back tomorrow, eh. Sort those account books out for you. Stay safe.'

The door closed. She was alone.

Right! No moping. On with life. Do the next thing. The next thing, obviously, was a bowl of hot chocolate and a honeycake. She set the milk to heat. As she waited, her eye roamed once more round the room. She doubted it had ever been so tidy.

Tscha! A perfectly decent sheet of blotting paper in the bin, though. Enobar. Fine for him to use a pristine sheet of Dame Bharossa's paper for every new message he wrote. She plucked it out and looked at the backwards scrawl. What had she last written all those months ago, back in her old life? Out of curiosity she crossed to the mirror over the fire and held it up. Looked like some kind of urgent warning: '[something something] *he's coming for you. He's going to kill you!'* The rest was too faint to make out. Probably a message for Mooby about Golar. Well, it was all over now, whatever it was.

She shrugged and laid it back on her desk, then went to fetch down her favourite bowl from the dresser. But what was this? Money?

She weighed the leather purse in her hand, peeped inside. Gilders. Lots of twenty gilder pieces. She ground her teeth. Grandmama. Yes, she needed cash. But for God's SAKE! *Please give me at least the opportunity to be a responsible adult!*

She dumped the gold out on the table and began to count it. Sixty, eighty, a hundred. I *wish* she wouldn't keep doing this—hundred and forty, hundred and sixty—it's *so* bloody patronizing—hundred and eighty, two hundred.

Two hundred gilders. Her hand went to the amulet. *You will pay me no wages until I have paid back your two hundred gilders.*

Paran. He'd been here! Her heart leapt. But then she realized what this meant. *Trust me: I always repay in the end.* She took a deep breath. Squared her shoulders. So that was it. The end. Butros was wrong: he wasn't coming back.

As she stood with her hot chocolate, looking out across the street, she waited for the tide to wash over her, grief for Paran. But it didn't come. She watched the old familiar world go by again. Signs creaked. The wind flutes sang. Washer-wenches flounced past. The big Minstery bell began to toll for Morning Prayers. Then one by one, all the little shrine bells joined in. She really ought to get herself up to the Precincts for prayers some time. Say thank you to old Pel. Or bawl him out for the mess he'd landed her in. Probably both those things.

Laundry snapped on a hundred lines. Far off the blacksmith's hammer, clang-clang-clang. She tossed the last crust of her honeycake out on to the cobbles. A gull swooped down and snatched it.

So. No more tears. She shrugged. All back to normal.

But deep down something warned her there wasn't going to be any such thing as normal from now on. This was not the end at all. It was another beginning.

THE END

Made in the USA
Charleston, SC
29 October 2013